When I Lie With You

(A Millionaire's Love, 2)

Sandi Lynn

When I Lie With You (A Millionaire's Love, 2)

Cover Design by Cover It Designs

Photography by Philip Flores @ Flores Photography

Models: Storm Bailey & Sara Mikkelson

Editing by B.Z. Hercules

Dedication

To my amazing and wonderful fans. Without you, these books wouldn't be possible. Thank you from the bottom of my heart for your love of romance and all your support. Your kind messages touch me every day and inspire me to keep writing. So, thank you from me to you. I hope you enjoy the conclusion of Ian & Rory's story.

Ian & Rory took a trip to Nocking Point Wines in Walla Walla, Washington. It's real and it does exist.

Go show Nocking Point Wines some love on their Facebook page at:

https://www.facebook.com/nockingpoint

You can also visit their website at:

http://nockingpointwines.com/

Twitter: https://twitter.com/nockingpoint

Table of Contents

Chapter 1
Rory

Our flight was scheduled to leave Paris at ten a.m. Ian didn't bring his dad's plane because Richard had taken a trip for the holidays. It was New Year's Day and we were both hung over, not only from the alcohol, but from all the sex we had last night. Ian and I rang in the new year on a perfect note, and now it was time to get back to reality and head back to Malibu.

"Happy New Year, sweetheart," Ian said as he kissed my head.

I lay wrapped tightly in his arms since it was only the two of us, naked on the bed, sheets torn off from last night's escapades.

"Happy New Year." I smiled as I lifted my head from his chest and kissed his lips. "I don't want to go back to Malibu. I like Paris and I want to stay."

"We can come back here any time you want to. If I could move here, I would. I would pack you up, keep you all to myself, and forget family and friends. But we have to live in reality, sweetheart, and unfortunately, we have to work, or at least I have to."

I gave him a confused look before nipping his bottom lip. "What do you mean by *you* have to? Am I not working for you anymore?"

"No, you're not. I'm firing you." He smiled.

"Mr. Braxton, I'll have you know that I've never been fired before. Would you care to explain to me the reason why you're firing me as your assistant?"

A small smile graced his face as he placed his hand on my cheek. "I want you to do something that you want to do and being my assistant isn't it. Pursue a career in music, take some classes. The world is your oyster, my love, and I'll do everything I can to make sure you're happy."

"I love you so much, Ian," I said as I kissed his soft lips.

"I love you too, Rory, and I want to make you happy."

"You do make me happy."

"But one day, I might not, and I don't ever want you looking at me with regret that you didn't do what you wanted with your life."

I didn't like that he said that. I knew our relationship wasn't going to be perfect. If it was, then something was wrong. But, I loved him, and I'd do everything I could to make him as happy as he made me. He rolled me on my back and stuck his hand down the front of my panties, cupping me below and inserting his finger.

"You're wet." He smiled.

"I'm always wet when you're around." I smiled as I took my bottom lip between my teeth.

He stared into my eyes while he hovered over me. "You're so special, and I will never get tired of telling you how much I love you. Now, spread your legs, sweetheart. I need to fuck you before we leave for the airport."

As Ian was shaving, I walked up behind him and watched him through the mirror. He looked so sexy and smelled so good. He stopped the blade and looked at me.

"What are you doing?" he asked.

"Watching you shave."

"Why?" He smiled.

"Because you're sexy and I can't help it."

"I know the feeling, sweetheart. That's how I feel when I look at you," he said as he went back to shaving.

His eyes, once again, looked over at me through the mirror. He set down his razor and turned around so he was facing me. He slowly undid the tie to my robe and slid it off my shoulders, letting it fall to the ground. He let out a low growl as he smiled.

"You're begging me to fuck you, aren't you?"

"Is that what you picked up from me staring at you shaving?" I asked.

"Yes. I know your look and you have that 'I need you to fuck me right now' look."

He stood there, shaving cream still on his face as he plunged a finger inside me. I gasped as I tilted my head back.

"I knew you wanted it. You're already soaking wet." He smiled as he grabbed me by my hips, turned me around, and set me up on top of the sink.

I wrapped my legs around him and he wasted no time thrusting into me as he held onto my hips and fluently moved in and out.

"God, sweetheart, you're so amazing." He panted. "I'll never be able to get enough of you."

My moans grew louder as he pushed in and out of me and my body jerked with excitement. He placed his finger on my clit and moved it in circles. My body tightened as a warmth of fluid gripped his cock.

"Fuck, Rory," he said breathlessly as he lifted me from the sink and turned me around so I was facing the mirror. "Look at me through the mirror, sweetheart. Watch me fuck you from behind."

I did as he asked as my heart pounded and my skin became moist. The sexiest part was that his face was still covered in shaving cream. He pounded into me as he grabbed my breasts and pinched my erect nipples with his fingers, causing the warmth to return between my legs. My body geared up for another orgasm as he pushed into me with force and spilled his come inside me, causing me to come again. He closed his eyes as he stood there, inside me, pushing out every last drop and then he wrapped his arms around me and held me tight.

"I love you," he whispered.

"I love you too," I said as I tilted my head back and looked up at him.

****

"Shit…shit…shit," Ian said as he grabbed my hand and we ran through the airport to our gate. "This is your fault, sweetheart. If you would've left the bathroom instead of watching me shave, I wouldn't have had to fuck you and we wouldn't be missing our flight home."

"It's not my fault you can't keep your dick in your pants, Mr. Braxton."

"Is that so? I'll show you later how I can't keep my dick out of you." He winked.

I silently laughed because I knew we were going to miss our flight. They already made the last call for boarding. I didn't mind if we stayed in Paris one more night. The truth was, I didn't ever want to go back to Malibu and deal with Richard and Andrew. Ian pulled me along and, when we finally reached our gate, the door closed.

"We need to get on that plane," Ian said sternly.

"I'm sorry, sir, but it's too late. We've already closed up," the woman spoke in her French accent.

"It's never too late, darling." Ian smiled as he pulled out a wad of cash from his pocket. "You call the pilot and tell him you have two passengers that are getting on the plane and he needs to wait. If you do that for me, you'll be very well thanked." He winked.

I rolled my eyes at his charm. I could see the woman swooning over him already. She picked up the phone and I guess she called the pilot, because before I knew it, the door opened and we were escorted to first class. I sat down in my seat and looked over at Ian.

"What?" he asked.

I sat there, shaking my head. "I can't believe you were able to get us on this plane."

Ian chuckled as he placed his finger under my chin. "I can do anything, Rory. Haven't you figured that out by now?"

"Yes, I've figured it out. But I think the first thing you need to do when we get back to Malibu is you need to buy your own plane." I laughed.

"I am." He smiled.

My eyes widened and my laughter subsided. "I was kidding."

"I'm not. I'm buying my own plane. It's something I should've done a long time ago, but I always used my dad's. Now that you're with me, we'll be traveling more and I think it's best to have our own."

He said "our," meaning it would be mine and his. That made me so happy to hear him say that. The feelings of insecurities were gone and I felt complete. We each had a couple glasses of wine and I fell asleep with my head on Ian's shoulder.

"Your father – your deadbeat, lousy cheating father – fucked my sister, got her pregnant, and ruined my life. You and your brother are nothing but a constant reminder of that."

I jumped and sat up straight. My eyes were wide and it took me a minute to focus on where I was at.

"Sweetheart, are you okay?" Ian said as he grabbed my hand.

I took in a deep breath. "I'm fine. It was just a dream."

"About what? You haven't had a nightmare in a long time. Have you?"

"It was just about my aunt. Nothing to worry about. I'll continue to see Dr. Neil when I get back."

He brought my hand up to his lips and softly kissed it. "That's a good idea."

"I kept meaning to ask you something. If I'm not your assistant anymore, are you hiring someone new?"

Ian gave me a small smile and ran his finger down my jawline. "Are you worried I'll hire another beautiful woman to take your place?"

"Yes. I need to know so I can train harder to kick her ass when she steals you away from me." I smiled.

"No one will ever steal me away from you, Rory. And to answer your question, no, I'm not hiring another assistant."

"Why?"

The corners of his mouth curved up slightly when I asked. "I created that position for you because I wanted to see you every day. After you moved out, I felt alone, and it made me realize how much I wanted and needed you around."

"Ian," I whispered.

"I wanted to take care of you without having to admit that I was in love with you, and hiring you as my employee allowed me to do that. You'll still be considered my employee. You'll get paid every week and you'll still be on my health insurance, but you won't be doing any secretarial work."

"Then what will I be doing to earn all that?" I smiled.

"Nothing. Just you being around is enough," he said as he leaned over and kissed my lips. "Try to get some more sleep, sweetheart. We should be landing in about three hours."

I propped my pillow against his shoulder and laid my head down. *What the hell was with that nightmare?*

Chapter 2

As soon as we walked through the door, Ian picked me up and carried me up the stairs.

"What are you doing?" I laughed.

"Something I should've done a while ago. I'm taking you to our bedroom."

He kicked the door open lightly with his foot and laid me down on the bed. He pushed a few strands of my hair back as he looked into my eyes.

"This is *our* bed, sweetheart. Our bed to sleep in, fuck in, and relax in. There has never been a woman in this bed until now." He smiled.

The butterflies started to flutter when he said that. My mind instantly wondered about the other room. *Do I ask him about it? Or just leave it alone?* I decided to leave it alone, since it was our first night back.

"Hold on a second," Ian said as he got up from the bed and grabbed his phone.

"What are you doing?" I laughed.

"I'm taking a few pictures of you on our bed. I like the way you look in it." He smiled.

I knew this was a big step for Ian, and being the only woman that ever sat or lay on this bed made it more surreal. I posed for him and he took in a sharp breath. He set his phone down and crawled towards me on the bed, licking his lips the whole time and staring at me with that carnal look. As I bit down on my bottom lip and smiled, he pushed me flat on my back and hovered over me with a smile.

"You make me happy. I've never been happy like this. When you're with me, I'm happy. When you're not, I'm sad. I just wanted you to know that."

I brought my hands up and ran my fingers through his hair. "You make me happy too, and I don't want anything else in my life but you. I need you, Ian."

He leaned down and locked his lips with mine, parting my lips so his tongue could enter my mouth. Our kiss became deep and passionate as he fell on top of me and held my head with his hands. He broke our kiss so his lips could explore my neck. As I wrapped my legs around him, I felt his erection pressed against me. Our breathing became rapid and so did our hearts. I wanted to make love to him. His hand traveled up my shirt as his fingers tugged at my hardened nipple.

"Fuck me, Ian," I said with bated breath.

"I will, right now," he whispered as he tugged at my pants.

Suddenly, we heard a voice calling from downstairs. "Hello. Ian, Rory, where are you? I know you're home, so I'll give you five seconds to get decent and come downstairs!" Adalynn exclaimed.

Ian looked at me. "Seriously?"

I couldn't help but laugh. "Yeah, seriously."

Ian climbed off me and went into the bathroom. I got up from the bed, looked in the mirror, ran my fingers through my hair, and straightened my clothes. As soon as Ian emerged from the bathroom, he took my hand and we walked down the stairs.

"Perfect timing as always, Adalynn," Ian said.

"Sorry, but you two have the rest of your lives to fuck. Come here, darling." She smiled as she held her arms out to me.

I welcomed her embrace. It was so good to see her again. "It's good to see you, Adalynn. Happy New Year."

"Happy New Year to both of you," she said as she kissed Ian's cheek. "Now, I want to hear all about Paris!" She smiled.

"We just got home less than an hour ago. Do you think we can tell you about it tomorrow? Rory and I are exhausted," Ian said as he looked at her.

"No. I'm here now and I want to hear all about it. In fact, Ian, you can go upstairs. Me and Rory have some catching up to do."

"That reminds me, Adalynn. The two of us are going to have a little talk about a certain lie," Ian said as he pointed his finger at her.

"Oh, please. It all worked out in the end anyway, and with your dysfunctional behavior, I wasn't about to give you any information."

Ian sighed as his eyes stared into hers. He looked at me and then kissed my lips.

"Go ahead and have some girl talk. I'm going to go take a shower."

"Okay." I smiled.

"Bye, Ian. It was good to see you," Adalynn said with a smirk.

"Whatever, Adalynn," he replied as he walked up the stairs.

Adalynn grabbed my arm and led me straight into the kitchen. She told me to have a seat at the table as she reached in the cabinet and pulled out two wine glasses.

"So? I want details! Lots of details." She smiled as she pulled a bottle of wine from the wine rack.

"It was so romantic. He's so romantic and we're officially in love."

She walked over to the table and handed me a glass of wine.

"I knew he'd come around. Okay, I really didn't, and for a while, I was worried. But, I'm happy he did," she said. "I knew he loved you."

"Did you talk to him when you came back from Paris?" I asked.

"No. I didn't. I didn't get a chance to, and to be honest with you, I was secretly hoping he'd come around on his own. So now what?"

I picked up my glass and took a sip. "I guess we're living together and we're going to start building a life together. Did I mention that he fired me as his assistant?"

"What?!"

"He wants me to take some music classes or do something that I want to do. He doesn't want me to have any regrets."

"Ian said that?" she asked with surprise.

"Yes." I smiled.

"Girl, you took a seriously fucked up man and turned him around. You're my hero." She smiled as she held up her glass.

As I brought my glass up to hers, Ian walked into the kitchen. He was freshly showered and wearing nothing but pajama bottoms. He looked so sexy and I wanted him so badly.

"What are the two of you toasting?" he asked as he reached in the cupboard for a wine glass.

"We're toasting your return home. I'm glad you brought my girl home because I really was hating the fact that she was going to stay in Paris and not come back."

"The only place she's staying is right here with me." He smiled as he kissed the top of my head.

Adalynn drank the rest of her wine and got up from her chair. "It's been fun, but I must leave now. The two of you must be seriously jet-lagged, and I have some wedding plans to go over."

"Have you set a date yet?" I asked as I got up from my chair to walk her out.

"Not yet. That's what Daniel and I are going to discuss as soon as he gets home."

She walked over to Ian and gave him a kiss on the cheek. "You're a smart man, Mr. Braxton, and thank you for bringing her home." She winked as she looked at me and gave me a light hug.

"You should be thanking her because I thought she'd tell me to fuck off and I'd be coming home alone."

Adalynn turned around and smiled at him before walking out the door. I sat down on Ian's lap and wrapped my arms around him.

"You look tired, sweetheart," he said as he stroked my cheek.

"I am. I'm exhausted."

"Then let's go to bed. As much as I want to finish what we started earlier, you need your rest."

I pouted as I put my forehead against his. "You're right, but there will be plenty of time for rest after you make love to me."

The corners of his mouth curved upwards before his lips brushed against mine. "You're so sexy and you're all mine."

"I was always yours," I whispered as our kiss became passionate.

He lifted me off his lap and then picked me up and carried me to the bedroom. He set me down on the bed and took down his pajama bottoms as I lifted off my shirt. I ran my hand up and down his hard shaft and a low moan came from deep inside him. He lifted me from the bed and slowly took down my pants. His mouth crashed into mine, pushing me back on the bed as he hovered over me while plunging his finger inside me.

"I want and need you so bad, Rory."

"I want you so bad too, Ian."

He growled as he inserted another finger, making sure I was ready for him. "You're so deliciously wet, sweetheart, and I need to taste you."

He removed his fingers as his tongue slid down my torso and to my aching clit. He wrapped his fingers around my wrists and lifted my arms above my head. A soft moan escaped my lips as he worked his tongue around my swollen area, which was begging for him to take me. I wrapped my legs around his neck as he continued to pleasure me, causing my body to tighten as he brought me to orgasm. As my body released itself, he let out a moan and released my wrists, taking my hardened nipples between his fingers.

"I need to fuck you right now. There's no more waiting. I need to be inside you," he whispered before crashing his mouth into mine.

The sensation going through my body was electrifying when I felt him push inside me. Every time we made love, the connection between us grew stronger. We were no longer two people; we were one.

Chapter 3
Ian

I stroked her hair softly as she lay in my arms. It felt good to hold her, and it felt more than right to have her in my bed. I needed her more than I would admit, and the pain it caused us both was more pain than I'd ever known in my whole life. Her scent was now embedded in my bed and this was where she belonged; not in the room down the hall or even in the room next door. But here, in my bed, where I could love her for the rest of my life. Now that we were back in Malibu, back to reality, there were going to be some issues we'd have to deal with, one of them being Richard.

I couldn't help but run my finger lightly across her cheek. She opened her eyes and looked at me with a smile on her face.

"Good morning," she whispered.

"Good morning. I'm sorry if I woke you."

"You didn't, and I wouldn't mind if you did. How long have you been awake?" she asked.

"About a half hour. I just laid here and couldn't help but stare at you."

Her smile grew wider as she lifted her head and softly kissed my lips. "I love you."

"I love you more, sweetheart. Are you up for a run?" I asked.

"Yes. I miss our runs along the beach," she said.

We climbed out of bed and threw on our running clothes before heading downstairs to see Charles. I could smell the fresh blueberry muffins Charles had made and they were making my mouth water.

"Stop salivating, Ian. You can have one when we get back." Rory smiled.

She already knew me way too well. When we walked into the kitchen, Rory walked over to Charles and gave him a hug.

"Charles, it's good to see you, friend. Miss Sinclair will be moving in permanently, so you are to accommodate her and her requests."

"Welcome home, Rory. It's good to see you." Charles smiled.

"Thank you, Charles. It's good to see you too," she replied.

I walked over to the counter by the stove where Charles had the blueberry muffins cooling. Just as I picked up one, Rory walked over and took it out of my hand.

"Hey! What are you doing?" I asked.

"You can wait to eat that when we get back." She smiled. "It will give you something to look forward to."

I placed my hands on her hips as I kissed her nose. "I'm already looking forward to something else."

"Me too! So we better get running so we can hurry up and get back." She winked.

"Damn you, woman. You've already started getting—"

Rory put her hand over my mouth and whispered in my ear, "Not in front of Charles."

I kissed her head and ran out the door. She followed behind me, laughing. We ran down along the shoreline and kept our usual steady pace. I looked over at her and smiled.

"What?" she asked as she caught up to me.

"Nothing. I was just thinking about how this is our first run together in Malibu as a couple."

"Yes, it is. Do you like it?" she asked.

"I love it, Rory, and there's something I need to tell you."

I didn't want to tell her, but she'd eventually find out and she'd be pissed. So I thought it better to come clean now. She had a look of worry on her face as she stopped.

"What is it?"

"Keep running, sweetheart. It's nothing bad. It's just something I did that I think you should know about."

"Ian, just tell me," she said as she started jogging again.

I took in a deep breath. "I bought the building that was the bakery and your apartment and I called in a favor to a friend of mine that works for the city and had him put the note on your door."

"You did what? Why the hell would you do that, Ian?" she asked as she stopped behind me.

This was the hardest part for me. I could no longer just tell her because I could. I owed her an explanation because she was my girlfriend and simple little answers wouldn't work anymore.

I ran my hands through my hair as I turned around and stood a few feet in front of her. She had her hands on her hips and her head cocked, waiting for my answer.

"I did it because I hated you living in that tiny little room. I wanted you at my house, and if I would've asked you to move back, you would've said no."

"So you just lied to me?"

"I didn't lie, I don't think. I just didn't tell you," I said as I walked closer to her.

"No, Ian. I think that classifies as a lie."

"Sweetheart, listen to me. I wanted you with me, in my house, where I could keep you safe. I wanted to save you from your nightmares, and I wanted you in my arms at night. At that time, it was the only way to get you back home." I smiled as I held her face and lightly kissed her lips.

"Since you're so free with telling me things, I have some questions that I want answers to, and I feel like you owe me since you lied to me."

"Rory, I didn't lie to you. But I will answer any questions you have." I smiled as I kissed her again.

"The blonde you took to the gala; did you bring her home and fuck her that night?"

I couldn't believe she asked me that. It obviously was bothering her, and I wasn't going to lie. I wasn't starting off our relationship on a lie.

"No, Rory. I didn't sleep with her. In fact, I left the gala early and left her there with Andrew. Seeing you before I left made me feel like complete shit. I came home that night, alone, and went to bed." A small smile graced her face after I gave her my answer. "Was there something else you wanted to ask?"

"Yes, actually, there is. When I came over the morning after you and Andrew went to dinner, I saw Andrew and the two women walking down the stairs. One of them said to thank you for last night and then Andrew said you were out running, but he didn't know how, since you only got a couple of hours sleep. Did you fuck one of those women?"

"That explains your attitude that morning when I asked if you were pissed at me. I knew something was bothering you." I pulled her into me and held her head against my chest before pulling her back and giving her another kiss. "I swear to you, Rory, on my life, that I did not sleep with any of those women. I let Andrew use the room. He was with the both of them, not me. They were telling him to thank me for letting them use it. Andrew wanted you to believe that I slept with one of them. God, I wish you would've asked me about it that day."

She wrapped her arms around my neck and hugged me as tightly as she could. "Thank you, Ian, for being honest. I love you so much."

"I love you more, sweetheart, and don't ever forget it. Now, can we finish our run because I can't stop thinking about those blueberry muffins?"

"You bet." She smiled as she took my hand and we finished our run.

****

"Damn, Charles, I think these are the best blueberry muffins you ever made," I said as I took a bite.

Rory looked at me and laughed as she walked over to where I was standing and wiped a crumb from my mouth.

"You should have heard him when we were in Paris, Charles. He was telling the people at the French bakery that they needed to get the recipe from you for blueberry muffins because theirs weren't cutting it."

"Ian, seriously?" Charles smirked.

"It's true, Charles. The muffins over there are shit."

I sat down at the table with my muffin and coffee and stared at Rory as she looked out the window. She was sweaty from our run and she never looked more perfect. I was getting hard just staring at her.

"I think we need to go shower now. I have to go into the office for a while."

She looked at me with a smile and got up from her chair. She walked over and stood behind me, wrapping her arms around me and whispering in my ear. "Taking a shower is a good idea because I'm dirty, and I want to be even dirtier with you in the shower."

She ran her hot ass up the stairs as I jumped up from my chair and ran up after her. She lifted her top over her head before she reached the bedroom and threw it behind her. Damn, she was hot and I couldn't wait to get her in the shower. She had it started before I fully stripped out of my clothes. I stepped into the shower and grabbed her hips as she wrapped her arms around my neck.

"I'm afraid that I'm going to have to punish you."

"Why's that, Mr. Braxton? I didn't do anything wrong."

"But you did, Miss Sinclair. You didn't let me finish my blueberry muffin."

"I do believe I taste better than your blueberry muffins. So if you're still hungry, then by all means, help yourself." She smiled at me.

Not only did she awaken the beast inside, she welcomed it, and I was more than happy to do as she wished.

Chapter 4
Rory

I kissed Ian goodbye as he walked out the door and headed to the office. Since he came to Paris, we spent every waking moment together, and it felt strange that he left, even if it was only for a while. Tomorrow was visiting day over at Hudson Rock and I couldn't wait to see Stephen. We Skyped every Thursday when I was in Paris, but I still missed him and I couldn't wait to hug him.

I walked over to the piano and ran my finger along the top. I sat down, positioned my fingers on the keys, and played some Chopin. I lost myself in the melody, but this time, I didn't need to be transported to another reality. The reality I was in was perfect, and I was happy. As Mandy walked into the room with a smile on her face, I stopped playing and gave her a hug.

"Rory, I'm so happy you're back. It was awful while you were gone. Mr. Braxton was miserable and I was so afraid I wouldn't ever see you again," she said as she hugged me tightly.

"I missed you, Mandy, and I'm here to stay." I smiled.

"I was so worried that you weren't going to take Mr. Braxton back. He knew I missed you because he came up to me the day he left for Paris and he told me not to worry because he was going to bring you home."

"And he did. How were your holidays?" I asked.

"They were good, thank you."

"How's your daughter?"

"She's really good. Just between us, Mr. Braxton gave me a raise as a Christmas gift. He said that I do a really good job and I deserved it."

My heart melted at the thought of Ian doing that for Mandy. He was finally opening up and becoming the person he was meant to be before his mom left him.

"That's wonderful, Mandy. I'm so happy for you. Now, when am I going to get to meet that daughter of yours?"

"Oh, I don't know. I don't think Mr. Braxton would want me to bring her here. He's not fond of children."

I was stunned to hear Mandy say that. Ian and I had never talked about kids in general, so I guess I wasn't aware of his feelings. My mind went back to that day when Connor and Ellery were here and he was holding Julia. He looked very uncomfortable and, when he saw me, he handed her to me right away.

"Don't worry about Ian. I can handle him. I really would love to meet your daughter. What's her name?"

Mandy looked at me and smiled. "Her name is Molly."

"Molly is a pretty name."

"Thank you, Rory. I better get back to work," she said as she turned and walked away.

I headed upstairs to move some of my things from my room to Ian's. As I reached the top of the stairs, I started down the hall and stopped and stared at the door to "the room." I put my hand on the doorknob and, surprisingly, it turned. I slowly pushed the door open and gasped when I saw the inside. The walls were no longer gray. They were a light yellow with white crown molding. There was a queen-sized bed with a beautiful duvet cover across it. A white-washed dresser sat on the wall where the hooks used to be and a beautiful matching armoire sat quaintly in the corner. I was in shock and had to look around and be sure this was the same room I had seen not too long ago.

"Do you like it?" Ian's voice said from behind.

I jumped and placed my hand over my heart. "Ian, you scared me."

"I'm sorry, sweetheart," he said as he clasped my shoulders.

"Why are you home already?" I asked.

"Don't you want me here?"

"Of course I do. I just thought you'd be gone longer."

"I grabbed what I needed to and I left. Truth be told, I missed you, and I can do some work from home."

"Aw, baby," I said as I turned around and hugged him. "I missed you too."

"Answer my question. Do you like it?"

"Yes. The room looks great. But why?" I asked as I looked up at him and placed my hand on his cheek.

"I wanted it gone. The memories, what it represented; everything. The room was an outlet for me; a way to release the pain I felt inside. The women I brought here were used to this kind of sex. But, you." He smiled softly. "You were different. I had no desire to do any of those things to you or with you. You were so innocent, and all I could imagine whenever I looked at you was making love to you as passionately as I could."

"Oh, Ian," I whispered as I softly stroked his cheek.

He leaned in and kissed my lips and then turned around and shut the door.

"What are you doing?" I asked.

He didn't have to say anything; his smile said it all. "I want to make love to you in this room right now. I want to create a new memory in here and I want to do it with you."

"I would love that." I smiled as my fingers deftly lifted his shirt over his head.

After we made love, Ian had to do some work in his study, so I put on my workout clothes and headed downstairs to the gym. The first thing I did was run on the treadmill for a while before switching over to the punching bag. Now that everything was settled and perfect with Ian, my mind wouldn't stop wondering about what my Aunt Nancy said about my dad. He left my mom when he found out she was pregnant and abandoned his children. Desperation was settling in, and I wondered if my life would've been different if he'd stuck around. I felt an overwhelming need to confront him because I was pissed and hurt by a man I'd never even met. I stepped off the treadmill, wrapped my hands, put on the gloves, and started jabbing at the bag. *Jab. Jab. Punch. Punch.* The more I thought about him, the harder I punched. I bet he didn't even know he had twin children. The thought consumed me as I continued to punch. The sweat was dripping from my forehead with each punch and kick I made.

"Remind me never to piss you off."

I gave the bag a few more punches and then stopped and stood there, trying to catch my breath. Ian walked over to me and handed me a towel.

"What was that all about? Don't get me wrong, sweetheart; watching you do that was fucking hot, but seriously, it looked like you were about to rip the bag from the ceiling."

"I was just thinking about my dad," I said as I wiped my face with the towel.

"I wondered how long it would take for what Nancy said to sink in."

"It's been there since she told me, but I had someone else on my mind and there wasn't any room for any other thoughts," I said as I kissed him on the lips.

"You're getting me hard, Rory. I'm standing here staring at you and wishing that I was the reason for you sweating." He winked.

"You're sexy, Mr. Braxton, but I do have to take a shower. I'm starting to stink."

"Yeah, I know."

I playfully punched him in the arm. "You ass."

Ian picked me up and put me over his shoulder as he slapped my ass and carried me up the stairs. "Now I'm going to punish you, Miss Sinclair, and you're not going to like it."

I couldn't stop laughing each time he slapped me. "Somehow, I think I'm going to fully enjoy your punishment."

****

"It's good to see you, Rory. I was a bit worried that you stopped coming to our sessions," Dr. Neil said.

"I'm sorry, Dr. Neil. I should've called you, but things happened so fast."

"So, tell me how you and Ian are doing?"

Dr. Neil and I talked about my relationship with Ian instead of my past. I thought that I had put closure on it after I went back to Indiana, but the thoughts of my father consumed me. After we finished talking about Ian, I told her about what Nancy had said about my father.

"What are your feelings towards your father right now?" she asked.

I looked down at my hands and began playing with my nails. "I'm angry at him."

"Why?" she asked.

"Because he abandoned not only my mother, but his kids. I don't think he knows that there are two of us."

"You mean twins?"

"Yes."

"If you were to see him, what would you say to him?"

I looked up at her and didn't say anything. I knew what I wanted to say, but I was too afraid, because if I did say something, the hurt and abandonment would become too real.

"Rory, what would you say to him if he was standing in this room?" she asked again. "It's all right."

I got up from the couch and walked over to where a picture hung over the fireplace. It was a painting of two women looking at each other through the glass. One was dressed in black and the other was dressed in white, but it was the same person.

"I would tell him that I hate him. I would tell him what a horrible person he was to leave like he did and abandon his own flesh and blood."

"Okay, that's a start," Dr. Neil said. "Do you think that you would want to find him and tell him how you feel? Maybe find out his reason for leaving."

"I've thought about it. I want him to know what he's done and how his children grew up," I said as tears started to fall. "I just want to know if he has any regrets. I need to know the truth."

I turned around as the clock chimed, alerting us that my session was over. Dr. Neil got up from her seat and handed me a tissue.

"It's okay, Rory. We'll talk more about this at our next session. Perhaps it would be beneficial for you to talk to Ian about it. Considering his mother left him when he was a child, it seems like this is something the two of you could really help each other with."

I grabbed my purse from the couch and gave Dr. Neil a light hug. "Thank you, Dr. Neil. I just might do that."

As I was walking out of the office, my phone rang. I pulled it from my pocket and saw that Ian was calling.

"Hi, honey."

"Hello, sweetheart. Are you on your way home?"

"Yeah. I just left Dr. Neil's office and I'm getting in the car as we speak."

"Good. We're going to go out to dinner with Adalynn and Daniel tonight. She wants to discuss the wedding."

"Sounds like fun. I'll be home soon. I love you."

"I love you too, sweetheart. Hurry home. I miss you."

"I miss you too," I said as I hit the end button.

All the way home, my mind kept going back and forth about my father and what Dr. Neil said about finding him. Things with Ian were so good right now and I was settling into my new life. *Did I really want to fuck it up by bringing my father into it?*

After I pulled into the driveway, I walked through the door and headed straight to the kitchen. Ian was standing at the counter, eating a blueberry muffin, and Mandy was at the sink, washing some dishes.

"Welcome home, sweetheart." He smiled.

I walked over to him and kissed his lips, tasting nothing but blueberries. "Thank you, my love. You look like you're enjoying that muffin."

"Always do."

I gave him a smirk as I said hi to Mandy.

"How did your appointment go?" Ian asked.

"It was okay. If you don't mind, I really don't want to talk about that right now."

"Sweetheart, what's wrong?" Ian asked as he took my hand.

"Nothing. We just talked about my father. I don't want to think or talk about it right now."

"Okay. We can talk about it when you're ready."

Ian tore off a piece of his blueberry muffin and handed it to me. "Here, blueberry muffins always make things better." He smiled.

"Your obsession with blueberry muffins is starting to worry me."

"Is that so? Well, I have another obsession," he said as he picked me up and carried me through the kitchen and up the stairs to our bedroom.

Chapter 5
Ian

"As much as I don't want to get out of this bed, we do need to get cleaned up to meet Adalynn and Daniel for dinner."

"I know," Rory whined as she rolled on top of me. "But first, I need to kiss your lips," she said as she kissed me. "Then I need to kiss your sexy chest." She smiled as her lips traveled to my bare chest. Then I need to kiss your—"

"Whoa," I said as I stopped her. "Sweetheart, do me a favor and save that for later tonight. If you do that now, we won't be meeting Adalynn and Daniel for dinner; that I can promise."

"You're no fun," she whined.

I kissed her soft lips as she stared into my eyes. "I'm so in love with you, Rory, and I need you to believe that. No matter what you want to do about your father, whether it be find him or forget about him, I'll be here for you, and I'll help you get through it."

"I do believe you love me, and I'm so in love with you too. We'll be here for each other." She smiled.

I pulled her down onto me and held her tight. "I'm happy; so happy and I don't want anything to ruin it."

"Nothing will, Ian. I promise," she whispered.

Somehow, I got the feeling that all was too good to be true and something was coming our way.

We both got up and got dressed. Rory freshened up her makeup and we headed to Cabot's for dinner. Joshua had the night off, so I drove. We were stuck in typical Los Angeles traffic and when I looked over at Rory, I noticed she'd been staring at me. I took hold of her hand and softly kissed it with a smile.

"You're beautiful. I want you to know that."

"You're sexy, and I want you to know that." She smiled.

We pulled up to the curb and I had the valet park the car. As we walked into the restaurant, the hostess took us over to our table, where Adalynn and Daniel were sitting.

"It's about time!" Adalynn said as she hugged me and then Rory.

"Traffic was terrible," I said as I shook Daniel's hand.

"Somehow, I don't think the traffic had anything to do with it." She smirked.

After we looked over the menu, we placed our dinner order and then Adalynn began talking about the wedding. She took hold of Daniel's hand as she looked at both of us.

"We set a date!"

"When?" Rory asked in excitement.

"April 19$^{th.}$"

"That's in three months. Is that enough time to plan a wedding?" I asked.

"That's what I asked." Daniel chuckled.

"I'll have plenty of time, plus now that you're not going to be Ian's slave anymore, Rory, you can help me, since you'll be my maid of honor. You *will* be my maid of honor, right?" she asked.

I looked over at Rory and she was glowing with excitement. "Are you serious, Adalynn? You really want me to be your maid of honor?"

"Yes, Rory, I do," she said as she reached over and patted Rory's hand.

"And I would like you to be my best man, Ian," Daniel said.

I looked over at him and felt honored. "Thank you, Daniel. I'd be honored to be your best man." I smiled.

Rory hooked her arm around mine and laid her head on my shoulder. "This is so exciting, Ian. I've never been in a wedding or even been to one."

Adalynn and Daniel sat across the table and smiled as I kissed Rory on the head. "I'm happy you're happy."

The truth was I was a little worried. Marriage wasn't my thing. It's only a little piece of paper that officially states that you're a couple. Who needed that? From what I'd seen in the world, relationships were perfect until that little piece of paper came into play. Then everything went to shit. There was no reason why two people needed to get married. I was happy living and sharing my life with Rory as we were. I was concerned that all this wedding planning with Adalynn would make Rory want to get married. I couldn't do that. I wouldn't do that.

Adalynn and Rory continued to talk about the wedding during dinner, and Daniel and I talked business and politics. It was nice to be out as a couple. After enjoying our dinner and having a few drinks, we called it a night. All I kept thinking about was getting Rory home and into bed.

"After you, Madame," I said as I opened the passenger door for her.

"Thank you." She smiled as she stepped in.

"Dinner was great, and I'm so excited to be a part of Adalynn and Daniel's wedding. Aren't you?" she asked.

I took hold of her hand and kissed it. "Of course I am. I couldn't be happier."

God, I had to keep praying that she didn't mention marriage to me. I felt that she wouldn't yet because it was too soon in our relationship for any kind of talk like that. The less we talked about Adalynn and Daniel, the safer I'd be.

"So, tell me what Dr. Neil had to say about your dad."

Rory looked at me strangely. "What made you think of that? We were just talking about the wedding and you instantly changed the subject."

"I'm sorry, sweetheart. I've just been thinking about how upset you were when you came home earlier from your appointment. It really bothered me."

She brought her hand up to my cheek and softly stroked it. "I don't want you to be bothered by it, honey. She just asked me about what I would say to him if I met him."

"Do you want to meet him? I can find him for you."

"I don't know, Ian. I'm just really confused about the whole thing."

"Well, just let me know, sweetheart, and I'll make some calls."

We pulled up to the house and I got out and opened the door for her. As I took her hand and helped her out, I picked her up and carried her into the house and up to the bedroom.

"What are you doing?" She smiled.

"I'm taking you to bed because it's all I've been thinking about all night."

"Oh, okay!"

I kissed her lips before putting her down. "I want you to strip for me, but not until after I get undressed and get in bed."

I took off my clothes as she carefully watched me. Just watching her watch me was getting me hard. I climbed into bed and smiled at her. "Your turn. Nice and slow, sweetheart. Go nice and slow. I want my own private show."

She turned around so her back was facing me and she slowly unzipped her dress. She took the zipper all the way to the end so I could see her v-string. Fuck, she was hot and sexy. She moved her ass back and forth in a sexy tease that drove me wild. She slowly took down one strap of her dress and then the other, holding it up over her breasts. She turned around and faced me, letting the dress drop to the floor. She stood there with a sexy look on her face as she licked her lips in only her so-called panties and bra.

"Get over here and let me slap that sexy ass of yours."

Her smile grew wider as she bit down on her bottom lip and walked over to me, bending over so I could slap her.

"God, sweetheart, I could come right now just watching you."

I lightly slapped her on the ass. She loved it. I didn't do it hard and I never left a mark. I would never physically hurt her, even if it was for play.

"Now go back across the room and take off your bra, slowly," I commanded.

She leaned over and lightly licked my lips with her tongue before strutting across the room like I asked. Her back was turned as she unhooked her bra and slowly took down the straps as she turned to me and winked, letting it fall to the floor. I could no longer wait. I wanted her now.

"Get over here." I smiled.

She took her hands and grabbed her breasts as she walked sensually over to the bed. She climbed on it and crawled up to me with a sexy smile on her face.

"That's my girl," I said as I grinned at her.

She rubbed my hard cock through the fabric of the sheet. "Now, where was I earlier?"

I looked at her and took in a deep breath as she pulled the sheet back and wrapped her mouth around my cock. She had me coming in no time and she had me feeling oh-so-good. My hands fisted her hair while her head moved up and down. I always let her know when I was about to come so she could decide how she wanted to handle it. This time, she surprised me and didn't pull out. Jesus Christ, she was fucking hot, and I couldn't believe she had just swallowed. I reached over and pulled her up to me as my mouth crashed into hers.

"I love you so much," I said as I paused and broke the kiss.

"I love you too." She smiled.

"I want you to lie back and let me pleasure you, sweetheart. I want to make you come all over this bed."

And that was exactly what I did. I brought her to two orgasms before completely devouring her with my cock.

Chapter 6
Rory

After our morning run, Ian and I showered and he got ready to go to the office. We walked down to the kitchen, where Charles had omelets waiting for us. I said good morning to Charles as he poured coffee for Ian and me.

"Where are the blueberry muffins?" Ian asked.

"I'm sorry, Ian, but there are no muffins today."

The look on Ian's face was priceless. This was a change for him and it didn't look like he was going to handle it well.

"You're kidding, right? That's really not funny, Charles."

"I'm sorry, sir, but the blueberries I bought yesterday had a funny taste to them and I didn't feel comfortable using them."

I walked over to Ian and grabbed his hand. "Come on, love; it's okay. You're going to be okay. You don't need a blueberry muffin every morning."

"Sweetheart, yes I do."

Just as he was whining, Mandy walked in with a brown bag and set it on the counter. "I picked up some blueberry muffins on my way over. Charles said he couldn't make them today."

Ian smiled as he walked over and opened up the bag. The air instantly filled with the aroma of fresh blueberry muffins.

"Mandy, you're the best." He smiled at her. "Thank you."

"You're welcome, Mr. Braxton."

I gave Ian a look as I shook my head. "What?" he asked.

"You're spoiled."

"You still love me, though." He smiled as he bit into the muffin.

I rolled my eyes and took a sip of my coffee. I cut into the omelet that Charles made and Ian sat down next to me.

"I wish I could go with you to see Stephen, but I have so much work to do."

"That's okay." I smiled. "I can't wait to see him. It feels like it's been forever."

"Are you going to talk to him about your father?"

Speaking of fathers, Richard breezed into the kitchen.

"Welcome home, son," he said as he patted Ian on the back.

Richard glanced over at me. "Hey," he said.

I responded by holding up my coffee cup with a smile. Ian looked at me and mouthed, "Be nice."

It irked me to no end how he was always telling me to be nice, but I never heard him say that to Richard.

Richard poured a cup of coffee and sat down at the table with us. "How was Paris?" he asked Ian.

"Paris was great. Why don't you ask Rory about it?"

"No need, Richard. Paris was wonderful. Ian and I had the best time and now we're back home and everything is perfect."

He looked at me and tried to crack a smile, but he failed miserably. I leaned over and kissed Ian on the lips before I got up from my chair. “I’m going to go get ready and then I’m leaving.”

“Oh, no need to leave on my account,” Richard said.

“Trust me, Richard, I’m not. I’m going to visit my crazy brother in the looney bin.” I smiled.

“Rory,” Ian said.

“I love you, honey. I’ll see you later,” I said to him as I walked out of the kitchen.

That man was still an asshole. I had an ounce of hope that when Ian told him that he was in love with me, his attitude towards me would be different. I was wrong. He’d always be an asshole.

****

I walked through the double doors of Hudson Rock, signed in, and headed straight to the visitors’ room. As I walked in, Stephen looked up from his book and smiled. He stood up and I ran over to him, wrapping my arms tightly around his neck.

“I missed you so much, Stephen,” I said as a tear fell from my eye.

“Rory. You look beautiful. I missed you too.”

He led me outside to the courtyard, where we always had our visits. We took a seat at our usual little table under a tree.

“You look amazing, Rory. I can tell you’re really happy.”

"I am, Stephen. You look great. How is it going here?" I asked as I held his hands.

"Things are okay. Therapy is going good. My meds seem to be working, and I've made some new friends. The doctor said that maybe I could get out of here one day if I keep showing signs of improvement."

"Good. That's what I want to hear." I smiled.

"How are things with Ian?"

"Things are really good. In fact, things are perfect." I smiled as I gently squeezed his hands.

"He's a good guy, Rory. You're lucky to have him. He came here and talked to me before he left for Paris."

"I know. He told me all about your visit. There's something I've been wanting to tell you for a while, but then all that stuff happened with Ian and I left for Paris—"

"What is it, Rory?"

"Remember when I went back to Indiana to put closure on the past right before Thanksgiving?"

"Yeah, I remember."

"Aunt Nancy told me that our father was her boyfriend and that him and Mom slept together one night while they were both drunk."

"Are you serious?" he asked with concern.

"Apparently, he wasn't happy Mom was pregnant and took off, leaving all of us."

"What an asshole. How could he leave his own children?"

"How would you feel if I searched for him?" I asked.

I could tell that bothered him by the way he got up from his chair and pulled a leaf from the tree. "Why would you want to do that, Rory?"

"Because I want answers. I want that bastard to tell me why he abandoned our mother and us!"

Stephen turned around and looked at me. "You always wanted the answers to everything, Rory. I think some answers are better left not knowing."

I closed my eyes and slowly got up from the table. I walked over to Stephen and looped my arm around his, laying my head on his shoulder.

"He's our flesh and blood. He's a part of us and I want to know why he did what he did."

Stephen wrapped his arm around me and pulled me into him, kissing the top of my head. "If it means that much to you, then find him. But I don't want to know him and I don't want you bringing him around me. Okay?"

I nodded my head as I hugged him tightly. Visiting hours were over and it was time for me to leave.

"I wish we had more time," I said.

"Me too, sis."

I gave Stephen a kiss and waved goodbye. Even though I knew he was okay and doing well, my heart ached every time I had to say goodbye. Guilt settled in deep inside and I couldn't stop it. As I walked out the doors of Hudson Rock and over to the parking lot where I parked my car, I looked up and smiled at the handsome man in a dark gray suit who was leaning up against my car.

"What are you doing here?" I asked as I kissed Ian's lips.

"I came to drive you home. I had Joshua drop me off."

"How long have you been standing out here?" I asked as I hugged him.

"Just a few minutes. How is he?"

"He's doing well," I replied.

"What's wrong, sweetheart? You look sad."

I took in a deep breath as I looked into his eyes. "Guilt. Every time I leave here, I can't help but feel consumed with guilt."

Ian placed his hands on each side of my face before softly kissing me on the lips. "I understand the guilt, but I don't think Stephen would want you feeling that way. He knows you had no choice."

"I know and you're right. Let's go home." I smiled lightly before kissing him.

Chapter 7
Ian

It bothered me that Rory was struggling. Not only about her father, but about the guilt she felt with Stephen. I got up from my office chair and stood in the entrance of the living room, where Rory was playing the piano. Words couldn't describe the feeling that overtook me every time I heard her play. I walked to the kitchen and poured us each a glass of wine and then set her glass on top of the piano while I sat on the couch with mine. She stopped playing and looked at me.

"Keep playing, sweetheart. I just want to sit here and watch you."

She flashed me a smile and continued playing. As I stared at her, I remembered the first time I saw her, when Joshua opened the door to the limo and set her in my lap. The pain on her face and the fear in her eyes as she looked at me unleashed a part of me I didn't know I had. I instantly wanted to protect her. I'd never felt that way with anyone before and, to be honest, it frightened me. That was why I brought her to my house instead of the hospital. I feared that once they took her, I'd never see her again and I wouldn't be able to protect her. I stared at her intently as her fingers hit the keys, and I watched her lose herself in the music. She possessed such talent and it made her happy. This girl, the woman who made me fall in love with her, was now a vital part of my life.

She finished her song, grabbed her glass of wine, and walked over to the couch. As I held my hand out to her, she gracefully accepted it and sat down beside me. After taking a sip of my wine, I set my glass down and wrapped my arms around her.

"I'll never get tired of hearing you play the piano," I said as I kissed her cheek.

"I hope not, because I plan on playing for you forever." She smiled.

"You better keep that promise."

I gently sucked her bottom lip as she continued smiling at me. I wanted her. I took her hand and softly kissed each finger.

"I love these hands. They're very talented in more ways than one." I smiled.

She closed her eyes and I knew she was highly aroused. I slowly laid her back and hovered over her as my erection was jammed between her legs.

"I need to fuck you, Rory," I whispered.

"I want you to fuck me, Ian," she whispered back.

My hand traveled up her shirt and under her bra. Cupping her bare breast, I smashed my mouth into hers, passionately, letting her know how much I wanted her. She wrapped her leg around my waist and returned the kiss with her tongue exploring my mouth.

"Hey, welcome back, bro," Andrew said as he shut the door.

I broke our kiss and looked over the back of the couch. "Andrew, I didn't know you were stopping by."

"I called you a few times, but you didn't answer your phone. Hey, Rory."

I got up from the couch and gave him a light hug. "Good to see you, man."

Rory sat up on the couch and gave Andrew a small smile. I wasn't exactly sure what was going on with the two of them. Andrew had talked to me a couple of times and expressed his opinion that he didn't feel Rory was good for me. I basically told him to mind his own business and that he needed to get to know Rory better.

"I think I'll head upstairs and leave the two of you alone," she said.

"You can stay, sweetheart."

"No, it's okay. Have your bonding time." She smiled as she lightly kissed my lips.

As I watched her walk out of the room, Andrew poured himself a drink. "Glad you're back, Ian."

"It's good to be back," I said as I walked over to the bar and poured myself some bourbon.

"I take it things with you and Rory are good."

"Things with me and Rory are great. I've never been happier. You should try it." I smiled as I held up my glass.

"No thanks. Women just fuck you over at some point and end up ruining your life. I thought you and I were on the same page about that?"

"Yeah, well, maybe we've been wrong about that. Rory walked into my life and she changed everything for me."

Andrew rolled his eyes as he walked over to the bar and poured another drink. "Whatever, Ian. She has you so pussy whipped already that before you know it, you'll be a daddy and you'll be shoveling out millions in child support."

I sighed as I sat down on the couch and glared at him. "First off, don't tell me I'm pussy whipped because that's not the case. I love her and she loves me. Second of all, there will be no kids. You know that's the one thing I'm firm on. There's no way in hell I'd bring a kid into this world."

Andrew chuckled. "Really, Ian? You don't think that little woman of yours is going to secure her future and trap you?"

"No. Rory isn't like that. She doesn't care about my money. She cares about me and the person I am," I said angrily.

"All women are like that and you're stupid to think otherwise. That girl came from nothing. You took her in and showed her this life and now she won't leave it. Why do you think she came back with you? Any secure woman would stay away from a man like you after the things you said. But the minute you ran after her in Paris, she was seeing those dollar signs, a rich husband, and three little kids running around this mansion with a future so secure she'd never have to worry again."

I shifted myself and took in a sharp breath. Andrew and I had always been close and always had each other's backs, but I didn't like him talking about Rory like that.

"You're wrong, Andrew. Very, very wrong. Rory and I love each other deeply. I love her for who she is and she loves me for who I am."

"She's in love with what you represent, Ian. Fuck, get your head out of your ass."

I shot up from couch and pointed my finger at him. "That's enough, Andrew. I will not sit here and let you talk about Rory like that. You're the one who needs to get your head out of your ass and go find someone to love. It's time to grow up, man."

Andrew chuckled as he threw back his bourbon and slammed the glass down on the bar. "You're making a serious mistake, Ian. Don't come crying to me when she takes you for everything you're worth," he said as he shook his head and walked out the door.

I stood there, pissed, enraged, and a little surprised by his attitude. He needed to see and understand that Rory changed me, my life, and my views. She knocked sense into me when I thought I had everything in life figured out.

"Did Andrew leave?" I heard Rory ask behind me.

I turned around and smiled when I saw her standing there. "Yes, sweetheart, he left."

"He wasn't here very long."

"He just wanted to stop by and say hi. He had somewhere to be," I lied to her.

There was enough tension between the two of them already. I wasn't about to tell her his concerns and what he had said. As I walked towards her, she gently bit down on her bottom lip. She must have known what I wanted because she had that sexy smile on her face. I wanted Rory Sinclair every second of every day, and I couldn't get enough of her. She was my girl, my woman, and my partner. I was no longer Ian Braxton, and she was no longer Rory Sinclair. We were now Ian and Rory, a couple, a team, and we were ready to build a future together.

Chapter 8
Rory

As soon as Ian and I got back from our run, we sat down in the dining room while Mandy served us breakfast. I looked at Ian as he picked up the blueberry muffin from his plate.

"Rory, why are you staring at me like that?"

"Do you think—" I stopped what I was going to say and took in a breath.

"Do I think what, sweetheart?" Ian asked.

"Do you think you could go one day without eating a blueberry muffin?"

I sat there, face twisted, waiting for his response. He put down his muffin, took a sip of his coffee, and flashed me that irresistible smile.

"Rory, blueberry muffins are like sex to me. I can never have enough." He winked.

I sighed because I knew I would forever watch my boyfriend eat blueberry muffins.

"Does it bother you that I eat these every day?" he asked.

"No, not at all. It's just that after you eat something for so long, you eventually get sick of it."

"Hmm, well if I ever grow tired of blueberry muffins, I'll let you know."

Just as I smiled at him, we heard the front door open.

"Good morning, my darlings," Adalynn said as she breezed into the dining room.

"Good morning, Adalynn."

"Morning, Adalynn. Muffin?" Ian smiled.

"God, no. I don't know how you can eat those things every day."

As I couldn't help but laugh, Ian looked at me and raised his eyebrow. I flashed him a smile and turned my attention to Adalynn. "So what you brings you by?" I asked.

"I was hoping that you would come with me and look for wedding dresses today."

The smile on my face grew wide. "I would love to go."

"You couldn't just call her on the phone and ask her that?" Ian asked.

"Ian, darling. I just had to see your beautiful, angelic face this morning before I could start my day." She winked as she looked at me.

The banter between the two of them always made me smile.

"Well, then. You've seen it and now I must head to the office," he said as he leaned over and kissed me and then kissed Adalynn on the cheek.

"Bye, darling." I smiled.

Mandy walked over and set a cup of coffee in front of Adalynn. "I'm so excited to go look at wedding dresses. I've only ever seen them in magazines."

"Good, because I'm going to be trying on a lot of them until I find the perfect one." She smiled as she sipped her coffee.

I ran upstairs and grabbed my purse while Adalynn finished her breakfast. As I took my phone from the dresser, I noticed a text message from Ian.

"I miss you already. Have fun with Adalynn today."

I smiled as I replied back.

"I miss you more and my fun will begin tonight when you're home with me."

"Rory, you're killing me."

"Love you, Ian."

"Love you too, sweetheart."

I was beaming from ear to ear as I walked down the stairs and over to Adalynn.

"I must say, Rory, you look like the happiest person I know."

"That's because I am. I've never felt such happiness, Adalynn, and I owe it all to Ian."

****

I stood in front of the rack of dresses in awe over their beauty. Adalynn was on the other side of the shop, working with a bridal consultant and explaining to her the vision she had for her dress. As I was lost in the world of elegant white, a sales woman approached me and handed me a glass of champagne.

"Thank you." I smiled.

Adalynn walked over to where I was standing with a smile on her face. "Pretty fancy, huh?"

"Everything is so beautiful," I replied.

"Have a seat over there on the couch. I'm going to try on the few dresses I picked out and I want your honest opinion."

"Of course I'll give you my honest opinion, Adalynn."

She walked into the oversized dressing room as I took my champagne and sat down on the couch. I pulled my phone from my pocket and sent Ian a text.

"I hope you're having a great day!"

"I am now."

I smiled.

"I'm off to a meeting, sweetheart. I'll talk to you later. Love you to pieces."

"Love you."

Adalynn cleared her throat to get my attention, and when I looked up, tears sprang to my eyes when I saw the beautiful bride standing before me.

"Adalynn, it's beautiful. You look so amazing."

"Nah, I don't like it," she said as she looked in the mirror.

"What! How can you not love it?"

"It's too much dress. I think I'm going to stick with the mermaid style. All this fluff isn't me."

I loved the fluff. I could see myself drowning in fluff and loving it every minute of it. Adalynn looked at me and smiled. "I want you to try this on."

"What? Are you crazy? I'm not trying on that dress!" I exclaimed.

She walked towards me with a wide smile on her face. "Yes, you are. You've never tried on a wedding dress and it's so much fun. Come on!" she said as she held out her hand.

I sighed as I got up. I secretly wanted to try on the dress. I followed her into the dressing room, where she changed out of the dress and handed it to the sales woman. She took me in the room next to Adalynn's and helped me into the wedding gown. I stepped outside the dressing room and stood in front of the large three-way mirror. Adalynn came out in a stunning Vera Wang, strapless, mermaid-style dress that was simply made for her.

"Rory, look at you. You look gorgeous. How do you feel?" she asked.

"Like a princess." I smiled. "I didn't realize how heavy wedding dresses are." I laughed.

"That they are. Well, what do you think?" Adalynn asked as she spun around.

"It's gorgeous and it's you. It's perfect."

She walked over to where the veils sat on a beautifully etched glass shelf. She picked one up that was a crown and set it on top of my head.

"There. Now you're complete." She smiled.

I gulped as I stood there, staring at myself in a beautiful wedding dress and veil. I remembered when I was a child, I would sit and look at magazines with my mom and sometimes there would be pictures of brides. She would look at me and say that one day that would be me and she couldn't wait to see me as a bride. My eyes started to fill with tears and I couldn't let Adalynn see me so emotional, so I went back into the dressing room to change out of the dress and back into my clothes.

"Are you okay, Rory?" she asked.

"Yeah, I'm fine. It's just overwhelming, you know. Getting married is something that I've always dreamed of and now that I've found the love of my life, he wants nothing to do with marriage."

"That was the old Ian, sweetie. I'm sure he's had a change of heart since he thought he lost you. I know it's way too soon, but has he mentioned marriage at all?"

"No." I softly smiled as I looked down. "We don't talk about it at all. We're just enjoying each other right now."

"And that's how it should be. You two have your whole lives ahead of you." She winked. "Now, I think I'm going to buy this dress."

****

"There you are," Ian said as we walked through the door.

"Hey, baby." I smiled as he kissed me hello.

"It's about time. I thought maybe you went and kidnapped my girl, Adalynn."

Adalynn looked at him and rolled her eyes. "Keep calm, Ian. You know us girls when we shop."

"Did you buy anything, sweetheart?" he asked.

"No, she didn't, but she tried on the most beautiful wedding dress. Oh, Ian, you should've seen her."

When Ian looked at me, I could tell he wasn't very pleased.

"It was nothing. I was bored," I said as I put my hand on his chest.

Ian gave me a small smile and walked over to the bar and poured himself a drink. "Adalynn? Rory?" he asked.

"No, thank you, darling. I have to get home. Daniel and I have invitations to go through. I'll call you later, Rory," she said as she leaned in and kissed my cheek. "Ta-ta, Ian."

"I'm sure I'll be seeing you at breakfast tomorrow," he said.

Adalynn turned around and looked at him before heading out the door. "Thank you for the invite, Ian. I'll be sure to stop by before I head to *Prim*." She smiled.

As soon as she left, I walked over to the bar and asked Ian to pour me a glass of wine. "We had fun today and Adalynn found the perfect dress."

"That's good," he said as he took a sip of his bourbon.

"Is something wrong, Ian?"

I could tell by his demeanor and the way he said "that's good" that something wasn't right with him. "Are you upset that I tried on a wedding dress?" I bravely asked.

"You really shouldn't be doing things like that. I don't want you to get your hopes up. You know where I stand on marriage, Rory."

And just like that, he brought me down from my high. A few words spoken from his mouth changed my entire mood. I could sense an argument brewing if I kept pressing it, so I simply told Ian what he wanted to hear.

"I know, my love. Don't worry. It was only for fun, nothing else." I smiled as I kissed him softly on the lips.

"Well, I'm glad you had fun." He pulled me into an embrace and kissed the top of my head.

I stood there, wrapped in his arms while a part of my mind was thinking about that wedding dress and the other part was thinking about how Ian wanted nothing to do with marriage.

Chapter 9
Ian

I was wrapped up in her. My arms were wrapped around her tightly and our legs were tangled around each other. She was sleeping soundly. I couldn't. I was up all night, thinking about Adalynn's wedding and what kind of effect it was going to have on Rory. I didn't want her getting any ideas and I didn't want it to tear us apart. She said she understood, but I did think she was lying. A girl like Rory deserved everything. I could give her anything she wanted. I could love her till death do us part. I could give her all of me. I just couldn't give her marriage.

I finally fell asleep, only to be woken up by the alarm clock. I opened my eyes and Rory wasn't in bed. She was always in bed. I turned off the alarm and got up to put on my pajama bottoms. I checked the bathroom first and she wasn't there. I walked down to the kitchen and smiled when I saw her bending over, taking something out of the oven.

"What are you doing, sweetheart?"

"I hope I didn't wake you," she said as she walked over and kissed me.

"No, the alarm did."

"Well, since today is Charles's day off, I thought it would be nice to make you some blueberry muffins."

I stood there. I couldn't believe she got up that early and made me muffins. My heart started to ache a little because this woman amazed me, yet again.

"Rory," I whispered as I pulled her into an embrace. "I can't believe you did this."

"Why, silly? I love you and I know how much you love fresh blueberry muffins in the morning." She smiled.

"You're amazing. I love you."

"I love you too. Now go sit down and I'll bring your coffee and muffin."

"No," I said as I led her to the chair and made her sit down. "You sit down and let me serve you."

I poured us each a cup of coffee and set two muffins on a plate and took it over to the table. The smile never left her face as she watched me the whole time.

"No run today?" she asked.

"I thought maybe we could use the gym downstairs today. It looks like it's going to rain," I spoke as I looked out the window.

"Yeah, it does look like rain."

I took a bite of the blueberry muffin and almost choked. It was the worst blueberry muffin I ever had. I tried so hard not to show it, but it was too late.

"What's wrong? You don't like it?"

I didn't know how to tell her it was awful. "It just seems different from how Charles makes them. Did you forget an ingredient? Maybe?"

A look of disappointment swept across her face and I felt like the biggest asshole around.

"I don't think I forgot an ingredient. Damn it!" she said as she got up from the table.

"Sweetheart, it's fine. Please don't worry about it."

She walked over and picked up the recipe card from the counter. "OH SHIT! FUCK! I forgot to put in the sugar." She pouted.

"Aw, baby, it's okay," I said as I got up and wrapped my arms around her. "You tried and that's all that matters."

"You don't understand. I wanted to do something special for you and, as usual, I fucked it all up. How could I forget the sugar?"

I looked over on the other side of the counter, where a measuring cup sat with sugar in it. "Is that it over there?"

"Ugh."

"Sweetheart, it's okay. It can happen to anyone. So what, you forgot to add the sugar. You had it measured out, which means you thought of it. It's the thought and I love your thoughts." I smiled as I brushed my thumb over her soft lips before gently kissing them.

I picked up Rory and set her on the counter. "I'm changing up our exercise routine today."

"Why? What are we doing?" she asked.

"First, I'm going to take you upstairs and fuck you fast and hard. Then, when I'm finished, you're going to get on top and fuck me fast and hard. It's going to be an awesome workout, sweetheart. I promise." I winked.

Rory smiled as she wrapped her legs tightly around my waist and her arms around my neck. "Let's go start that workout, Mr. Braxton."

The one thing I loved about my girl was that she was so easy to please. I picked her up from the counter, took her upstairs, and we both had one hell of a workout.

****

"Mr. Braxton, Mr. Black is on line two for you."

"Thank you, Jan. I'll take it."

"Connor. How are you, friend?" I answered.

"Good, Ian. How are you?"

"Things are great."

"How's Rory doing?" Connor asked.

"Rory's good. Thanks for asking. What can I do for you?"

"I ran across a piece a property here in New York City and I was hoping that you'd come out and take a look at it for me."

"Sure. When do you want me to come out there?"

"How about next week? And bring Rory with you. Ellery's been asking about her and wants to see her."

"I sure will. She'd love to see the two of you again. Rory visits her brother on Thursdays, but we can fly out after."

"Sounds good. We'll plan to meet Friday morning. Don't make plans for Friday night. Ellery and I are taking the two of you out on the town."

"Sounds good, Connor. We'll see you next week. Rory will be thrilled."

"Talk to you soon, Ian."

I hung up the phone and sat back in my chair. Rory was going to be thrilled that she was going to be able to see Ellery again. I thought about texting her or even calling her, but I decided to wait and tell her the news in person.

"Jan, do me a favor and call the florist. I want two dozen red roses sent to Rory Sinclair at my home address."

"I'll do it now, Mr. Braxton," she replied.

As I was looking over some legal papers, I heard the office door open. I looked up as Andrew walked in.

"Hey, bro," he said with smile on his face.

"Andrew," I replied and continued looking over the papers.

"Let's go hit the club tonight."

"Sorry, but I'm spending the evening with Rory."

"Shit, Ian. What's wrong, won't the little woman let you off the leash for one night?"

"That's enough, Drew."

"Whatever, man," he sighed.

I looked at him and saw the disappointment in his face. Andrew didn't have too many friends, because honestly, he was an ass. "Why don't we ask Rory, Adalynn, and Daniel to come with us and we can all go together?"

"Seriously, Ian? Just tell the bitch you're going out for the night. You don't owe her any explanations."

The one thing you didn't do was call my girl a bitch. I could feel the anger towards him building up inside. I stood up and slammed my hands against the desk.

"Don't you ever call Rory a bitch or any other demeaning name again! Do you understand me, friend?"

"Chill out, Ian. Fuck, man," he said as he got up from his chair. "All I wanted was to spend a little time with my best friend. Is that so wrong?" he said as he shook his head and walked out of my office.

I sat back in my chair and threw a pen across my desk. As long as he had a problem with Rory, he was going to have a problem with me. Maybe Adalynn could talk to him. I finished up what I had to do and walked out of my office.

"I'm out of here for the night, Jan. I'll see you in the morning."

"Good night, Mr. Braxton."

Andrew really had me fired up and he pissed me off. I needed to calm down. When I climbed into the back of the limo, I poured a glass of bourbon.

"Bad day, Ian?" Joshua asked.

"You could say that," I said as I threw back the bourbon.

I pulled my phone from my pocket and stared at our picture. When we were in Paris, we had a nice young woman take a picture of the two of us in front of the Eiffel Tower. Rory and I had the biggest smiles on our faces. I took pride in the fact that

I was the one responsible for making her smile like that. What Andrew didn't understand was that I wanted to spend every waking minute with Rory. I knew he was having a hard time, because growing up, we always talked poorly of relationships and women. But the one thing I realized was things change, and people can change. If only Andrew could find someone as special as Rory.

I could hear the sweet melody of piano music playing as I approached the house. A smile graced my face because, somehow, Rory erased any kind of bad day I had. As I opened the door, walked into the living room, and set my briefcase down, Rory stopped playing and walked over to me. I noticed the vase of red roses were sitting on top of the piano.

"Thank you so much for the beautiful roses, Ian. I was so surprised when they were delivered." She smiled as she wrapped her arms around me and planted a kiss on my lips.

"You're welcome. I'm glad you like them," I replied as I hugged her tightly.

"Have you been drinking?"

She could smell the bourbon on my breath. "I just had a drink on the way home, that's all."

"Bad day?"

"Kind of. I just had to deal with some real assholes today."

She tightened her arms around me and buried her face in my neck. "I'm sorry, honey."

"It's nothing for you to worry about, sweetheart. Let's go change and go to dinner. I want to hear about your day."

"I was thinking maybe we could order in some Thai food and eat on the patio. It's such a beautiful night out." She smiled.

"That's an excellent idea. I knew there was a reason I loved you so much." I smiled back as I kissed the tip of her nose.

We placed our order and, as we waited for it to be delivered, Rory grabbed two wine glasses from the cupboard and took them outside. I pulled a bottle of Pinot from the wine cellar, opened it, and took it outside, pouring some into each of our glasses. After our food arrived and we were sitting down and eating dinner, I decided it was the perfect time to tell Rory about our little trip to New York next week.

"We're going on a trip next week," I said as I ate my rice.

"We are? Where are we going?"

I looked at her and smiled. "New York. Connor called me today and needs me to fly out there to look at a piece of property for him. I thought we'd turn it into a mini vacation since you've never been there."

Her face lit up and her happy eyes did a little dance. "Ian, I'm so excited. I can't wait to see Connor, Ellery, and Julia again. Plus, I've always wanted to visit New York."

"I knew you'd be excited, sweetheart."

"When are we going?"

"Thursday, after your visit with Stephen. I'll go to the office in the morning and I'll have Joshua drive you to Hudson Rock. We'll pick you up after and head to the airport."

"How long are we staying in New York?" she asked with excitement.

"We'll fly back Sunday night. Sound good?"

"It sounds great," she replied as she reached over and took hold of my hand, which was on the table.

It felt great to see Rory so happy. She deserved to be happy and there was nothing I wanted more. The sun had set and it was getting dark. Rory excused herself and told me she'd be right back. I poured another glass of wine and stared at the ocean. As I was sipping it, Rory walked out onto the patio in a short, white satin robe. She was sexy and hot as hell.

"Are you ready for bed already?" I smiled.

"On the contrary, Mr. Braxton." She smiled back.

As she walked over to the pool, she had her back turned to me, and she slowly let the satin robe drop to the cement. She was completely naked and, instantly, I became hard. She climbed down the steps into the pool and went all the way under the water. I leaned back in my chair and watched her as she swam to the edge and looked at me. She held up her finger and motioned for me to come over to her. I got up from my chair, fully erect, and stripped out of my clothes, joining her in the pool as we made love under the moonlight.

Chapter 10
Rory

Ian and I were up in the bedroom, packing for New York, when Mandy knocked on the door.

"Mr. Braxton, your father is here."

I rolled my eyes. "Great." I sighed.

Ian chuckled as he kissed my head. "Be nice, Rory."

"I'm always nice. I'm going to finish packing and I'll be down after."

"Okay, sweetheart," he said as he walked out of the room.

I'd only seen Richard a couple of times since we'd been back from Paris and, each time, he wasn't any nicer to me. I wished he wasn't such an asshole and that we could have some kind of friendship, for Ian's sake. I finished packing and headed downstairs. Ian and Richard were sitting on the couch, having a drink and laughing.

"Seems like you two are having some fun." I smiled as I walked into the room.

"Rory," Richard said as he nodded his head.

"Richard," I replied.

"Hi, sweetheart." Ian smiled as he got up from the couch. "I'll go grab those papers for you, Dad."

Ian walked out of the room and left me alone with Richard. Talk about an awkward moment. But I was pleasantly surprised when he spoke to me.

"How are you doing, Rory?"

"I'm doing great, Richard. How are you?"

When he got up from the couch, he walked over to the bar and poured himself another drink. "I'm fine, and I owe you an apology for the things I've said to you in the past."

I almost needed to sit down. I couldn't believe these words were coming out of his mouth. Suddenly, I became frightened. Was this another one of his tricks? Was there some ulterior motive behind his apology?

"Thank you, Richard."

Just as I was about to say something else, Ian walked back into the room and handed his father some papers.

"Well, I'll let the two of you get ready for your trip and I'll see you when you get back."

"You don't have to leave, Richard," I blurted out.

Ian gave me a strange look.

"Thanks, Rory, but I have some things of my own I need to do. Have a safe trip and I'm sorry again, Ian, that I'm already using the plane."

Ian and his father hugged lightly. "It's okay, Dad. I'm looking into buying my own company plane anyway."

"Do me a favor and hold off on that purchase," Richard said.

"Why?" Ian asked in confusion.

"Because I may be buying a new one and you can have mine. I won't even charge you." He winked.

Something odd was going on. Why was Richard being so nice all of a sudden? It was like he became a new man overnight. Richard gave me a small wave and Ian walked him to the door.

"What's going on with him?" I asked.

"Nothing. Why?"

"Because he was being nice. He apologized to me for the things he said in the past."

Ian walked over to me and picked me up, carrying me up the stairs. "He can be a nice guy and that makes me happy that he apologized to you."

I kissed him on the cheek. "I'm so happy we leave for New York tomorrow. I can't wait to see baby Julia. She's so adorable."

"Yeah, she's a pretty cute kid," Ian mumbled.

****

I was restless. I could feel it as I was trying to wake from my nightmare.

"Rory, sweetheart, wake up. You're having a bad dream," I heard Ian say as his hands gripped my shoulders.

My eyes flew open as I sat up and tried to catch my breath. Ian reached over and turned on the lamp and then turned to me with concern.

"Are you okay?" he asked as he stroked my hair.

"I'm fine. It was only a dream," I said with bated breath.

"Your dad?" Ian asked.

"Yeah. I'm going to go downstairs and get bottle of water," I said as I turned to Ian and placed my hand on his cheek.

"Let me go for you."

"No. I'm going myself," I snapped. "I'm sorry, baby. I just need some fresh air. I'm sweating."

"Okay. Go do what you need to do, sweetheart."

I softly kissed him on the lips and got out of bed. The dreams of Jimmy O'Rourke stayed with me even after I'd woken up. I went downstairs and grabbed a bottle of water from the fridge. I looked over at the bottle of wine sitting on the counter that Ian and I shared earlier and put the water back. I grabbed a new glass from the cupboard and filled it with alcohol. I unlocked the patio door and stepped outside. The wind was light and the air was cool, but I didn't care. It felt good to breathe fresh air. I headed down towards the sand and stood there, staring at the water.

"You're worrying me," Ian's voice said from behind.

I turned around and smiled at him. He walked up behind me, wrapped his arms around my waist, and rested his chin on my shoulder.

"Hmm, is that wine?"

"Yes."

"I thought you were going for water."

"I was. Then I saw this and it sounded better. Would you like a sip?"

"No thanks, sweetheart. Tell me what you want to do about your dad. You can't keep going on like this."

"Can you find him?" I asked.

"Yes, I can."

"Then do it. I need to put Jimmy O'Rourke to rest."

Ian picked me up in his arms and carried me back to the house and up to our bedroom. He laid me down on the bed and covered me with the sheet. As he climbed in next to me, he wrapped his arms around me.

"As soon as we get back from New York, I'll look for your father. Until then, I don't want you give him another thought. Now, go to sleep."

"Thank you. I love you, Ian. I love you so damn much."

"I love you so fucking much, sweetheart. Good night."

****

As I was talking to Stephen in the courtyard, he looked over my shoulder and a smile spread across his face. I looked at him and then behind me and saw Ian standing by the door. As soon as I gave him a smile, he walked over to where Stephen and I were sitting, gave me a kiss, and then shook Stephen's hand.

"Ian, how are you, man?"

"I'm good, Stephen. How are you?"

"I'm okay. No complaints," he replied.

"Honey, what are you doing here?" I asked.

Ian sat down next to me. "I finished up early and I thought I'd stop by and see how Stephen's doing before we leave for New York."

"Thank you, Ian." Stephen smiled. "Look at the two of you. I'd be lying if I said I wasn't a little jealous."

"Stephen," I said as I looked sadly at him.

"Rory, don't give me that look. You deserve it. You took care of me your whole life and now it's time for someone to take care of you. You're taking care of my sister, right, Ian?"

Ian looked at me and smiled. "I think I'm taking very good care of her."

"You are taking very good care of me." I smiled back as I laid my head on his shoulder.

"That's all that matters to me," Stephen said.

The announcement that visiting hours were over came across the speakers. We all stood up and Ian and I hugged Stephen goodbye.

"Have fun in New York, sis."

"Take care, Stephen. I'll see you next week."

Ian took my hand and we walked out of Hudson Rock and straight to the limo where Joshua was waiting to take us to the airport. After we climbed in, Ian put his arm around me and pulled me into him.

"Are you all right?" he asked.

"I'm fine. Now let's go to New York City!" I said excitedly.

Ian chuckled as he tightened his grip around me.

****

Ian unlocked the door to our room and when I walked inside, I gasped. As I stood there, I looked around the suite.

"Rory, are you okay?" he asked with concern.

"This room, it's—"

"Welcome to The Trump, sweetheart." He smiled.

It was the most amazing hotel room I'd ever been in. Not that I'd been in many. Ian took our bags into the bedroom and I followed behind, throwing myself on the luxurious king-sized bed. Ian smiled as he sat down next to me and stroked my hair.

"I'm happy you like the room."

"I love the room. Would it be wrong if I never wanted to leave?"

"No, but this is New York City, sweetheart. We just can't sit in the hotel room the whole time we're here." Ian chuckled. "This is what we're going to do. We're going to make love first and then we're going to change and get ready for dinner. I want you to experience Jean Georges. It's one of the restaurants here in the hotel and it's one of my favorites." He smiled as he leaned over and his lips brushed against mine.

I wrapped my arms around his neck and pulled him on top of me. "I love that idea."

"I knew you would," he said as he began unbuttoning my top.

After a session of crazy sex that pretty much destroyed the bed, Ian and I showered and got ready to go down to Jean Georges. As I was putting the finishing touches on my makeup, I heard Ian on the phone.

"Can you send up the maid to fix our bed? We'll be leaving the room in about ten minutes. Thank you."

"Ian!"

"What?" he asked.

"How embarrassing!"

"What's embarrassing?"

"You having the maid come up here and fix the bed. She's going to know what we did and how crazy it was. Look at it," I said as I pointed to the bed.

Ian laughed and he wouldn't stop. "Rory, this is a hotel. People fuck in hotels. Half the time, that's why they come here. The staff is used to it and won't give it a second thought."

"Well, I don't want to be here when she gets here."

Ian walked over to me and wrapped his arms around me. "You're too cute and you make me laugh. I love you, sweetheart."

"I love you too," I said as I kissed him and then walked over to the bed.

"What are you doing?" he asked as I picked up the sheet from the floor.

"I'm trying to make the bed more decent."

"Rory, stop." He chuckled as he grabbed my hand.

Suddenly, there was a knock at the door. "Maid service."

"What the fuck! You told them ten minutes, Ian."

Ian laughed and walked over to the door and opened it. The maid walked in and straight to the bedroom where I was standing. I was so humiliated at what she must've thought, I looked at her and said, "I'm sorry, so sorry."

Ian sighed, grabbed my hand, and led me out of the hotel room. We walked down to the restaurant and were promptly seated. It was a beautiful restaurant and I was happy Ian wanted to eat here. As we were looking over the menu, a beautiful woman walked over to our table.

"Ian Braxton, how wonderful to see you." She smiled.

Ian looked up at her and then at me. I could tell he was nervous. "Michelle, nice to see you," he said as he got up and lightly kissed her cheek. "I want you to meet my girlfriend, Rory."

She looked at me, lightly shook my hand, and then turned her attention to Ian. "Girlfriend, eh? Ian Braxton doesn't do girlfriends. At least that's what you told me," she said.

"Things change, Michelle," Ian said calmly.

"Things may, but people don't." She smiled as she looked at me. "Nice seeing you again, Ian," she said as she walked away.

Suddenly, I was very uncomfortable. The waiter brought my cosmopolitan and I grabbed it from his hand before he had a chance to set it down on the table. I did more than take a sip.

"Rory, I can tell you're pissed."

"No. What gives you that idea?" I asked sarcastically. "One of your many women, I assume."

Ian rolled his eyes and leaned back in his chair. "Yes, I won't lie to you."

I nodded my head as I threw back my cosmo. "Okay. I guess it's something I have to learn to deal with around the world."

"Rory, that's not fair."

"No, what's not fair is me having to be subjected to that every time we go out!" I snapped.

"It's not like I hid who I was before I met you, so you can't hold it against me."

In a way, he was right, but now that he was mine to keep, seeing the other women and knowing he fucked them in ways he probably would never fuck me burned the blood that ran through my veins. We ate our dinner in silence. It wasn't until after the waiter gave Ian the bill that he decided to say something.

"You need to stop behaving like this."

I took in a deep breath and looked at him. "I'm hurt and upset, Ian. I'm sorry if you think I'm behaving like a child. See, the thing is, you don't ever have to worry about running into someone like that from my past because there's only you."

"Rory."

I threw my napkin on the table, got up, and walked out of the restaurant. I walked out of the hotel and onto the busy streets of New York City. I didn't care where I was going, I just needed some fresh air. Was I being ridiculous? I think so. This was all new to me. As I was walking, I felt someone grab my arm.

"You will never walk away from me. Do you understand?"

I stopped dead in my tracks and the people that were behind us ran right into us. I turned around and apologized to them.

"You will let go of my arm now!" I said through gritted teeth. "Or I will scream and make a scene."

"Right. That I know you will do." Ian sighed as he let go of my arm. "Talk to me, sweetheart."

Chapter 11
Ian

Rory walked across the street and over to Central Park. I followed behind because I knew she needed space. This was killing me because she was upset. She sat down on a bench in front of the fountain and I sat down next to her. We both just stared at the fountain and didn't say a word. I had asked her to talk to me, and I knew she would when she was ready.

"I'm sorry," she finally spoke. "It's just hard when you're so in love with someone and you feel threatened by another woman."

"Sweetheart," I whispered as I took hold of her hand. "Why do you feel threatened?"

"Because, there's always going to be someone prettier than me and more entertaining."

My heart ached when she said that. Insecurity was still deep inside her and I hated that she felt that way.

"Sometimes, I still can't believe that you picked me over all those millions of women you've dated and slept with."

"Rory, first of all, it wasn't a million, so please get that number out of your head. Second of all, I think you are the most beautiful woman on the face of this earth."

She turned her head and looked at me as I placed my hand on her cheek. "I love you, and I'm sorry that you have to deal with those other women. Unfortunately, I had to go through a lot of them before I found my soul mate." I smiled. "You're perfect and you're you. You'll always be beautiful and entertaining to me. You keep me on my toes and you keep my soul alive. You've changed me, and I thank you for that."

A tear fell down her cheek and I gently wiped it away with my thumb. "I love you too, Ian, and it scares me to think I might lose you someday."

"I don't ever want you to be scared. You're never going to lose me."

I pulled her into me and held her tight. I needed her to feel safe and secure. "All better?" I asked.

She looked up at me and smiled. "Yeah, all better."

"Good. Now let's go back to the hotel so I can make love to you for the next few hours."

"Next few hours?" She laughed. "Are you taking Viagra?"

"I don't need Viagra when I'm with you, sweetheart. Just your look keeps me hard for hours."

****

I rolled over and the Rory's side of the bed was empty. I opened my eyes and looked around the room. As I glanced at the clock, I noticed it was six a.m. and the sun was starting to rise. I got out of bed, put on my pajama bottoms, and walked into the living area of the suite. That was where I saw Rory standing and looking out the window. I walked up behind her, wrapped my arms around her, and softly kissed her neck.

"What are you doing out here?"

"Just looking out into the city. It's so amazing here, Ian. Just to be able to look at all the cars, the people on the streets, the tall buildings; it's just incredible."

"Well, I'm glad you're enjoying the city so far, sweetheart," I said as I kissed her cheek. "Are you hungry?"

"A little."

"Why don't you go take a shower and I'll order us room service? Connor is sending his driver, Denny, to pick us up at nine-thirty."

Rory turned around and smiled at me. "I can't wait to see Ellery and Julia."

"I know, sweetheart."

She gave me a kiss and then went in the bathroom to take a shower. I called our breakfast order in and then checked my voicemail messages from last night.

"Hey, Ian, I wanted you to know that we found Rory's father. Mr. Jimmy O'Rourke is living in Los Angeles. He owns the Piano Bar in Hollywood. Good luck."

I sighed as I sat there, debating when I was going to tell Rory. I told her that I would look for him when we got back from New York. I honestly didn't think he'd be that easy to find. God, wait until Rory finds out that her father lived less than an hour away from us. I didn't want to ruin our trip for her, so I'd tell her as soon as we got back home. I looked up and saw that she was standing in the doorway, looking at me.

"You looked like you were in deep thought," she said.

I held out my arms to her, motioning for her to come sit on my lap. She smiled as she walked over to me and sat down.

"I was just thinking about some business stuff." I smiled as I kissed her head.

"Is everything okay?" she asked.

"Everything is fine, sweetheart. It's just business; nothing for you to worry about."

Just as I leaned in to kiss her beautiful lips, there was a knock at the door.

"Room service."

Rory got up and I walked over to the door. I wasn't wearing anything but my pajama bottoms and the young girl that delivered our food gasped when I opened it. I held the door open as she pushed in the cart.

"Here's your breakfast, Mr. and Mrs. Braxton."

Instantly, I spoke up. "We're not married."

Rory shot me a look and the girl looked at Rory.

"Oh, I'm sorry. I didn't—"

"Don't worry about it," I said as I reached in my wallet and pulled out some money for a tip.

She quietly left the room, shutting the door behind her.

"Wow, Ian," Rory said.

"Wow what, sweetheart?"

"That was rude."

"Well, we're not married and I don't want her thinking we are."

"Of course not, because that would tarnish your playboy reputation," she said with a big attitude.

"Rory. Stop it and come eat your breakfast." I sighed. "I'm not going to argue with you over something stupid like that."

"It's just the way you said it, Ian. You said it with an authoritative tone. Big deal if she thought we were married. You didn't have to be so rude about it. Better yet, maybe I should get my own room so people won't make that mistake again and maybe when we go out, I can walk a few feet behind you so people won't get the wrong idea."

I rolled my eyes at her and took in a deep breath. "Sweetheart."

"No! This is not okay," she said as she grabbed her tray and stomped off into the bedroom, slamming the door behind her.

Great, now she was eating alone in the bedroom. I was starting to believe that Adalynn's wedding was getting to her. I walked over to the bedroom and opened the door. She was sitting on the bed with her knees up. I stood in the doorway and stared at her, since she wouldn't look up at me.

"Can I come in?" I asked.

"No. I just want to be alone right now."

I knew I needed to apologize to her, but I was afraid it would come out wrong. "Rory, please. I'm coming in, and I don't want you throwing something at me."

I saw a small smile grace her face. I walked over and sat down on the bed. "There's a little bit of a smile. I'm sorry. I'm really sorry for what I said and how I said it. I'll be honest with you, Rory, I didn't realize it came out that way. Please forgive me, sweetheart."

She looked up at me with her sad eyes and nodded her head. I let out a deep breath and wrapped my arms around her. "For the record, you're not staying in another room and you're not walking behind me. Now let's eat breakfast and then head to Connor's and Ellery's place."

****

"Ellery, you're looking as beautiful as ever." I smiled as I kissed her cheek.

"Ian, good to see you, buddy," Connor said as we shook hands.

Ellery grabbed Rory and dragged her upstairs. Connor grabbed his coat and we climbed into the limo to go look at the property he was interested in. Once we arrived, I looked at the empty field.

"This is it?" I asked.

"Yep, this is it. What do you think?"

"I think it's a field, Connor." I chuckled.

"Good eye." He winked. "Look beyond the field, Ian. I want to build one of the largest art galleries in New York, and this is the place to do it."

I stood there with my hands in my pockets, nodding my head. "For Ellery?"

Connor looked over at me and smiled. "Yeah, for Ellery."

I started walking forward towards the field. "You two are a perfect couple. You give me hope," I said.

"Hope is what Rory should be giving you, Ian. She's an amazing woman."

"Yes. She is an amazing woman."

Connor walked up and placed his hand on my shoulder. "Relationships aren't easy. I almost lost Ellery a few times over things I never should have done. She's my first and last love. Me and you aren't that different, Ian. From what I can see, she's completely changed you as Ellery did me."

I laughed softly. "She's changed my views on a lot of things and she's changed my life. I don't know what I would've done if she hadn't come back with me from Paris."

Connor sighed. "Yep, I know what you mean. I don't know what I would've done if Ellery hadn't come back with me from California."

"I guess we're lucky." I smiled.

"We sure are. Now, what do you think about the property?"

"It's a field, Connor. It's really not property yet. But I'll turn it into a property and you can go and build Ellery the biggest art gallery in New York." I smiled.

"Thank you, friend," he said as he patted me on the back.

Chapter 12
Rory

"Would you like to feed her?" Ellery asked.

"Really? I would love to feed her."

Ellery handed the baby to me and I laid her in my arms and put the bottle in her mouth. She grabbed hold of my finger and stared up at me with her beautiful blue eyes.

"She's so beautiful, Ellery. You and Connor make amazing babies." I smiled.

"You and Ian will make beautiful babies too. You're drop dead gorgeous, and Ian, well, look at him."

"Thank you, but, I don't think Ian ever wants children. Hell, he gets pissed off when you *mention* the word marriage."

Ellery cocked her head and looked at me. "Why?"

"I don't know. He's totally anti-marriage. He wants nothing to do with it and we got into an argument this morning in the hotel room because the girl that brought up our breakfast thought we were married and Ian snapped at her. He was totally out of line and he saw nothing wrong with it."

"Are you two okay now?" she asked.

"Yeah. He apologized after I yelled at him and locked myself in the bedroom."

Ellery laughed. "Sounds like something I would do."

I looked down at Julia as she was drinking her bottle. It felt so good to hold her and so natural. "Ian still has a lot of issues, and a lot of them have to do with his mom. He feels betrayed and I think she just really left her mark as far as he's concerned with relationships."

"Help him work it out. Connor was a hot mess before I stepped into his life. You need to peel away the layers until you find the man Ian truly is."

I smiled at Ellery. "Thank you."

The elevator doors opened and Ian and Connor walked into the living room. Ian stopped and looked at me as I was holding Julia. Connor and Ellery went upstairs for a moment to freshen up before we headed out. Julia finished her bottle and I sat her up to burp her.

"Aren't you going to say hi to Julia, Ian?"

He gave me a small smile and sat down next to me. He looked at Julia and smiled.

"Hey, Julia."

She screeched and laughed at the same time. "Do you want to hold her?" I asked.

"No. You keep holding her. She's happy with you."

"Here, just take her," I said as I started to hand Julia to him.

"No, Rory. I don't want to hold her. I'm not a fan of children."

His words startled me. I sort of knew that already, but to hear him say it made it very real. "How can you not like children?" I asked.

"I don't want to discuss this now, sweetheart."

I sat there and stared at him in disbelief.

"Why are you looking at me like that?" he asked.

I couldn't say a word to him. His issues were on a deep, unreachable level. I looked down at Julia, because at that moment, I couldn't look at the man I deeply loved.

"Rory, please. We're going to have a great night with Connor and Ellery. Please, don't be upset with me right now. I promise, you can punish me later." He smiled as he reached over and lifted my chin with his finger.

He was right; we were going to have a great night with great friends and I didn't want anything to ruin it. His issues were something that I was going to have to forget about for tonight and deal with later. I gave him a small smile as the elevator doors opened and Mason stepped out.

"There's my princess. Come to Uncle Mason, sweetie." He smiled as he walked over to me. "Hi, Rory, Ian. It's good to see you."

"Hi, Mason. It's good to see you too." I smiled as I stood up and handed Julia over to him.

Ian said hello and he got up and lightly shook Mason's hand. Connor and Ellery walked back into the room and asked if we were ready to leave. I kissed Julia's head and stepped onto the elevator as we took it down to the parking garage where the limo was waiting for us.

"Ellery really wants to take Rory to Times Square, since she's never been to New York," Connor said.

"She'd love that. Wouldn't you, sweetheart?" Ian asked with a smile.

"Yes, I've always wanted to see Times Square." I smiled at Connor and Ellery.

"Great! You're going to love it, Rory!" Ellery exclaimed.

We walked around the streets of Times Square, and I was in awe. The crowds of people, the street vendors, and the variety of things to do amazed me. Being from a very small town, this was something I wasn't used to. Ian and I held hands and, every time he looked over at me, he smiled. The words he had said earlier about children and how he wouldn't hold Julia still consumed my mind. Connor didn't make dinner reservations because Ellery said she just wanted to go eat somewhere that was unplanned. I really liked her. She was a fly-by-the-seat-of-your-pants kind of girl and I admired her. As we were walking across the street, Ellery saw Ellen's Stardust Diner and told Connor and Ian that was where we were eating.

"Elle, are you sure?" Connor asked with a look on his face.

"Of course I'm sure. Rory is going to love it! The wait staff sings!" She smiled as she grabbed my hand and we walked ahead of the guys.

"I thought maybe we could go somewhere a little more quiet and—"

"And what, Connor? Classy? No, not tonight, babe. I'm sure Rory gets enough class in Malibu. Tonight, she's going to experience New York City at its best!"

"Okay." Connor sighed.

The line was long and the hostess told us there was about an hour wait. Ian and Connor both reached in their pockets and Ellery grabbed their hands.

"Oh no you don't, you two. No trying to buy our way in. We're going to wait in this line like everyone else."

"But, Ellery, I really need a drink and I'm hungry," Connor said.

"There's a bar right there. You and Ian go and have a drink and Rory and I will wait in line."

"No. We aren't leaving the two of you here alone. We'll wait."

Ellery looked over at me. "Connor has safety issues," she said.

I couldn't help but laugh. I looked at Connor and smiled as he rolled his eyes. As we were waiting in line, there were two women standing behind Ian and Connor and they were whispering. I couldn't hear exactly what they were saying, but I did hear the words "sexy and hot." I leaned over and whispered to Ellery what I heard.

"I think those two are talking about our guys," I said.

Ian and Connor were oblivious to it all because they were too busy talking about stocks. "I'm sure they are. Women hit on Connor all the time and I'm sure Ian gets it too. I mean, look at them." She laughed.

I turned around and saw the one woman with the long, blonde hair tap Ian on the shoulder.

"Excuse me. Could you please take a picture of me and my friend?" she asked.

"Sure, no problem." Ian smiled.

I watched him take her phone as the two women smiled and he took their picture.

"Thank you so much." She giggled.

She took her phone back and I thought she pulled up the picture to look at it. She smiled and turned her phone around for Ian and Connor to see.

"You take great pictures," she said as she showed them a picture of her tits.

Connor and Ian both smiled. "I don't think we took that picture," Connor said.

"Oops, wrong one. Sorry." She smiled.

Ellery and I both smacked Connor and Ian on the arm. "What a whore," I said.

The blonde looked at me. "Excuse me? Who are you calling a whore?"

Ian grabbed my hand as Connor grabbed Ellery's. I turned around and ignored her, but it didn't last when she continued to speak.

"I said, who are you calling a whore?"

"We can take her down together," Ellery said to me.

"Rory, let it go," Ian whispered.

I stared the blonde right in the eyes. "Next time you want to show off your tits to a guy, make sure they aren't with their girls. Okay? Because we women have a code. You know the code that says we won't try to steal another woman's man? We women have to stick together and follow that. How would you like it if you were with your husband or boyfriend and someone did that to you? You'd be pissed, right? Well, am I right?"

The blonde sighed and nodded her head. "Yeah, I'd be pissed. I'm sorry. I really am."

"I appreciate your apology. Enjoy your dinner," I said as I turned around.

The hostess called our name and we were seated at our booth. I slid in and Ian slid next to me. He leaned over and kissed my head.

"You're amazing. I just wanted you to know that." He smiled.

"I would have ripped her head off," Ellery said.

"Yes, she would have." Connor nodded.

"You're a classy woman, Rory." Ellery smiled at me.

"She sure is," Ian said as he put his arm around me.

****

Denny dropped Ian and me off at our hotel and we said our goodbyes to Connor and Ellery. I hugged Ellery and told her to give Julia a big kiss for me. She smiled and told me to call her. After I hugged Connor, and Ian said his goodbyes, he helped me out of the limo and we made our way to the elevator. Ian pushed the button and, as we waited for the door to open, he pulled me into him and kissed me on the head. When I looked up at him and smiled, it seemed like everything for which I was mad at him earlier was gone. It was the little things he did that made me swoon over him. The elevator doors opened and we took it up to our room. As soon as Ian unlocked the door and we walked into the room, my phone chimed. I pulled it from my purse and smiled as I read a text message from Andre.

"How is my beautiful American girl?"

"I'm good. How is my sexy French man?"

"The sexy French man is good. I was just checking in with you. Talk to you soon."

"Really, Rory?" Ian said.

I set my phone on the table and looked at Ian. "What?"

"It seems to me that you're flirting with the French guy."

"Are you jealous, Mr. Braxton?" I asked as I bit my bottom lip and began unbuckling his belt.

"Jealous of a man with an accent? Never." He smiled as lifted my shirt over my head.

"You're not even a little jealous that the sexy French man sent me a text?" I said as I took down his pants.

"You'll know when I'm jealous, sweetheart," he said as he leaned in and kissed my neck while he unhooked my bra.

I gasped as his hands cupped my breasts. "How will I know?" I said with bated breath as I stroked his hard cock.

He moaned. "I'll do this." He pushed me up against the wall. "Then I'll do this." He ripped my panties right off of me.

I was excited and my heart was pounding in anticipation.

"Then I'll do this." He plunged two fingers inside me. "Then I'll do this." He grabbed my wrists and pinned them above my head with his other hand. "Then I'll do this," he said as he removed his fingers and pushed himself deep inside me, banging my ass against the wall with each thrust.

He brought my leg up around his waist and held onto me tight. I wrapped my other leg around him as he held me up with one hand and the other still had my wrists pinned to the wall. He was so strong. He thrust in and out of me as growls escaped from deep within his chest. Each thrust was harder and longer than the one before. I was out of breath and the last thrust inside me sent my body into pure bliss as he pushed me over the edge and into an amazing orgasm. My body shuddered as did his as he released himself inside me, spilling into me every last drop of pleasure he had in him. He moaned as he finished off and then buried his face into my neck.

"Yes, I'm jealous," he whispered.

He let go of my wrists and I wrapped my arms around him, holding him tight. He carried me to the bedroom, still buried deep inside me and laid me down on the bed. He hovered over me and stared into my eyes.

"You're mine and don't ever forget it," he said.

"How can I when you fuck me like that?"

He smiled as he leaned down and kissed me on the lips.

Chapter 13
Ian

We boarded the plane and took our seats in first class. I always let Rory have the window seat because she said it calmed her to look at the clouds. I sat there, thinking about what my father said about his plane. There was no need for him to buy a new one because there was nothing wrong with the one he had. It wasn't like him just to buy things like that.

"You look like you're in deep thought." Rory smiled as she took hold of my hand.

"I was just thinking about my father and him buying a new plane. It's just odd to me."

"Why? The man can afford it," she said.

"I know he can, but that's not the point. The plane he has now is practically brand new. It's only a few years old. It's just out of character for him."

"Well, maybe Richard is having a change of heart about things. He was very nice to me that night he came over, for the first time ever."

"I'm happy he's finally warming up to you. He has no choice, really," I said as I brought her hand to my lips. Did you enjoy New York, sweetheart?"

"I did. Thank you for taking me." She smiled.

One of the many things I loved about Rory was the fact that she was always thanking me for things. She didn't expect anything from me except my love, and I knew Andrew was dead wrong about her.

"You're welcome. There are going to be many more trips in our future. I'm going to show you the world, Rory Sinclair. Just the two of us." I smiled.

She smiled back and rested her head on my shoulder. I rested my head on hers and closed my eyes, remembering our day yesterday, when it was just her and me spending the day touring New York City. She was so excited about everything; like a big kid. She fell in love with the art museum and, of course, all the shopping we did. We were only interrupted by Adalynn a couple of times when she was face timing Rory and showing her maid of honor dresses that she liked. I made a comment and she told me to shut up. I loved Adalynn and nothing pleased me more than her and Rory becoming best friends. Rory needed someone like Adalynn in her life. I lifted my head and so did Rory. She looked at me and then leaned over and gave me a kiss.

"I love you," she said.

"I love you." I smiled.

Those words. Those three words that I never spoke to anyone except to my mother when I was just a child. Those three words that meant nothing to me and had no meaning. My mother had told me she loved me every day, but she left and never came back. As far as I was concerned, she showed me that those words didn't have any meaning. But, when I almost lost Rory, I found that those three words meant everything to me.

****

We pulled up to the house and I saw Adalynn's car in the driveway. I looked at Rory.

"Did you know she was coming over?" I asked.

Rory looked away and then made the cutest face that I'd ever seen. "Well, she texted me and said she wanted to show me some dresses, so I said okay. I'm sorry, Ian. It's just that—"

"Shh, sweetheart. It's okay," I said as I kissed her.

How could I be mad? Rory was so excited to see those dresses and who was I to deny her that? We had a beautiful few days alone and now it was time for her to help Adalynn with the wedding. As soon as we walked into the house, Adalynn came strolling out of the kitchen. She ran right to Rory and hugged her.

"I'm so happy you're back. I can't wait to show you the dresses! Oh, hi, Ian." She smiled.

"Hi, Adalynn. Good to see you, darling." I smiled as I kissed her cheek.

"Good to see you too." She smiled before grabbing Rory's hand and taking her into the living room.

While Rory was looking at dresses, I went into my study to catch up on some work. I pulled my phone from my pocket and noticed I had a missed call from Andrew. I punched in my password and listened to his message.

"Hey, Ian. Hope you had a good time in New York. Give me a call when you get back. I'm not sure if you remember, but that event we committed to about six months ago is coming up next week and you have to be there. Call me."

Shit, I forgot about the event for K Corp. Damn it. I dialed Andrew's number.

"Hey, buddy," he answered.

"Hey, Drew. I completely forgot about the K Corp event."

"Good thing I reminded you. We both sponsored it, so we have to be there."

"No problem, Rory and I will be there. I suggest you bring someone along."

"Don't worry, friend. I intend to. I knew there was no way you would leave Rory at home."

"Good, as long as we're clear on that."

"Are you up for some golf tomorrow? It's Sunday."

I did miss playing golf and maybe it was a good idea to spend some time with Andrew so he'd get off my back about Rory. "Sure. How about nine?" I said.

"Great, Ian! I'll pick you up tomorrow morning. See ya, buddy."

I hung up and continued going through my messages. I was going to have to tell Rory about her father and I was still trying to decide when to do it.

"You look like you're in deep thought," Rory said as she stood in the doorway.

I looked up and gasped when I saw her standing there in a floor-length red dress. She looked like an angel.

"Do you like?" She smiled as she spun around.

"You look gorgeous, sweetheart, simply stunning. Is that the one?"

"Yeah, I think so. I love it and so does Adalynn."

"It's perfect." I smiled.

"I'll be sure to tell her. I'm going to go change."

"Okay. I'll be done here in a few minutes."

I watched her beautiful body turn around and walk away. I decided that maybe it was best to tell her about her father tonight, over a couple of drinks and some Thai food out on the patio. I unlocked my top right hand drawer to get out my checks and, as I pulled them out, I stared at the white envelope that I'd kept tucked away for the past five years. A white envelope that was addressed to me. There was no return address on it, but I knew who it was from and I had no desire to or intention of reading it. I didn't even know why I kept the damn thing. I shut the drawer just as Adalynn walked in.

"When you get a chance, Ian, we need to go over a couple things regarding *Prim*."

"Okay, Adalynn. When's good for you?" I asked as I pulled the calendar up on my phone.

"How about Monday morning at ten?" she replied.

"Ten it is." I smiled at her.

She stood there and looked at me with a cocked head. "I like that you're happy. You're a different man, Ian Braxton."

"Thanks, Adalynn," I said as I got up, walked over, and hugged her. "It looks like we both are getting everything we want."

"Ahem," Rory said as she stood in the doorway. "Are you flirting with my best friend?" she asked me.

"Why? Are you jealous?" I replied with a smile.

"No. You'll know when I'm jealous, my love." She smiled back and winked.

"Adalynn, as much as I love you, you need to get the hell out of here now!" I told her.

"How rude, Ian."

"Not rude, darling, it's called desperation. I am desperate for my beautiful girlfriend over there to show me what happens when she gets jealous."

Adalynn sighed and rolled her eyes. "Good lord, you two make my head spin."

She turned around and gave Rory a light hug. "I'll see you soon. Try not to hurt him too much." She winked.

****

"I swear that I'm going to make you jealous every day," I said as I kissed her lips.

The bed was in shambles and we were both drenched in sweat. Still trying to catch her breath, Rory looked at me with that smile. The smile that told me she wanted me to fuck her again.

"Sweetheart, are you trying to kill me?"

"Of course not." She laughed.

"You need to remember that I'm ten years older than you."

"Not a full ten for a couple of weeks. What do you want to do for your birthday?" she asked as she ran her finger down my chest.

"I don't know. I haven't given it any thought. I do know that I don't want a party."

"Why?"

"Because I want to spend my birthday with you and only you. How about we take the yacht out for a couple of days?"

"I would love that."

I kissed the tip of her nose. "Good, then that's what we'll do. Now, let's get these sheets off the bed, shower, and then order dinner. How's Thai sound?"

"Thai sounds great. Are we taking a shower together?"

"Do I ever shower alone anymore, sweetheart?"

She jumped up out of the bed and went into the bathroom to start the shower. I grabbed hold of my semi-hard cock and looked down.

"Here we go again."

Chapter 14
Rory

Ian was already waiting for me outside on the patio with an open bottle of wine and the table set.

"Our food should be here shortly." He smiled as he poured some wine into my glass.

"Great. I'm starving."

"We sure did work up quite an appetite," Ian said as he walked by and lightly kissed my neck.

As I sat down at the table and took a sip of my wine, Ian walked back with the Thai food. He set the cartons on the table and then took his seat across from me.

"There's something I need to talk to you about," he said.

"What is it?"

"I found your father."

I almost choked on my food. "What? Where is he?"

"That, my darling, you're never going to believe. He lives in Los Angeles."

"What? You mean like less-than-an-hour-away Los Angeles?" I asked in utter shock.

"Yeah, that Los Angeles, sweetheart." He chuckled. "He owns a bar called the Piano Bar in Hollywood."

I felt sick to my stomach and I put down my fork. It was hard to believe that my father lived so close, but yet so far. A man I knew nothing about except that he was a coward who abandoned his children.

"Are you okay, Rory?" Ian asked.

I sighed as I stared down at my food. "I don't know, Ian. I'm not going to lie to you. It really upsets me that he's so close and I'm scared, but I need to see him, talk to him, and get some answers."

Ian got up and walked over to me. He grabbed my hand, helped me up from the chair, and wrapped his arms around me.

"Listen, I know you're scared, but I'll be with you every step of the way. If you feel that strongly about seeing him, then do it. If you feel like you just can't, then I'll support you. It's your decision, sweetheart, and only you can make it. You need to do what's best for you."

My grip around him tightened. I never thought in a million years that I would have found someone who loved me and supported me like Ian did. "Have I told you how much I love you?"

"Yes, but please tell me some more." He smiled.

Ian broke our embrace and grabbed our wine glasses. "Come on; let's go down by the water," he said as he held out his arm.

I smiled as I looped my arm in his and we walked down to the beach. As we were sitting in the sand, Ian told me about his golf date with Andrew tomorrow. As much as I didn't want him to go, I didn't dare tell him that. I didn't like Andrew and I didn't like Ian hanging out with him.

"Oh, by the way, I have an event dinner to go to next week and you'll be joining me. I want you to go shopping and find a nice dress to wear. But nothing too sexy, understand?"

"Yeah, whatever, Ian."

"No whatever, sweetheart; nothing sexy."

I was silently laughing to myself. If he didn't want sexy, then he'd get frumpy. That would teach him to tell me what I could and couldn't wear.

"Okay, my love. Nothing sexy."

"Thank you." He smiled as he kissed my head.

****

Another restless night between thinking about my father, and Ian's command about not wearing a sexy dress to the event we were going to. Ian was already in the bathroom, getting ready for his golf day with Andrew. I got up, walked into the bathroom, and wrapped my arms around him, laying my head against his bare back as he shaved.

"Good morning, sweetheart. I hope I didn't wake you."

"Good morning, and no, you didn't."

I gave him a soft kiss on his back and then went downstairs for some coffee. Since it was Sunday, Charles had the day off, so I made a pot of coffee. As I was waiting for it to brew, Ian walked into the kitchen.

"What are you doing today?" he asked.

"I don't know. I really hadn't thought about it."

The coffee finished brewing and Andrew walked into the kitchen. "Good morning, all." He smiled.

"Andrew." I nodded.

"Look at you, Rory. Looking sexy, even with the 'I just rolled out of bed' look."

"Would you like a cup of coffee, Andrew?" I asked because I wanted nothing more than to throw it in his face.

"Nope. Ian, let's go. We can stop on the way and grab some breakfast."

"Sounds good, man. Bye, sweetheart. Have a good day and I'll be home later," Ian said as he gave me a kiss goodbye.

"Have fun."

I ran up the stairs to get dressed and to give Mandy a call.

"Hello."

"Hi, Mandy, it's Rory. I was wondering if you and Molly would like to come over today and go swimming. Ian is out with Andrew for the day and I thought it would be fun to hang out."

"That sounds like fun, Rory. Molly and I would love to come over. Thank you for the invite."

"You're welcome and I'll see you later."

I was excited. I really liked Mandy and it was going to be nice to visit with her as friends and not on work time. I decided that we needed a treat. I went through the cupboards and gathered all the ingredients for chocolate chip cookies. As soon as the first batch came out of the oven, Mandy arrived with Molly.

"Oh my gosh, Rory, it smells so good in here." She smiled.

I smiled back and looked at Molly. "She's beautiful, Mandy."

"Thank you, Rory."

"Come on; let's go out to the pool."

Mandy climbed in with Molly and I followed behind. The sun was shining, and it was overall, a perfect day.

"So Mr. Braxton is with his friend?" she asked.

"Yeah, he's with douchebag Andrew. I can't stand him and I wish Ian wouldn't see him anymore."

We had Molly in a baby float that Mandy brought over and I pulled her around the pool. She was laughing and splashing her little hands in the water. Mandy confided in me that she was seeing someone and that he was really good with Molly.

"What's going on here?" Ian asked as he stood by the pool.

"Ian, you're home already?" I asked.

"Hi, Mr. Braxton."

He looked at Mandy and said hi. "I've been gone four hours, Rory," he said with an attitude.

Now I was pissed. There was no reason for him to come home the way he did with an attitude.

Mandy and I climbed out of the pool and I took Molly from her float and held her on my hip. "Ian, meet Molly, Mandy's daughter." I smiled.

He stared at me with a not-so-pleased look. "I said, meet Molly," I whispered through gritted teeth.

"Hey there," he said as he looked at her.

"Let me take Molly inside and get her changed," Mandy said as she took her.

I took the towel from the chair and began drying myself off. It seemed that Ian thought it was a good idea to start with me.

"What the hell are you doing, Rory?"

"Having a lovely afternoon with my friend," I replied.

"Mandy is the staff, not your friend."

As I stared into his serious eyes, anger began to brew inside me. "So let me get this straight. Because she works for you, I can't be friends with her? So now you're choosing my friends?"

"Don't be ridiculous, sweetheart."

"The only one being ridiculous here is you, Ian. I don't care if she works for you or if she's homeless. She's my friend and we're hanging out whether you like it not," I snapped and stormed into the house.

Mandy changed Molly back into her clothes and, before they left, I gave them a hug goodbye. Ian walked over to the plate of chocolate chip cookies and, as he grabbed one, I snatched it out of his hand and threw all the cookies in the garbage.

"What the fuck, Rory!"

"You don't deserve one of my cookies. You're rude and I don't want to talk to you right now."

"How the hell am I rude?" he asked as he threw his hands up in the air.

"Mandy may be your employee, but she's also a human being and she's my friend, and if I want her to come over on her day off to hang out, then I'll have her over. I don't know if she really has many friends, considering she puts in long hours working for your ass and then going home and taking care of her daughter."

He stood there and stared at me. "I'm going to take a shower and then I think I'll go to dinner with Andrew."

"Go to dinner with Andrew, Ian. I don't fucking care."

He shook his head and walked upstairs. I wanted to tell him so bad what Andrew said to me on Thanksgiving, but somehow, I didn't think he'd believe me. I sat down at the piano and began to play. After a short while, Ian walked into the living room.

"I'll be home later," he growled.

I didn't even look up at him. I couldn't bring myself to. He walked out of the room and out the front door. I slammed my hands down on the keys as hard as I could and tears began to fall from my eyes. As I lightly pressed the keys, one at a time, I thought about what Ian said about my father. I ran upstairs to change, grabbed my keys, and drove away.

Chapter 15
Rory

I stood outside and looked up at the sign that read "*Piano Bar*." My stomach was twisted in knots as I pulled the door open and stepped inside. I looked around at the people that were gathered at the table; talking, laughing, and having a good time. A man was playing the piano that sat in the corner of the room. As I walked over and took a seat at the bar, a red-haired woman came over and set a napkin down in front of me.

"Welcome to the Piano Bar. What can I get for you, honey?"

"I'll have a cosmopolitan please," I replied.

"One cosmo coming right up."

The bar was simple. Nothing fancy and certainly not uptight.

"Here you go. Enjoy." The bartender smiled as she set down the drink in front of me.

I gave a polite smile as I picked up the drink and sipped it. As I reached in my purse to pull out my phone, I heard a man say, "Rosie makes the best cosmos in the world. You're lucky she's working tonight."

I looked up at the man and gasped. He looked exactly like Stephen; almost a spitting image of him. I gulped and forced a small smile. My heart was racing and my skin started to sweat. It was him; my father. I knew it. I could feel it. I needed to know for sure.

"I agree. This is the best cosmo I've ever had. Hi, I'm Rory S—" I immediately stopped myself. If I gave him my last name, he would know. "Sanders. Rory Sanders."

"Nice to meet you, Rory Sanders. I'm Jimmy O'Rourke, the owner of this bar." He smiled.

I was right; it was him, and suddenly, I just wanted to throw my arms around him and tell him that I was his daughter. After all these years, I finally met my dad; a man who didn't even know who I was.

"Nice to meet you, Jimmy O'Rourke."

I scanned his hands to see if he was wearing a ring. He wasn't.

"Are you new in town?" he asked. "I haven't seen you around here before."

"Yeah, I am."

"Welcome to the Piano Bar. Now if you'll excuse me, I have some piano to play." He winked.

I watched him as he walked over to the piano and took a seat. He stretched out his fingers before he began to play. His fingers delicately stroked each ivory and black key. The melody he made was amazing.

"He's the best there is," the redheaded bartender spoke. "I've never seen anyone play with more passion than him."

"Yeah, he's great." I smiled. "Do you know him well?" I asked.

"I've worked for him for over ten years. We've been through a lot together."

I was starting to get the impression that they were a couple. "Is he married?" I blurted out.

"That's an odd question to ask," she said.

"I'm sorry. That came out completely wrong. I was only asking because someone as talented as him would certainly have a significant other. Can I have another cosmo, please?"

"Sure. Coming right up." She smiled. "By the way, I'm Rosie or Rose. Jimmy likes to call me Rosie."

"Nice to meet you. I'm Rory," I said as I threw back the last of my first cosmo.

It was starting to get really packed in the bar. As soon as Jimmy hit the last key, everyone in the bar applauded. He stood up and took a bow. Rosie set down my second cosmo just as Jimmy walked back behind the bar. I picked up my glass and held it up.

"That was really cool. You're really good."

"Thank you, darling." He smiled.

I had my phone sitting next to me and I saw the screen light up with a text message from Ian.

"Where the hell are you? I came home, you're not here, and you didn't say you were going out."

"It's none of your business."

"You are my business. Now tell me where you fucking are!"

I didn't feel like arguing with him, so I lied.

"I'm at Jordyn and Ollie's place, visiting. I'll be home in a while."

"Come home now."

What the hell was his problem?

"No, Ian. I will come home after I'm done visiting."

"Don't expect to get fucked tonight."

Really? Did he really just say that to me? Now, I was pissed as hell.

"Don't worry. I won't."

I waited for a response and one never came. He was pissed. I was pissed, and at that moment, I didn't care. As Rosie was walking by, I asked her if anyone could play the piano. She told me that it was open to anyone that had the talent. I asked her if she could watch my drink for me, and then I got up and walked over to the piano. I stretched my fingers, just like my father did, and gently placed my fingers on the keys. I began play a song that I felt was very fitting for the moment, "Only Human." I closed my eyes and lost myself in the melody. After hitting the last note, I went right into Chopin. The bar grew quiet and all eyes were on me. I didn't have to look up; I could feel it. I breathed life into the music and, when I finished, the patrons of the bar applauded and whistled. I smiled as I got up and walked back to my seat. Jimmy walked over and stared at me for a moment before speaking.

"Wow. That was amazing, Rory. Where the hell did you learn to play like that?"

"Thank you. I've been playing since I was a kid. I learned the basics and then pretty much taught myself the rest."

"You don't learn talent like that, honey. You were born with that gift." He smiled.

I looked down at my drink. I finished it off and asked for another.

"You are welcome here to play any time you want."

"Thanks, Jimmy." I smiled.

Rosie brought me over another cosmo. I was already starting to feel the effects of the last two. "Round of shots on me," Jimmy said as he looked at me and Rosie.

He grabbed the bottle of vodka and poured us each a shot. Jimmy held up his glass.

"To a very talented woman." He smiled.

"Cheers," I said as I threw back the vodka.

As I sat on the bar stool, I was feeling really good. Too good, in fact, and there was no way I could drive home. It was now midnight and my phone chimed with a text from Ian.

"Are you coming home or do I have to embarrass you and come get you?"

I couldn't respond because I couldn't type, so I dialed his number.

"What the fuck is going on, Rory?" he answered.

"I need you to come get me," I slurred. "I'm sorry I lied to you, Ian."

"What are you talking about? Are you drunk?"

"Yeah, and I can't drive unless you want me to kill me and someone else."

"Don't be fucking stupid, Rory. Give me Jordyn's address."

"I'm not at Jordyn's."

"WHERE THE FUCK ARE YOU?" he screamed into the phone.

My head was already pounding. I started to cry.

"I'm at the Piano Bar."

"Stay inside. I'm on my way."

I finished the last of my cosmo and held up my glass for another one. "There's no way you can drive home, honey."

"Well, now we don't have to worry about that, Rosie, because my sexy boyfriend is on his way to pick me up," I slurred. "Bring on the cosmos." I smiled.

"One more and only if he's picking you up," she said with seriousness.

"He is. I just called him."

She made another cosmo and set the glass down in front of me. *What was I doing? Did I even know?* Between Ian being a prick about Mandy coming over and seeing my father for the first time in my life, it was too much. I picked up the glass, brought it to my lips, and drank as much as I could before Ian took it away from me. I turned my head and looked at him. He stared at me and shook his head.

"Rory, why?"

I held up my finger to him. "Don't ask me questions I can't answer."

"You're drunk off your ass."

"So what."

"Can I get you anything?" Rosie asked Ian.

"No, thanks. I'm good."

I looked up at Rosie. "Rosie, this is my boyfriend, Ian. Ian, this is my new friend, Rosie. She makes the best cosmos in the world."

Suddenly, Jimmy walked behind the bar. "Excuse me, sir, but you best remove your hand from her."

Rosie put her hand on his arm. "It's cool, Jimmy. He's her boyfriend. He came to pick her up."

"Oh, I'm sorry about that."

"Nah, it's okay. And you are?" Ian asked as he cocked his head.

"Jimmy O'Rourke, the owner," he said as he stuck out his hand.

Ian turned and looked at me and then back at Jimmy as he shook his hand. "Nice to meet you, Jimmy. I'm Ian Braxton. Thank you for looking out for my girlfriend."

"No problem. She's a real talented woman. You should be proud of her." He smiled.

"I am and I know she is. Come on, sweetheart, let's go home," Ian said as he helped me from the chair, picked me up, and carried me outside.

The cool air felt good, but I still felt sick to my stomach. Ian put me in the car and helped me buckle my seat belt. As I laid my head against the window, Ian looked over at me, but didn't say a word the entire ride home. The only thing I wanted to do was curl up, go to sleep, and forget tonight ever happened. Ian pulled into the driveway and told me not to move. He walked around to the passenger's side, opened the door, and helped me out of the car. I was really dizzy and I felt like I was going to throw up.

"Ian, I'm not feeling so good," I said before he picked me up.

"Not feeling good as in you're going to be sick?"

"Yes. Like right now!" I exclaimed as I ran over to where some bushes were and began vomiting.

"Really, Rory? There?"

Ian walked over to where I was on my knees and pulled back my hair. "This is what happens when you drink too much. It was unnecessary."

Unnecessary to him, maybe, because nothing seemed to bother him. "This is no time for a lecture," I said as I threw up again. He softly rubbed my back until I was finished.

"Are you done?" he asked.

"I think so."

"Come on; let's get you in the bathtub. You smell, sweetheart."

Ian picked me up and carried me into the house. He set me down on the bed and told me to wait there while he started the bath. He walked over to me and undressed me, then helped me up and walked me to the tub.

"Be careful. I have you," he said as he helped me into the tub.

I sat down in the hot water and brought my knees up to my chest. Ian took my chin and lifted it so I was looking at him.

"Look at you. You're a mess." He smiled as he took the wet washcloth and wiped the mascara stains from under my eyes. "Why, Rory? Why did you go there without me?"

"I don't know, Ian."

I leaned back my head while he wet my hair and then closed my eyes as he shampooed it.

"Why did you lie to me about where you were?"

I took in a deep breath. "I didn't want you to get mad."

"But, sweetheart, you were going to tell me eventually, right?"

I nodded my head.

"Then I would have been triple mad because you lied to me, and one thing I will not tolerate in a relationship is lying. Do you understand me?"

I turned my head and gave him a stern look. "Why do you think it's okay for you to talk to me like that?"

I'd had enough of him and his commands. He was really pissing me off and I didn't deserve to be talked to like that.

"Excuse me?" he said.

"Sometimes, you talk to me like I'm a child. I'm not a fucking child, Ian."

"Sometimes, I beg to differ."

God, why did he have to be such an asshole right now? Of all times, why when I'm drunk and not feeling good.

"Get the fuck out!" I yelled.

"Rory, stop."

"Don't tell me what to do!" I yelled as I raised my hands to him and he grabbed them.

"Rory."

I couldn't hold it back anymore. I broke down and sobbed as I stared at him. He took his hand and placed it on my cheek. "Sweetheart," he said as he looked into my eyes. He wrapped his arms around me and held me while I cried into his shoulder. When I began to calm down, Ian helped me up and out of the tub. He wrapped a large towel around me and walked me over to the bed.

"Let's get you in your pajamas and into bed."

He dried me off and pulled my nightshirt down over my head. After he towel dried my hair, he pulled back the covers and I got into bed. He climbed in next to me, wrapped his arms around me, and pulled me into him.

"I'm sorry, sweetheart. I love you," he whispered as he kissed my head.

"I love you too," I whispered back before I closed my eyes and fell fast asleep.

Chapter 16
Ian

"Good morning, Charles," I said as I strolled into the kitchen.

"Good morning, Ian. Coffee for you and Rory?"

"Just for me. Rory is still sleeping. She had a very late night last night. Actually, I'll have that coffee when I get back. I'm going for a run."

"Very well. Your blueberry muffins will be waiting for you as well." Charles smiled.

"Thank you, my friend."

I put on my running shoes and headed out the door. It was a cool morning, but it felt good. I needed to think about yesterday and what had happened last night. For Rory to go and see her father for the first time by herself really angered me. As I was running along the shoreline, deep in thought, Rory ran up next to me. I looked over at her and smiled.

"I didn't think you'd be able to get out of bed this morning."

"It was hard, but I needed this run."

"Are you feeling okay?"

"Meh. Nothing a little bit of coffee and a blueberry muffin won't cure."

I shook my head at her and smiled. I loved her so much, regardless of how much she pissed me off sometimes.

"I'm sorry about last night," she said.

"Me too. It's just when I came home yesterday I was looking forward to being with you alone. When I walked in and saw Mandy, I just kind of got upset, and then seeing you in the pool with her kid. Rory, I love you more than anything in this world, but I don't want children, ever, and you need to understand that."

I had hoped this wasn't starting a fight, but I needed to be very clear about where I stood as far as kids were concerned.

"I know that, Ian," she said and I could sense a tone of disappointment.

I stopped running and asked her to please stop with me. As I turned to her, I put my hands on her hips and I pressed my forehead against hers.

"I'm sorry about yesterday. I promise you that I'll try to be a better boyfriend and not tell you what to do. I know sometimes I can come off harsh and I'm sorry about that. I'll work on it. We're going to say things and make mistakes along the way, but we'll figure it out and we'll learn from our mistakes."

Rory wrapped her arms around my neck and hugged me as tightly as she could. "I love you so much, Ian, but damn, stop treating me like a child."

"I love you too, Rory, and I promise I'll work on it. I seriously don't mean to."

She softly kissed my lips and smacked me on the ass. "Let's go; I need coffee." She smiled.

We ran back to the house and Charles poured us some coffee and set it on the table. As I grabbed the creamer out of the refrigerator, Mandy walked into the kitchen. She was wearing her sunglasses.

"Good morning, Mandy." I smiled.

"Good morning, Rory. Mr. Braxton," she said nervously.

"Good morning, Mandy," Rory said.

"If you don't mind, I'm going to start on the upstairs today," she said.

"No, that's fine," I replied.

I needed to shower and head over to *Prim*. Rory and I took our coffee and went upstairs. When we walked into the bedroom, Mandy was taking the sheets off the bed. She looked up at us and I was startled. She had a very noticeable black and blue bruise across her cheek.

"Mandy, what happened?" Rory asked.

"Oh, I'm sorry. I should have come in here last," she said.

"What happened to your face?" I asked.

"It's nothing. I ran into the door. Thank you for your concern. I'll come back and finish later."

Something was off with Mandy. She seemed like a nervous wreck and it was like she couldn't get out of here fast enough.

"Poor girl. Look what you did to her," Rory said as she started the shower.

"What I did? What the hell did I do?"

"Your behavior yesterday towards her. You make her nervous."

"Rory, that's not true."

I stripped out of my clothes and Rory did the same. We made love in the shower and I was late meeting Adalynn at *Prim*.

****

"You're late!" Adalynn exclaimed as I walked through her office door.

"I know. Damn traffic." I smiled.

"I don't think the traffic had anything to do with it."

I took a seat in the leather chair across from her desk. "What's going on?"

"Can you be more involved here at *Prim*?"

I looked at her in confusion as I shifted in my seat. "Why?"

"Daniel and I are going on a month-long honeymoon to Europe and I need you here."

"A month? Who goes on a honeymoon for a month, Adalynn?"

"Two people who are in love with each other, get married, and want to spend time alone before coming back to reality and all the bullshit. Maybe you should try it some time?"

"I don't need to be married to go away on vacation for a month with the person I'm in love with."

"Says you." She smiled. "Anyway, you're going to need to be here to oversee things while I'm gone."

I once again shifted in my chair. "Why? You have capable staff here that can oversee things."

"Renee is going on maternity leave right before the wedding and she's my right hand."

"Then maybe she should stay and not go on a maternity leave," I said.

"Ian, you're an idiot."

I put my hands up. "Okay, okay. I'll be here."

"Don't worry about any of the creative stuff. Just be here for the business end of things. How are things going?" she asked.

"Good. Things are good."

Adalynn looked at me and smiled. "Don't fuck things up with Rory. She's good for you and you're good for her. Love her, Ian."

"I do love her, Adalynn."

"I mean *really* love her."

I gave her a half smile as I got up from the chair. "Don't worry about me and Rory. I'm doing everything possible to make sure she's happy. Why are you so concerned?"

"Because I know you'll do something to fuck it up."

"Thanks for the vote of confidence, Adalynn," I said as I walked out of her office.

As I slid into the back of the limo, my phone started to ring. I pulled it from my pocket and saw Rory was calling.

"Hi, sweetheart."

"Hi, Ian. Listen, I just got a call from Hudson Rock and they're taking Stephen over to the ER. They said he's sick. So, I'm heading over there now."

"I hope it's nothing serious. Do you want me to meet you there?" I asked.

"No. I just need to be there to make sure he's okay. I'll keep you posted. I love you."

"I love you too, sweetheart. I'll talk to you soon."

I hung up and concern washed over me. If they were transferring him to the ER, then something serious must be wrong because the doctors at Hudson Rock were more than capable of treating an illness.

"Joshua, take me to the ER instead of the office. Rory's brother is being taken there."

"Sure thing, Ian."

Even though Rory said it wasn't necessary for me to come there, I was doing it anyway. I didn't want her there alone and with no support. As I walked into the ER, I asked the nurse at the desk where Stephen was. She took me back to the curtained room, where I saw Rory sitting in the chair and holding his hand.

"Hey, sweetheart," I said as I walked over and kissed her head.

"Ian, what are you doing here?"

"Hey, buddy." I smiled at Stephen. How are you?"

"Not too good, Ian," he whispered.

He was pale and he looked weak. "Don't worry; the doctors here will take good care of you."

I grabbed a chair and set it down next to Rory. She grabbed my hand and smiled at me.

"Thank you for coming."

"No problem, sweetheart. What did the doctor say?"

"They haven't been in yet. The nurse came in and drew some blood and said the doctor will be in shortly."

"He probably just picked up a virus or something."

"Yeah, you're probably right."

The doctor walked into the room and introduced herself as Dr. Kullen. She walked over to Stephen and examined him.

"Stephen has all the symptoms of the flu virus. We'll keep him here overnight for IV fluids and we'll monitor him. The virus just needs to run its course and he should be fine in a couple of days."

"Thank you, doctor," I spoke.

"Yes, thank you."

"You're welcome. Get better, Stephen." She smiled as she gave his arm a light squeeze.

"We should go, sweetheart, and let Stephen get some rest," I said.

"I don't want to leave him just yet. You go. I'll be home later."

"I'm not leaving you here. I'll stay with you. I'm just going to run to the office and grab a couple of things and then I'll be right back," I said as I kissed the top of her head.

I could see the worry in her face and in her eyes as she sat there and held Stephen's hand. I called Joshua and had him come pick me up from the hospital and drive me to the office. Once I grabbed what I needed, I headed back to the hospital and stayed with Rory until she felt comfortable enough to go home.

Chapter 17
Rory

I tossed and turned all night. Even though the doctor said not to worry, and the virus would run its course, I couldn't help it. Ian had his arm around me as I wiggled my way out from under him as carefully as I could so I didn't wake him up. The clock read four a.m. I made my way to the bathroom, shut the door, turned on the light, and looked at myself in the mirror. The bags under my eyes were not a pretty sight. As I splashed cold water on my face, there was a light knock on the door.

"Sweetheart, are you okay?"

Shit. I didn't mean to wake him up. I opened the door and looked at Ian. "I'm fine. I just couldn't sleep. Go back to bed. I'm sorry if I woke you."

He wrapped his arms around me and held me tight. "If you can't sleep, then neither can I," he said.

I looked up at him and ran my hand lightly down his cheek. He always looked so sexy in the morning. I softly kissed his lips, and then my soft kiss turned passionate. He picked me up and carried me over to the bed. Before laying me down, he took down the straps of my nightgown and it fell to the ground. His mouth instantly gravitated to my breasts as he forcefully took them in his mouth. I hooked my thumbs in the waistband of his boxers and pulled them down, feeling his hard cock, which was ready and waiting for me. I knelt down and softly wrapped my lips around the tip, gently sucking before letting my tongue lick around it in circles. He gasped and then moaned as his hands gripped the sides of my head.

"I can't have you make me come this way, sweetheart. I need to come inside you," he said as he lifted my head.

I lay down on the bed and he hovered over me, not hesitating to plunge two fingers deep inside me. "You are incredible, baby," he whispered as he kissed me.

His mouth explored my neck and his thumb make small circular motions around my clit, exciting me more than I already was and bringing me to the verge of an orgasm. My body tightened and shook and one last stroke was enough to send me over the edge. I threw my head back and let pleasure take over my body. I opened my eyes as he stared at me, smiling with delight.

"Are you ready for orgasm number two?" he asked.

"Always," I whispered as I brought his lips to mine and kissed him passionately.

He thrust inside of me fast and hard without a moment of hesitation. He pounded himself in and out of me as if we hadn't had sex for a while, even though we did last night. Loud and deep groans escaped from his chest as he pushed me and himself into oblivion. I was always amazed at how fast this man could make me orgasm so many times in a row. He strained as he pushed every last drip inside me before collapsing on top and burying his face into my neck.

"I love you so much, Rory."

"I love you too, Ian."

Our heart rates began to slow and our breathing slowly returned to normal. He climbed off of me, got up, and went into the bathroom. When he was finished, he climbed back into bed and pulled me into him.

"We don't have to go back to sleep. We can talk if you want," he said as he kissed my head.

I wanted to talk to him about the bruise on Mandy's cheek because her story didn't settle right with me.

"The bruise on Mandy's cheek is bothering me."

"Why? She said she ran into the door. It happens."

"I guess. She told me she was seeing someone."

"Good for her," Ian said as he tightened his grip around me.

"I think we should get up. I really want to get to the hospital early and see how Stephen is doing."

"Okay, sweetheart. Let's shower, grab some breakfast, and then we'll go."

We both climbed out of bed and took an amazing shower together. A shower that was supposed to be quick, but ended up taking us longer as Ian couldn't keep his hands off me. We headed downstairs and as I grabbed two mugs from the cabinet, Charles told Ian that Mandy called in sick today.

"Really? She's never once called in."

"She said that she and her daughter both have the flu," Charles replied.

"Ah, well, it's going around."

I set our cups down on the table and Charles made me scrambled eggs and toast with a side of fresh fruit. As Ian sat down with his muffin and fruit, we heard Adalynn's voice coming from the foyer.

"Good morning. I have arrived." She smiled as she walked into the kitchen.

"Good morning." I smiled back.

"Adalynn, don't you think it's a tad early to be dropping by?" Ian asked.

"No. I know you're up anyway."

I laughed lightly and Ian looked at me and rolled his eyes.

"Eggs, Adalynn?" Charles asked.

"Of course, Charles. Soft boiled, please, with a side of wheat toast." Adalynn sat down next to me and grabbed my hand. "I received a call yesterday that all the bridesmaids dresses are in! I'm so excited. I did hire a wedding planner yesterday to tie up the odds and ends of the wedding. I feel like I'm running out of time."

"Gee, didn't we ask you if three months was enough time to plan a big wedding?"

"Shush up, Ian. Anyway, darling, I'm going to need you to go to the bridal shop for a final fitting."

"Okay. I'll go today after I leave the hospital." I smiled.

"Hospital? Why are you going to the hospital?"

"Stephen was admitted there yesterday. He has the flu virus."

"Oh, Rory, I'm sorry."

"Thank you, but the doctor said he'll be fine. The virus just has to run its course."

Adalynn, Ian, and I finished our breakfast and Adalynn left for *Prim*. Ian grabbed his keys and told Joshua that he would drive us to the hospital while he sent him on some other errands. I ran upstairs and grabbed my purse and Ian waited for me in the car.

"I'm sure Stephen's doing much better today," I said as I stared out the passenger window.

"I'm sure he is, sweetheart. We'll be there soon and you can see for yourself."

Ian pulled into the hospital and into the first parking space he saw. He walked around and opened the door, taking my hand as we walked into the hospital. We took the elevator up to the third floor where Stephen's room was. As the doors opened, we saw a team of doctors and nurses running down the hall. As we watched them from behind, I saw them go into Stephen's room. I grabbed Ian's arm and began running faster down the hallway. My heart was racing with fear. I couldn't remember if Stephen had a roommate. As I approached the room, I saw them. It was chaos. I looked at Stephen from across the room and he wasn't moving. I screamed as Ian grabbed me and pulled me into him, pressing my face against his chest.

"Get them out of here," someone yelled.

"Please, you need to wait outside. I promise we're doing everything we can," the nurse said as she guided us out of the room.

I started to shake uncontrollably as I began to pound on Ian's chest. "Do something, damn it! Do something. Please," I cried.

"Shh, sweetheart."

A few moments later, a doctor came out of the room. "Are you his sister?" he asked.

I turned around and looked at him with tears in my eyes as I nodded my head.

"We did everything we could but it was too late. We think that the virus he had attacked his heart. I'm so sorry."

"No. No. No," I said over and over as I shook my head in disbelief. "He's fine. He'll wake up you'll see. I'm going in there right now to wake him up!" I screamed.

"Rory," Ian said as he tried to pull me back.

I yanked my arm out from his grip and went into the room. "Stephen, it's time to wake up. Come on. We're going to be late for school," I said as I lightly shook him.

I stood there and stared at him as I ran my hand across his cheek. "You're so cold. Why are you so cold?"

My body was trembling and tears were falling from my eyes. Ian came up behind me and wrapped his arms around me.

"He's so cold, Ian. Ask the nurse to bring him a warm blanket."

"Sweetheart, that isn't going to help him. Rory, he's gone."

I knew it was true, but I didn't want to believe it. I felt like I was in a horrific nightmare and I couldn't wake up. I turned to Ian and looked at him.

"This isn't real, Ian. This is all a dream, a very bad dream. Please wake me up. Please," I pleaded with him as I grabbed his arms.

"It's not a dream, sweetheart. I'm sorry. I'm so sorry." He started to cry.

My legs were giving out and I began to sink slowly to the floor. Ian grabbed me and held onto me so I wouldn't fall. "You need to sit down, Rory," he said.

I turned around, and with Ian still holding me, I looked at Stephen. He looked so peaceful. I climbed up on the bed and snuggled into him.

"You're finally over the rainbow," I whispered. "There will be no more voices and no more pain. You're free, Stephen, and one day, we'll be together again."

I began sobbing as Ian placed his hands on me and sat me up. "Come on, sweetheart, the nurses need you to sign some paperwork."

He handed me a tissue and I wiped my eyes. The nurse was standing in the doorway with a clipboard in her hand. "I'm very sorry for your loss, Miss Sinclair."

"Thank you," I whispered as I took the pen from her hand and signed on the line.

Ian wrapped his arm around me. "We need to go home now, okay?"

I nodded my head as we slowly walked out of the room and out of the hospital. If Ian hadn't been holding me tight, I would've fallen to the ground. He was my support beam right now because, without him, I would fall to the ground. He opened the door for me and helped me into the car. As we drove down the road, I felt like I was suffocating. I couldn't believe Stephen had died. A feeling of loneliness crept up inside me. I silently chanted, "I can make it home. I can make it home."

Finally, Ian pulled into the driveway and, before he could even throw the car in park, I jumped out the car door and ran towards the beach. Ian yelled my name and ran behind me. When I got to the shoreline, I collapsed on my knees and screamed. Ian came up behind me and, instead of wrapping his arms around me, he knelt down beside me, but didn't touch me. He gave me my space. The space I needed at that moment. He didn't say word. He just sat there beside me and let me have my fit.

"Why? Why did you take him?" I screamed as I looked up at the sky. As I continued to sob, Ian slowly inched his hand towards mine, stopping just before he reached my fingers. I turned my head slightly and looked at his warm hand. The hand that reached out to comfort me. I placed my hand on top of him, letting him know that now I needed him. He let out a sigh and pulled me into him as we both fell back in the sand. He held me as I sobbed into his chest and told me to let it all out. I looked up at him as tears were streaming down his face. I raised my hand and softly wiped them away with my finger.

"I need to go inside now," I said.

"Okay, sweetheart."

Ian helped me up and placed his arm around me, helping me up to the house, up the stairs, and into our bedroom. I climbed on top of the bed and curled up in a ball. I couldn't deal with the reality of what happened, not yet. Ian covered me with a blanket and sat down on the edge of the bed, pushing my hair behind my ear.

"Get some rest, my love. I'll handle things. I'll be back to check on you later. I love you."

I nodded my head and whispered, "I love you too."

Chapter 18
Ian & Rory

Seeing Rory like that was the worst thing I'd ever seen. I wanted to make all of her sadness and pain go away, but there was only one thing that could do that, and that was time. I walked downstairs and told Charles what had happened. I made sure he was extra attentive to her needs. As I walked over to the bar and poured myself a bourbon, my phone rang; it was Adalynn.

"Adalynn, I'm glad you called. I was just going to call you."

"Ian, I can't get a hold of Rory. I wanted to know if she went to get her dress fitted."

"No, Adalynn, she didn't. Something happened."

"What's wrong, Ian? You sound funny," she asked.

"Stephen passed away this morning."

"WHAT?!" she screamed into the phone. "I'm on my way."

"No, Ada—" I started to say before she hung up.

Great. There was no way I was letting her see Rory today. I walked into my study and sat down. I rested my elbows on the desk and cupped my face in my hands. What a day. What a fucking lousy day. I debated whether or not to call Rory's Aunt Nancy. Maybe I should wait and see what Rory wanted to do. I didn't want to upset her any more. I reached in my pocket and pulled out my keys. I unlocked the drawer and opened it. When

I lifted out the box, I looked down at the white envelope. I sighed and slammed the drawer shut. Just as I was about to get up, Adalynn walked in.

"Ian, I'm so sorry. Where is Rory?"

"She's sleeping, Adalynn, and I want her to stay that way."

"My God, what happened?" she asked as she sat down in the chair across from my desk.

I took in a deep breath and ran my hand over my face. "The doctor thinks the virus attacked Stephen's heart. They're going to do an autopsy to be sure."

"Oh my God. Poor Rory. How bad is she?"

"She's bad. I'm really scared that she may not recover from this. You should've seen her, Adalynn. I was terrified."

"With the right support and time, she'll get through this. Ian, my God, she needs you more now than ever."

"I know that and I'm going to handle everything for her and do whatever it takes to help her get through this."

Just thinking about the road ahead scared me. Rory was a strong woman, but Stephen was her world. She spent her entire life taking care of him and now he was gone.

"Tell Rory I stopped by and I'll be back tomorrow."

I started to speak, but she interrupted me.

"Yes, Ian. I WILL be back tomorrow. I'm her best friend and I need to show her my support and love."

I sighed. "All right, Adalynn. I'll see you tomorrow."

I walked her to the front door, kissed her, and gave her a hug. "Thanks for stopping by."

"You know I'm always here."

I gave her a half smile as I shut the door. I walked up the stairs and slowly turned the doorknob. I peeked inside at Rory and she was still sleeping. As I went to shut the door, I heard her call my name.

"Ian?"

"Yes, sweetheart, it's me," I said as I walked into the bedroom.

I sat on the edge of the bed and ran my hand across her soft cheek. Tears began to fill her eyes again as she looked at me. I didn't know what to say to her. I was so scared that I was going to say the wrong thing. She took my hand and brought it up to her lips as she softly kissed my palm and then began to sob.

"I just can't believe he's gone."

"I know, sweetheart. I can't either."

I got up from the bed, lifted my shirt over my head, and took down my pants. I climbed in on my side and turned her around so she was facing me. I held her face close to my chest as she wrapped her leg around mine. We fell asleep for the rest of the night.

****

I woke up. Rory's side of the bed was empty. Instantly, I panicked. The bathroom door was open and the light was off. She wasn't in there. I looked over at the clock and saw that it was five a.m. I pulled on a pair of gray sweatpants and walked downstairs. I noticed the door off the kitchen was unlocked. I stepped onto the patio and looked down at the beach, where I saw Rory sitting in the sand, looking out into the water.

"Ian, I'm sorry, babe. I didn't mean to wake you up," she said as I sat down next to her.

"You didn't wake me. I woke up and you were gone. I got nervous. What are you doing out here?"

"I needed some fresh air," she said as she softly took my hand.

"Talk to me, Rory. Tell me what you're feeling," I said.

"You don't want to know what I'm feeling, Ian."

"Yes I do. Talk to me."

She closed her eyes as she began to speak softly. "I feel alone. I feel like a part of me was ripped away and it's a part that I'll never get back. I feel lost, Ian. I spent my entire life taking care of my brother. It's all I knew and now it's gone; he's gone. What am I going to do on Thursdays?"

"You'll go on, Rory. You'll do something else on Thursdays. It's going to be tough for a while, but you're one of the strongest women I know and, with time, you'll begin to heal."

She wiped a tear that fell from her eye. "Heal. Does anybody ever really heal? There will always be an empty place inside me. A place where Stephen and I were connected. A place where we were not only twins, but we were one. We shared a bond and a connection on a deeper level than you could ever imagine."

"I know you did, sweetheart, and I want you to hold onto his memory for the rest of your life. As hard as this is, you need to think of Stephen and how he is right now. He's no longer locked up in a psychiatric hospital. He doesn't hear voices anymore and he's free. In some way, that has to make you feel a little better."

She looked at me and gave a small smile. "I know all that, but I want him here with me." She began to cry.

I wrapped my arm around her and pulled her into me. "I know you do, sweetheart, so do I."

Rory

A few days had passed and we had a very small funeral service for Stephen. I didn't contact my Aunt Nancy because, as far as I was concerned, she didn't care about him anyway when he was alive. The event dinner was tonight and Ian chose not to go. I had already told him that I wasn't up for going out and he agreed. The autopsy had confirmed that the virus Stephen had attacked his heart and that was his cause of death. I hadn't done anything since he died except stay in bed and sleep. Ian told me that I needed to make an appointment with Dr. Neil and talk to her about everything. But, to be honest, what was she going to do to make me feel better. Every day was a struggle for me just to get out of bed. Tomorrow was Ian's birthday and I felt horrible that I didn't get the chance to buy him anything. I climbed out of bed and walked downstairs to his study, where I knew he was working. I stood in the doorway and stared at him for a moment before he realized I was there.

"Hey, sweetheart." He smiled.

"Can I come in?" I asked.

"Of course you can. Come here," he said as he held his arms out to me.

I walked over and sat down on his lap. He wrapped his arms around me and gave me a soft kiss.

"Did you have a nice nap?"

"I guess. I'm hoping that we're still going on the yacht for your birthday tomorrow."

His eyes lit up. "Are you up for it? Do you really want to go?"

"Yes." I smiled as I ran the back of my hand across his cheek.

"Then yes, we're going."

I hugged him as I buried my face in his neck. The scent of his cologne was making me horny. It always did, but today, it was stronger than ever. We hadn't had sex in three days and I missed him being inside me. Even though I felt close and connected to him, I needed him in another way. I softly began tracing his neck with my tongue.

"I need you to make love to me," I whispered.

"It would be my pleasure, sweetheart," he whispered back.

He lifted me up and carried me upstairs. We made love three times that night. He knew how much I needed him.

Chapter 19
Ian & Rory

Rory and I spent a couple of days on the yacht. There was no other way I wanted to spend my birthday than with her. After everything she'd been through, she seemed to be doing okay. We had beautiful meals, wonderful conversations, and made love multiple times a day. My favorite part of the trip was when Rory played "Happy Birthday" on the piano and sang to me. She talked a lot about her father and wanted to pay another visit to the Piano Bar. She said she wanted to tell him who she was and what had happened to Stephen. I didn't know if that was such a good idea, but it was her decision and I'd support her. Andrew was pissed off that I was spending my birthday with Rory and he wanted to take me out to the club when we got back. I didn't know if Rory was up to going. I thought maybe if Adalynn and Daniel came with us, she'd be more willing to go. I didn't want to push too much. She was slowly trying to feel normal again. As we were on our way home and sitting in the limo, I pulled my ringing phone from my pocket and saw that Andrew was calling.

"Hello, Andrew."

"Ian, my friend. How was your birthday on the yacht?"

"It was a lot of fun, and quiet."

"Well, don't get too used to the quiet because we're hitting the club tomorrow night. I talked to Adalynn and she and Daniel are coming. We're going to celebrate your birthday big, bro. Oh, you can bring Rory if you want."

"I'll talk to Rory about it. I'll see you tomorrow night. Bye, Andrew."

I sighed as I hit the end button and then grabbed Rory's hand. "Andrew has planned a small get together at a club with Adalynn and Daniel for my birthday. Are you up for going?"

"Of course. If it's to celebrate your birthday. It'll be fun with you and Adalynn and Daniel there."

"And not Andrew, right?" I asked.

"Ian, Andrew doesn't like me for some reason."

"Nah, I think he does. Like I told you before, I think he's jealous," I said as I kissed her temple.

When we arrived home, I carried the bags upstairs and Rory followed. She sat down on the bed and sighed.

"I want to go to the Piano Bar tonight."

I turned around and looked at her. "Are you sure?"

"Yeah. I may not say anything to Jimmy, but I just need to go. He's the only family I have left."

I climbed on the bed and leaned into her. "I'm your family."

She brought her hand up to my cheek and smiled. "Yes, you are my family, but I'm talking blood related."

"You know that blood doesn't always make a family, sweetheart."

"I know, but he's my dad."

I smiled at her as I ran my finger along her jawline. We were interrupted by Richard's voice calling my name from downstairs.

"Great, my dad is back from his trip. He and Adalynn always have perfect timing."

Rory laughed and we both got up from the bed and walked downstairs. Richard was at the bar, pouring himself a drink. "Hey, you two. How was your little trip?"

"It was great, Dad. Glad you're back. How was your trip?"

"It was productive, to say the least. Rory, I'm so sorry about your brother," he said with open arms.

Rory walked over and thanked him as they lightly hugged. I was happy they were starting to get along. My phone rang and as I pulled it from my pocket. It was a business call that I'd been waiting for.

"If you'll excuse me, I have to take this. It's important."

Rory

Richard didn't look well. He looked tired and different. "Are you feeling okay, Richard?" I asked.

He looked at me and cocked his head. "Yes, I feel fine. Why do you ask?"

"You just look tired. That's all," I replied.

"Nah, I'm good." He winked.

He reached in his pocket to pull out his phone and a small, white piece of paper fell to the floor. I reached down to get it and Richard tried to stop me.

"No, Rory. I'll get it."

It was too late; I already had it in my hand. I glanced at the paper. At the top, it said John Hopkins Medicine. I looked at him as he stared at me while taking the paper from my hand. Ian walked back into the room and Richard lightly shook his head at me.

"What's going on?" he asked.

"Nothing. I just dropped something and Rory was kind enough to pick it up for me."

I smiled at him and walked over to where Ian was standing.

"What brings you by, Dad?"

"I wanted to give you your birthday present, son," he said as he reached into his suit pocket and pulled out a long box.

Ian took it with a smile and opened it. Inside, sat a beautiful gold watch.

"Dad, this is Grandpa's watch," Ian said as he looked at him.

"Yes, it is, and it's time to pass it to you. You've wanted that watch ever since you were a kid."

Ian smiled and gave Richard a light hug. "Thank you. I don't know what to say."

"You don't have to say anything, Ian. Happy birthday, son," Richard said as they hugged again.

Ian looked at me as he showed me the watch. It was beautiful and you could tell it was an expensive antique. "It's beautiful, honey." I smiled.

Ian removed it from the box and put it on. As he was examining it, the strangest thing came out of Richard's mouth.

"Do you have any plans tomorrow, Rory?"

I looked at him in confusion, bewildered that he would even ask me that. "I'm not sure yet. I don't think so unless Adalynn needs help with the wedding."

"Well, I'm going to pick you up around noon tomorrow and take you to lunch," he said.

I was shocked and no words would come out of my mouth. "Uh, okay. I would like that."

"Great. I'll see you tomorrow then. I need to get going. I have a few business things I need to do."

Ian walked Richard to the door and thanked him again for the watch. As soon as he shut it, he turned and looked at me. "That's really nice of my dad to take you to lunch." He smiled.

"You don't think it's weird?" I asked.

"No, that means he's accepting you now."

"Ian, he seems different."

"Yeah, I noticed that too. But in a good way." He smiled.

As we stood and hugged in the foyer, Mandy walked through the front door. She was startled when she saw us, and Ian and I were just as startled when we saw a bruise on the other side of her face.

"I didn't know you were coming back today. Welcome home," she said as she quickly turned her cheek and began to walk away. I was surprised at Ian's response.

"Stop right there!" he commanded.

He walked over to her and looked at her cheek. "What happened to the other side of your face, Mandy?"

"Stupid door again. I swear I'm such a klutz. I don't know what's wrong with me lately." She smiled lightly, but her nervous tone gave her away.

"You're lying," Ian said abruptly and with rudeness. "Did someone do this to you?"

"Ian, stop," I said as I walked over to Mandy. I could tell she was on the verge of tears.

"Mandy." Ian's voice softened. "Rory told me that you're seeing someone. Is he hurting you?"

A tear fell from her eye that said it all. "He doesn't mean to. He always apologizes after and says how much he loves me and he doesn't mean to hurt me. I've tried to break it off with him, but he won't stay away. He keeps coming back and telling me how much he loves me and Molly.

I put my arm around her and led her over to the couch. Ian followed behind and poured Mandy a glass of wine. "Here, it's okay. Drink this to calm your nerves."

She took the glass and sipped the wine. I looked at Ian as he sat down in the chair across from us. "Mandy, who is this man you're seeing?" he asked.

"Just someone," she replied.

"I want his name," Ian snapped.

I looked at him and gave him my mean look. He took in a deep breath. "Mandy, no man should ever hit or harm a woman physically. You need to stop seeing him. Think of your daughter. Better yet, give me his name and I'll have a talk with him."

"No, Mr. Braxton. You can't get involved."

"Then how about if I fire you?" Ian said.

"IAN!" I yelled.

Ian sighed and rolled his eyes. "I'm sorry. I didn't mean that," he said as he got up and knelt down in front of her. "Listen, Mandy. You're my employee and you're a very good one at that. But you're also my friend, and I won't allow anyone to hurt my friends. So, I have an idea, if it's all right with Rory."

I looked at him in confusion. "Rory and I are going to the Piano Bar tonight. We would like you and your friend to join us."

"Really?" she asked. "You want to go out with me and Colton?" she asked with surprise.

"Yes. Right, Rory?"

"Of course. We would love for you to come with us," I said as I took hold of her hand.

"That way, when you break up with him tonight, I'll be there to have a few words with him if he gets out of line." Ian smiled. "I'll make sure he never bothers you again."

"Thank you both. I don't know what to say."

"There's no need to say anything. Why don't you text him right now and see if he'll come," Ian said.

Mandy pulled her phone from her uniform pocket and sent Colton a text message. I got up and brought her a tissue from the bathroom. Ian followed behind me.

"I'm going to beat the shit out of that guy when I see him."

"So am I. I feel so bad for her. Thank you for helping her," I said as I kissed his lips.

We walked back into the living room and Mandy said that they'd meet us at the Piano Bar around eight o'clock.

"Mandy, go ahead and take the rest of the day off and get ready for tonight."

"No, Mr. Braxton, I couldn't," she said nervously.

"Yes, you can, and I insist. I'll pay you for the entire day, so I don't want you to worry about that."

"Are you sure?"

"Positive." Ian held out his hand and helped her up from the couch.

I gave her a hug and told her not to worry. She smiled at both of us and left. Ian put his arm around me and I laid my head on his shoulder.

"Are you sure you want to go there tonight?" he asked.

"Yes, I'm positive."

"I have some work to catch up on before we go tonight, so I'll be in my study if you need me."

I gave him a soft kiss. "I think I'm going to go downstairs and work out for a while."

"Sounds good, sweetheart. I'll join you in the shower later." He winked.

I smiled and went upstairs to change into my workout clothes.

Chapter 20
Ian

We arrived at the Piano Bar thirty minutes before Mandy and Colton were supposed to meet us. It was pretty crowded, but we were lucky and found a table that sat four people. I led Rory over to the table and pulled out her chair for her. She looked beautiful, but I could see she was nervous. I told her to stay at the table while I went up to the bar to order our drinks.

"Hey, how are you?" Rosie asked. "Is your girlfriend with you?"

"Yes, we're sitting at that table over there." I pointed. "One beer and one cosmo, please."

"Coming right up. Go back and sit down with your girl. I'll bring your drinks." She winked.

I gave her a smile and went back to the table. "Came back empty handed?" Rory asked.

"Rosie is going to bring our drinks over herself."

"Any sign of Jimmy?"

"I didn't see him, sweetheart."

Rosie walked over and set our drinks on the table. "Welcome back, Rory. It's good to see you again."

"Thank you. It's good to see you too." Rory smiled.

I saw Jimmy walk through the bar and over to the piano. Rosie looked at her watch.

"Right on the dot. He plays every night at seven forty-five."

Rosie walked away and Rory reached across the table for my hand. "Wait until you hear him play," she said.

Jimmy sat down at the piano, stretched his fingers, and began playing. He was good and I was impressed. It was clear where Rory got her musical talent from. When he was finished playing, he got up, took a bow, and walked over to the bar. I gave Rory a kiss and looked at my watch. It was eight o'clock and I kept an eye on the front door, waiting for Mandy and Colton to walk in. A few moments later, they both walked in and Rory stood up and alerted them to where we were sitting. Mandy looked nervous and she was holding her wrist. They walked over to the table and Colton introduced himself.

"If you'll excuse us, gentlemen, we girls need to use the ladies' room," Rory said.

While they were gone, I asked Colton what I could order Mandy to drink and I found it odd that he said water.

"She wouldn't want a glass of wine or something stronger?" I asked the asshole.

"No. I don't like her drinking," he said as he ordered himself a beer.

I was getting irritated just looking at him and knowing what he did to Mandy. A few moments later, the girls came back to the table and sat down. Colton leaned back and put his arm around the back of Mandy's chair. As I stared at the both of them, I could tell Mandy was nervous.

"Ian, I'm going to run up to the bar and order another cosmo," Rory said.

"I'll come with you. Can I get either of you anything? Mandy, would you like a glass of wine?"

"Dude, what did I tell you earlier?" Colton blurted out.

Mandy looked at me and shook her head. This asshole was pissing me off and it was taking everything I had in me not to jump across the table and knock him out of the chair. Rory grabbed my hand and led me to the bar.

"They got into an argument on the way here and he grabbed her wrist as hard as could and wouldn't let go. She has bruises already, Ian."

I shook my head as we grabbed our drinks from the bar and sat back down at the table. "So, how long have the two of you been dating?" I asked.

"About a couple of months. Right, babe?" he asked as he looked at Mandy.

"Yeah, a couple of months," she replied.

I hated this guy and I couldn't hold back anymore. "Those bruises Mandy has on her face are not very pretty," I said as I leaned back in my chair.

"Yeah, man, I know. I can't believe how clumsy she is sometimes."

Rory put her hand on my arm because she knew what was coming next. "Mandy, let me see your wrist," I said.

Mandy looked at me with fear in her eyes.

"Dude, what the fuck is your problem?"

"You want to know what the fuck my problem is," I snapped as I stood up and grabbed him by the shirt. "My fucking problem is that you don't know how to be nice to women."

"You have two seconds to get your fucking hands off of me," Colton said as he stared at me.

"Let's take this outside," I said as I yanked him out of the chair and dragged him through the bar.

Once we were outside, he got out of my grip and tried to deck me. I saw it coming and ducked, throwing him up against the brick wall with my arm pressing firmly against his neck. "You and Mandy are over and you are to never come near her again!" I yelled in his face. "You aren't to call her, text her, or go to her house. I'll have my men watching you and if I catch wind of you anywhere near her, I'll kill you myself. Do you understand me?" I said through gritted teeth.

Colton couldn't say anything. He stood there and tried to nod his head. I loosened my grip on him and pushed him away from the wall. "Now, get the fuck out of here."

He looked over at Mandy, who was standing there in tears. "Do you want me to leave, baby? Do you want us to end?"

"Yes. Don't you ever come near me again, you bastard!" she yelled.

He wiped his mouth on his sleeve and walked away. Rory ran and hugged me. "Are you okay?"

"Sweetheart, really?" I smiled. I walked over to Mandy and put my arm around her. "Come on; let's go inside and get you a drink."

****

I brought Mandy her second glass of wine. Jimmy saw us and walked over to the table.

"Hey, little lady. Welcome back." He smiled at Rory.

I could tell she was slightly uncomfortable as she downed the rest of her cosmopolitan. "Are you going to play tonight?" he asked.

"No, I don't think so." She blushed.

I reached over and placed my hand on hers. "You should, sweetheart. Do it for me."

Rory gave me a small smile, got up, walked over to the piano, and began to play. I sat there with a grin on my face, listening to every note.

"Very talented woman. Does someone in her family play?" Jimmy asked.

"Her father does," I replied.

I noticed the way Jimmy kept staring at her. Almost as if he knew or recognized her.

"Is that so?" he asked.

Rory finished her song and came back to the table. When she sat down, I leaned over and gave her a kiss.

"That was nice, Rory." Jimmy smiled.

"Thank you. If you'll excuse me, I'm going to use the ladies' room."

I could sense something was wrong. Rory seemed upset and on edge. Mandy went with her to the bathroom and Jimmy walked away.

Chapter 21
Rory

Mandy and I came out of the bathroom and started walking down the long hallway back to our table. I was startled when I heard a voice behind me.

"You look just like her."

I stopped and told Mandy to go ahead and that I'd meet her at the table. I slowly turned around and stared down the hall at the man who was my father.

"Excuse me?" I said.

He started to walk slowly towards me. "Your mother. You look just like her."

I looked down because I couldn't look him in the eyes. "She's dead, you know," I blurted out. "She died when I was ten years old."

"I'm sorry. I didn't know."

And here it came, all the anger and resentment that was built up inside me unleashed itself.

"How would you know? Huh? You don't know shit about me or Stephen."

He looked at me as water filled his eyes. "Stephen is your twin brother?"

How did he know about that? I felt a hand on my shoulder. "Rory, not here," Ian whispered.

I pulled away. "Was my twin brother. He just died."

"What?" Jimmy asked in shock.

"He's dead!" I screamed.

"I'm sor—" He began to speak and I instantly cut him off.

"Don't. Don't you dare," I said through gritted teeth as I pointed my finger at him. "Don't act like you care. You haven't cared about us in twenty-four years. I found you for one reason and one reason only; to find the answer to the question that has haunted me my entire life."

He stood there, nervous and without words. Ian placed both hands on my shoulders. "Sweetheart, let's do this another time. This isn't the place."

"You want to know why I left. That's your question," Jimmy said.

Tears started to stream down my face. The conversation I had played over and over in my head for so many years finally came to life.

"I'll tell you. But not here, and not tonight. My bar isn't the place to discuss this. This needs to be done in private."

"Then let's take it to your office," I said.

"Rory, we have Mandy out there, waiting for us. Let's not do this now," Ian spoke.

He was right. Mandy had her own problems tonight and I was sure she wanted to go home. "Fine, not here, not tonight,"

I said as I turned around and looked at Ian. "I'll leave it up to you to figure it out. I'm going out there to get Mandy and I'll meet you outside. I need some fresh air."

Ian nodded and kissed me on the head. I walked away from my father and didn't even give him a second look. I wanted peace. I needed peace. But most of all, I wanted him to know how much I hated him for abandoning us. Peace in my life would never exist as long as I carried that around with me. I told Mandy that we were leaving and she followed me outside. As we waited for Ian, I figured I'd better tell her what happened. So I did. Ian came out a few moments later and pulled the car around for us. As soon as I climbed in, Ian grabbed my hand.

"It's going to be okay, sweetheart. He's coming over the day after tomorrow to talk. I'll be with you the whole time."

I didn't say anything. I just laid my head on the window and went deep into thought. We dropped Mandy off at home and Ian told her that she didn't have to come to work tomorrow, but she insisted that she was fine and she wanted to. As we were driving home, Ian softly pressed his lips against my hand.

"Talk to me, sweetheart. Tell me what's going on in that pretty little head of yours."

"Confusion, sadness, uncertainty, anger, all of the above."

Ian chuckled. "You're adorable when you're confused." He smiled.

We pulled up to the house and, as soon as I walked through the door, I went upstairs and got ready for bed. Ian did the same and climbed in next to me.

"Come here, sweetheart. I don't want to do anything but hold you. You're safe with me, Rory, and I'll do anything to protect you."

"I know, Ian," I said as I snuggled against him.

****

I was sitting at the dining room table, drinking my coffee and waiting for Ian to come and sit down. He was on a business call with a company in Japan. I was nervous about my lunch with Richard today. Ian told me that I was being ridiculous and to enjoy myself. But somehow, I had a feeling that it wasn't going to be a pleasant lunch. As I was in thought, Adalynn strolled in the room and took a seat across from me.

"Good morning, darling." She smiled.

"Good morning. Coffee? I asked as I held up the carafe.

"Thank you. Can you believe I'm getting married exactly one month from today?"

"No." I smiled. "It's coming so fast."

"Where's Ian?" she asked.

"He's on a business call with Japan."

"Oh, what a big, important man he is." She winked.

"I heard that, Adalynn," Ian said as he walked over and lightly kissed her cheek.

"Of course you did, darling. How are you?"

"I'm good. Did Rory tell you she confronted Jimmy last night?"

Her mouth dropped as she looked at me. "WHAT!"

I picked up my coffee cup and took a sip of coffee before responding to her. "He told me I looked like my mother. So he basically confronted me."

Mandy walked over and handed Adalynn a fruit cup. "Thank you, darling. Wait, Mandy, what the hell happened to your face?"

Mandy looked at Ian and then at me. "Some douchebag she was seeing thought it was fun to hurt her. I kicked his ass last night and told him never to come near her again."

Adalynn looked at Ian and raised an eyebrow. "Wow. Go you."

Ian chuckled and Mandy smiled. "Well, I'm glad for your sake that bad man is out of your life. You deserve better, honey." Adalynn smiled at her.

Mandy walked away and Adalynn turned her attention back to me and my father. "So, go on. What else did he say?"

"Nothing much. He just said he wouldn't discuss it there, so Ian told him to come here tomorrow."

"Here? Are you okay with that?" Adalynn asked me.

"Yeah, I guess. At least here I can scream and yell and maybe throw a thing or two at him." I smiled.

"True. Well, get the answers you need and then move on. Speaking of moving on," she said as she looked at her watch. "I have to get to *Prim*. I'll see the both of you tonight. Get your dancing shoes out, Rory. We're going to tear up the dance floor."

I gave her a small smile as she got up from the table and left. I really wasn't up to going out tonight, but it was for Ian's birthday, so I had to go. I didn't want to disappoint him, plus I didn't trust Andrew.

Ian and I finished breakfast and he left for the office. "Call me after you have lunch with my dad and let me know how it went," he said as he gave me a kiss goodbye.

"I will, babe. Have a good day at the office."

I wanted to go visit Stephen's grave, so I texted Richard and asked him if I could meet him at the restaurant. He said it was fine and to be there around noon. I took a shower, got dressed, and drove my car to the cemetery after stopping at the florist and picking up some flowers. I parked along the curb, which sat a few feet away from a large tree that stood behind Stephen's grave. The black marble headstone looked beautiful in the sunlight. I knelt down and carefully placed the flowers on his grave.

"Guess what, Stephen. I met our dad last night. He knows who I am. He told me that I look just like Mom. The funny thing is that you were the spitting image of him. He's coming over tomorrow to explain to me why he left. I'm finally going to get the answers I've always wanted. I miss you, Stephen, but I know you're over the rainbow and that you're happy now."

I wiped my eye and looked at my watch. It was almost noon. I said goodbye to Stephen and drove to the restaurant to meet Richard.

****

Richard got up from his seat and gave me a light hug when I walked in. I sat down and ordered a glass of red wine as I admired the beauty of the Italian restaurant.

"How are you, Rory?" Richard asked.

"I'm okay. How are you?"

He pursed his lips together and gave me a small smile. "I'm sick, Rory, and I don't want you telling Ian about this."

I frowned at him and shook my head. "What do you mean, you're sick?"

"You need to promise me that you won't mention any of this to Ian. I'm not ready to tell him."

"Then why are you telling me, Richard?"

"Because you saw the paper from John Hopkins."

"I suspected something was wrong because of the way you reacted when I picked up the paper."

"You didn't say anything to Ian, did you?"

"No," I replied as I shook my head. "What's wrong with you?"

He pick up his glass of scotch and took a drink before answering me. "I have pancreatic cancer, stage four, and it has spread."

Instantly, that sickening feeling in my stomach appeared. "Richard," I said as I placed my hand on his. "My God, are you sure?"

"Of course I'm sure and so is every doctor at John Hopkins."

"You're getting treatments, though, so you'll be fine," I said.

"No, Rory. There's nothing they can do for me. It's too far spread at this point."

Tears started to fill my eyes. "No, Richard. There's got to be something. You're not going to die. Ian needs you."

He placed his other hand on mine. "Rory, I need you to listen to me. I know we got off to a rough start and I'm so sorry about that. There are things about me you don't know, so I don't expect you to understand. What I do know is that you're the best thing that has ever happened to my son. I've never seen him happy like he is. At first, I thought you were just another woman after his money, but you're not. You're a kind and warm woman. You're selfless and you're genuine. My son is one lucky man to have found you. To be honest, I knew right away you were the one because I saw it every time Ian looked at you and it scared me. I didn't want his heart broken like mine had been."

I didn't know if Richard was talking about Ian's mother with that remark, but I felt incredibly bad for him. I just wanted to hug him and tell him that everything was going to be okay, but I had the feeling it wasn't going to be.

"When are you going to tell Ian about this? And how can you expect me to keep this secret from him?"

"You'll do it for me. I trust you. Ian will never know that you knew. I'll tell him when all my affairs are in order."

"But—"

"No buts, Rory. I've made peace with it and I need you to as well. Ian is going to need you in a way he's never needed anyone before."

Richard went on to eat his lunch. He had put me in an awful position and I hated it. I couldn't lie to Ian and now I was forced with a decision I didn't want to make.

Chapter 22

Ian & Rory

I set down my briefcase and walked upstairs to see if Rory was getting ready to go out to the club. When I walked into the bedroom, she had just gotten out of the shower and she was standing naked in the closet, looking through her clothes.

"Hot damn, that's what I like to see when I come home after a long hard day at the office."

She turned her head and looked at me with a smile splashed across her face. "How long and hard is it? I mean, did you have a nice day?"

I smirked and walked up behind her, placing my hands on her breasts and gently giving them a squeeze. "I like your first line better, sweetheart, and I'll show you how long and hard it is."

She gasped, and I knew in that moment that I had her. She could never resist me, just like I could never resist her. My fingers made their way down to the area that she told me constantly ached for me. Feeling how wet she already was turned me on even more. As my tongue began to explore her neck, she reached behind and stroked my hard cock through the fabric of my pants. My finger made its way inside her, causing her to let out a sexy moan. As I turned her around, I passionately kissed her lips before they trailed down to her breasts, torso, and then finally her pussy. She brought her leg up over my shoulder as I had a tight grip on her hips. She ran her fingers through my hair as her body tightened and she yelled my name. Her legs shook as she came. I stood up, tore off my shirt, and took down my pants as fast as I could. There was no waiting. I wanted her and I needed her now. I kissed her lips as I led her to the bed. After I laid her on her stomach, I took her from behind. I clutched her tight beautiful ass as I thrust in and out of her rapidly. I could feel her swelling again and preparing to come.

"Come again, sweetheart. I need you to come one more time for me."

"Please don't stop, baby. I'm so close."

Her moans grew louder and I felt her coming. I gave one final thrust as the buildup in me released and pure bliss took over. As I collapsed on top of her, I reached under her and softly held her breasts while we tried to catch our breath.

"I love you," I whispered and kissed the side of her face.

"I love you too. More than you'll ever know."

While I was in the shower, Rory was putting on her makeup.

"How did lunch go with my dad?" I asked.

"It was nice. I think he really likes me now," she replied.

"I know he likes you, Rory. What did you talk about?"

"Nothing much. Just small talk."

"About what?" I asked as I turned off the water and slid the glass door open.

"He was just asking me about my childhood."

She was lying and I knew it. I wrapped the towel around my waist and walked over to her, wrapping my arms around her waist and looking straight at her through the mirror.

"You would never lie to me, right?" I asked.

"Of course not, Ian," she said with nervousness. She stared at me and I could see the sadness in her eyes. She turned around, looked at me, and then started to walk away. "I'm sorry, I can't do this."

"Do what, Rory?"

"Lie to you. I can't. I love you too much to lie to you," she said as she turned around and looked at me. "Ian, your dad is really sick."

I cocked my head as I looked at her from across the bathroom. "What? What do you mean?"

"He told me not to tell you because he's going to tell you when he has everything in order. He has stage four pancreatic cancer and it spread. I'm so sorry."

I walked over to her and wrapped my arms around her. "I already know, sweetheart."

She pushed back. "What? How?"

"I just found out a couple of days ago. He'd been acting strange lately and he wasn't looking well, so I had someone find out what was going on." I put my hands on her face. "Thank you for telling me the truth when I asked you. You have no idea how much that meant to me," I said as I kissed her warm lips.

She broke our kiss and looked at me with knitted eyebrows. "What the fuck, Ian? You knew and you didn't even bother to share it with me?"

"Sweetheart, listen to me. I just found out the night he came over. I was going to tell you about it that night, but I saw the look on your face when you picked up the piece of paper from the floor."

"You saw that?"

"Yes. I was on my way back into the room and I saw his reaction when you went to pick it up. Then, when he asked you to lunch, I found it odd and that was when I suspected he was going to tell you."

"So basically, you waited to see if I'd lie to you or not?" she asked with an attitude.

"No, not really. But I did want to see if you'd tell me."

Rory sighed and walked to the bedroom. "You really suck, Ian."

"I'm sorry, sweetheart."

"Do you have any idea how much it's bothered me all day that your father put me in that position?"

I walked over to her and grabbed both her hands. "I'm sure it did bother you and he was wrong, but I'm so proud of you for telling me. I love you so much, Rory," I said as I pulled her into me.

"I love you too. You're not going to say anything to him, are you?"

"No. I'm just going to pretend I know nothing. I'm really upset about it. But we can talk about it later. We need to finish getting ready for the club."

Rory

We met Andrew, Adalynn, and Daniel at the club. Andrew wanted to pick us up, but Ian told him that we'd all meet up there. We walked inside and, instantly, Andrew flagged us down. Ian had a tight grip on my hand as he led us to a booth.

"Hi, darling. You look amazing!" Adalynn said as she gave me a hug.

"So do you." I smiled.

Andrew leaned over and gave me a light kiss on the cheek. "You look nice, Rory."

I forced a small smile to amuse him as I said thank you. I said hello to Daniel with a kiss and we all sat down. Ian put his arm around me. It was almost as if he was letting everyone know I was his. He wasn't thrilled with the short dress I was wearing. We, or should I say he, had a discussion about it before we left the house. Naturally, I won and he didn't say another word about it. The music was loud and people were everywhere. Andrew ordered appetizers and had a round of drinks brought to the table every thirty minutes.

"Come on; let's go dance!" Adalynn said with a grin.

"Do you want to come?" I asked Ian.

"No, you go ahead. I'll just sit here and watch you." He smiled.

Adalynn and I tore up the dance floor. I had a couple of drinks and I was feeling really relaxed. I caught Ian staring at me as I danced. He was biting his bottom lip and shaking his head. I was pretty sure he was turned on and so was I just by looking at him. After a couple of songs, Adalynn and I went back to the table and sat down. Ian already had another drink waiting for me.

"You looked amazing out there," he whispered in my ear. "Wait until I get you home. In fact, we may not even make it until we get home," he said as he grabbed my hand from underneath the table and put it on his hard cock.

I removed my hand and giggled as I kissed his lips.

"Okay, you two, that's enough," Andrew said. "It's time for your birthday present. Follow me."

We all got up and followed Andrew into a private room. There was a TV, two couches, a loveseat, and a couple of chairs.

"You sit in this chair, Ian."

I looked at Ian and he shrugged his shoulders. I didn't like this because I knew douchebag Andrew way too well. He was up to something. Whatever he had planned, I wasn't going to let it bother me. He was doing it to hurt me.

Suddenly a tall, blonde-haired girl walked in, wearing a box. She was dressed as a present and had a bow on top of her head. She was wearing thigh-high black stockings and black high-heeled shoes. She walked over to Ian.

"Are you the birthday boy?" she asked.

"Yeah." Ian smiled.

I sat there because I knew damn well she was a stripper. I glanced over at Andrew, who sat on the couch with a smirk on his face.

"I need you to unwrap me," she said.

Ian didn't hesitate as he took the bow off her head. I sat there with a raging fire inside me. A fire so hot that it was making my skin burn from inside.

She took the bow from him and stuck it on his head. Adalynn got up and sat down next to me.

"Don't let it get to you," she whispered.

"It already has," I replied.

The stripper told Ian that he needed to finish unwrapping her by pulling down the zipper in the back. She turned around and he did.

"Now that you've unwrapped your present, it's time to see what's inside." The stripper smiled.

She shimmied out the box only to reveal a black baby doll nightie that was fully opened in the front with a matching string up her ass. I looked over at Andrew and he was smiling at me. I shook my head as I glared at him. He threw back the rest of his drink.

The stripper gave Ian a lap dance and when she turned around, she grabbed his hands and planted them firmly on her ass. Ian looked at me and he knew how pissed I was. He immediately removed his hands from her. After her little dance, the stripper slowly stripped out of her nightie and shoved her tits in Ian's face. That was the last straw as I bolted up from the couch and walked out of the room. I heard Ian yell my name. I was in tears as I ran down the hallway. I found the ladies' room and stepped inside. A few moments later, the door opened, and when I looked over, Andrew was standing there with his hand on the knob.

"Get the fuck out of here!" I yelled.

"Rory, calm down. I came to apologize to you."

"Where's Ian?"

"I told him I'd come find you and bring you back."

"You are an asshole. Now get the fuck out of here!" I yelled.

Andrew smiled at me as he started walking towards me. "Come on, Rory. We're friends. You always forgive your friends."

"WE.ARE.NOT.FRIENDS! I would never be friends with a scumbag like you."

"Now, Rory. That's not nice," he said as he grabbed my hair. "I like you, and I want to fuck you. I've wanted to fuck you since the first day I saw you in Ian's basement, punching away at that punching bag. But then Ian had to go and fall in love with you. I warned him you were trash and only using him for his money," he said as his grip on my hair grew tighter.

I was scared, but I needed to remain calm. I could handle him. Suddenly, I heard Adalynn on the other side of the door.

"Rory, why is the door locked? Are you okay? Are you in there?"

"Adalynn!" I yelled as Andrew put his hand over my mouth.

"Rory, what's wrong?" she asked.

I struggled as Andrew had me tight in his grip. "Just let me fuck you one time. Ian will never know. I have to know what it feels like to be inside you."

I bit his hand and he yelled as he removed it from my mouth. I turned around and kneed him in the balls. He grabbed himself and fell to the ground. I ran to the door and unlocked it, but as I tried to turn the knob, Andrew grabbed my leg and pulled me down. He threw me on my back and pinned my arms above my head with one hand while the other hand covered my mouth. I was trying to kick, when suddenly, the bathroom door flew open and Ian grabbed Andrew off of me and threw him up against the sink, punching him and then throwing him to the ground.

"What did you do?" Ian screamed at him.

"She's a fucking whore, Ian. Ever since she walked into your life, you've given up everything, including our friendship," he said as he punched Ian in the mouth.

Adalynn ran to me and hugged me. She helped me up and I stood there and watched Ian beat the shit out of Andrew.

"You piece of shit. You were like a brother to me!" he screamed with each punch. "How could you do this to me and to the woman I love?"

Andrew didn't say a word. He couldn't. Daniel went over and pulled Ian off of him.

"That's enough, Ian. I think he got the message."

"Don't you ever, and I mean ever, come near me or Rory again. Do you understand me?!" Ian yelled at Andrew. "Our friendship is over forever!"

Ian wiped the blood from his mouth as he turned around and looked at me. His breathing was rapid. He walked over to me and placed his hands on each side of my face, checking to see if I was hurt.

"Are you okay?" he asked with sadness in his eyes.

I couldn't cry. Normal people would cry in a situation like this, but I couldn't. I felt nothing but rage. The rage I used to feel growing up. The numbness was back and it took over my body as if it never left.

"I'm fine," I whispered as I looked at Ian.

"See, she's fine," Andrew said as he stood up.

The rage inside consumed me and I pushed Ian out of my way. I stared at Andrew as I began to walk towards him.

"Rory, what are you doing?" Ian asked.

I approached Andrew and, for a moment, we just stared at each other. I hated him. I hated everything about him. The words that kept going through my mind were "*Focus all your energy into your hands. Let it build and then focus when you're ready to strike.*" And that was exactly what I did. I threw a punch across his face and broke his nose. He fell to the ground and held his nose. Blood spilled everywhere. I looked down at him and then I spit on him. "Go to hell, you asshole," I said and then turned and looked at Ian. "I want to go home."

Ian put his arm around me and I moved out from under it.

"I'm still pissed at you about the stripper," I said as I walked ahead of him and out of the bathroom. "Someone needs to call 911 for that asshole in there," I said to the line of women that were waiting to get inside.

Chapter 23
Ian

"Rory, stop!" I commanded. But she didn't listen. She kept walking ahead of me and acted like I didn't exist.

"Ian, now's not a good time to have an attitude with her. She's been through a horrible ordeal tonight and, if anything, she just needs you to be calm and take care of her."

"I do take care of her and I will continue to do so, Adalynn."

We both said goodbye to Adalynn and Daniel and we walked to the car. I opened the door for her and she climbed in, grabbing the handle and slamming it shut. After I climbed in, I looked at her and she wouldn't look at me. After I slammed my hands on the steering wheel, she turned her head and looked at me.

"You have no right to be angry with me," she said. "I'm the one who has the right. I've been hurt and humiliated on all levels tonight and I just want to go home."

The only thing I wanted to do was grab her and hold her tight. But I knew if I tried to touch her, she'd either slap me or she'd get out of the car.

"I'm sorry about the stripper. But that wasn't my fault. I had no clue that Andrew had hired her. I know now the only reason he did it was to hurt you. Sweetheart, please talk to me. We are not leaving this parking spot until you talk to me."

She turned her head and looked at me. Her eyes were full of sadness and hurt. I slowly reached for her hand and she let me hold it. "Andrew is out of our lives for good. In fact, tomorrow morning, I want you to press charges against him."

"No, Ian. I think he learned his lesson. I just want to forget about tonight and go on with my life. He isn't going to come anywhere near either of us anymore. Can you please drive us home now?"

"Can I have a kiss first?" I asked hesitantly.

She leaned closer and I gave her a warm, loving kiss. As I ran my hand down her cheek and stared into her eyes, I whispered, "I love you and only you."

"I'm still mad about the stripper," she said.

"Ugh, Rory. I'll tell you what. I'm going to get you a male stripper, then we'll be even, okay?"

She finally gave me her beautiful smile. "The only stripper I want is you."

I let out a breath. Finally, she wasn't so pissed off at me anymore. "You got it, sweetheart. I'll strip for you every night." I winked.

I started the car and, as I drove us home, I held her hand the whole way. I still couldn't believe the events of tonight. I knew Andrew was a little emotionally fucked up. But I had no idea he would do something like this. Every time I thought about it, I wanted to go and kill him.

When we arrived home, Rory went upstairs and started the bath. I walked over to the bar and poured some bourbon for me and a glass of wine for her. I took them upstairs and into the bathroom. I set the glass on the edge of the tub as Rory lay back and looked at me.

"Join me," she said.

"You really want me to?" I asked in disbelief because I thought she wanted to be alone.

"If I didn't, I wouldn't have asked."

I gave her a smile and stripped out of my clothes. She scooted up so I could climb behind her. I wrapped my arms around her and she rested the back of her head on my chest. "We have so much to talk about, Ian. So much has happened in the past few days between my father, your father, douchebag Andrew."

"I know, sweetheart," I said as I kissed her head.

"I want to go back to Paris where it was peaceful and quiet and just the two of us."

"We'll go back there soon. I promise. Let's deal with one issue at a time. We've already dealt with Drew, so we can cross him off our list."

"I wish you'd talk to me about your dad," she said.

"What's there to talk about? I'm obviously upset and I'm pissed that he hasn't told me. It's hard to take it all in, you know?"

"I know it is, babe. I didn't tell you earlier, but I love you too," she said as she turned her head and kissed my lips.

Those words, at that moment, meant everything to me. I kissed her back passionately and we made love in the bathtub before heading to bed.

****

"I was so worried about you all night," Adalynn said as she stormed into the dining room and hugged Rory.

"I'm okay, Adalynn. Thank you for your concern." She smiled.

"And him? The two of you?" she said as she pointed to Ian and me.

"We're fine, Adalynn, and good morning to you," I said.

"Whew, thank God. I thought maybe Rory was going to kick you out on your ass or something because of that stripper whore."

I looked at her and cocked my head. "That stripper was not my fault, and Rory and I already discussed it and we really don't want to discuss it again."

"Fine," she said as she waved her hand at me. "Coffee, I need coffee."

"You know where it is. Go get some," I said.

Adalynn looked at me and rolled her eyes. "Can you believe I was married to this guy?" She winked at Rory.

"Why do you keep bringing that up?" I asked as I walked to the kitchen.

"Because I think it's funny and I know it bothers you." She laughed.

I poured her a cup of coffee and set it down in front of her. "Speaking of marriage, yours is coming quick and you'll be going on your honeymoon, which means I'll need to be at *Prim* to oversee things." I smiled.

"The business end of things, Ian. Not the creative side of it," Adalynn responded.

"Oh, but, darling, I'm very good at the creative side of things. Ask my beautiful girlfriend over there."

"Ian, I'm warning you. Just the business side. I've got the creative end covered."

"We'll see." I smiled as I finished my breakfast and got up from my chair.

"Damn you, Braxton. If I have to worry about my company on my honeymoon, I'm going to have your head."

"Our company, Adalynn. Our company." I smiled before I walked out of the room.

I knew it was mean to tease her like that, but it couldn't be helped. The truth was that I could have cared less about the creative side of things over at *Prim*. As long as it was making me money, I didn't care. I went upstairs, grabbed my briefcase, and kissed Rory before I left for the office.

"I'm only going to be there a few hours. I'll be back in plenty of time before your dad gets here. I don't want you to worry, sweetheart."

"I'll be okay. Have a good day. I'll see you in a few hours." She smiled.

I headed for the limo with worry on my mind. I'd told her not to worry, yet I was consumed with it. I was worried about the effect the meeting between Rory and Jimmy would have on her long term. Then there was the worry about my own father.

Chapter 24
Rory

I was nervous, very nervous as I sat on the bed and folded my clothes. I needed to keep busy to keep myself from going crazy. *Was I ready to hear Jimmy out? Was I ready to accept the reason he'd abandoned his children? Was I ready to talk about Stephen?* I wasn't sure of anything anymore after what had happened over the past few days. I just wanted to escape. I didn't want to deal with reality anymore, at least for a while. I finished putting my clothes away and went down to the beach. I stood down by the water and thought about Stephen. He would have loved it here. There were so many things he would have loved to have seen and done, but now, he wouldn't be able to.

"What are you doing out here?" Ian asked from behind.

I smiled. Every time I heard his voice, I felt a sense of peace and protection. I turned around and saw him standing there with a bouquet of flowers in his hand and a smile on his face. I walked up to him and gave him a kiss as he handed me the flowers.

"They're beautiful, Ian. Thank you."

"You're welcome. They're for a beautiful woman." He smiled as he pushed a few strands of my hair behind my ear.

He put his arm around me and we went back up to the house.

"Those are beautiful, Rory," Mandy said as she sniffed them.

"Thank you. Do you know where a vase is?" I asked.

Ian grabbed a bottle of water from the refrigerator and, as Mandy handed me the vase, the doorbell rang. Instantly, I felt sick to my stomach. My reaction must have said it all because Ian kissed me and rubbed my back before answering the door.

"Just come into the living room when you're ready, sweetheart."

I nodded my head and filled the vase with water. I could hear them talking in the foyer.

"It'll be okay, Rory. You can do this. Keep your head up and be confident. You're one of the strongest women I've ever met." Mandy smiled.

I took in a deep breath. "Thank you, Mandy."

I walked out of the kitchen and into the living room. Jimmy was sitting on the couch and Ian was sitting on the loveseat across from him. Ian looked at me and gave me a small smile. Jimmy stood up and turned around.

"Hi, Rory," he said nervously.

"Hey," I replied.

I sat down next to Ian, feeling as awkward as shit. I picked up the glass of wine that was waiting for me on the end table. I took a sip and a deep breath.

"The only thing I can do right now is apologize, Rory," Jimmy said.

I sat there and stared at him. God, he looked so much like Stephen. I wanted to burst into tears, but I refused to do it in front of him, at least for now.

"Why? And how did you know that my mother had twins? From what Aunt Nancy told me, you took off the minute you found out she was pregnant."

"There's a lot more to it than just that. Things Nancy never knew about," he said as he sipped his water.

Ian took hold of my hand and held it, trying to offer me some comfort and reassurance. "Do you even know what kind of childhood Stephen and I had? Do you even want to know? If you had stuck around, things could've been different. We were raised by an alcoholic and drug-addicted prostitute after my mother died. I was the one who had to take care of Stephen and me. I raised both of us because Nancy couldn't even look at us, and I never knew why until I went and paid her a little visit. That's when she told me about you. Do you know that her drug dealer cared more about me and Stephen then she did?"

He sat there and shook his head. "I'm sorry."

I couldn't stand listening to his apologies anymore. I bolted up from the loveseat and got in his face. "You're *sorry*! Sorry doesn't cut it anymore, Daddy!" I yelled.

Ian got up, grabbed my arm, and led me back to the loveseat. "Sweetheart, keep calm."

Jimmy reached into his pocket and pulled out his wallet. He smiled as he looked at a picture and then handed it to me. It was a picture of my mom. Tears started to fill my eyes when I looked at it. Ian rubbed my back as I tried not to cry.

"Your mother is beautiful. You look just like her," Ian said.

"When I came out of the storage room that night and saw you sitting at the bar, I almost had a heart attack. It was like your mom was sitting there. I wasn't sure at first, but then when you came into the bar the other night, I knew. I could feel it, especially when you played the piano."

He reached into his wallet and pulled out another picture and handed it to me. It was a picture of me and Stephen as babies. I gasped and the tears I tried to hold back fell down my face, one at a time.

"Your mom sent that picture to me after you were born."

"She knew where you where?"

He nodded his head as he looked down. "Yes. Your mom and I had a relationship together."

"But you were with Aunt Nancy," I said.

"She's what made everything so hard. I left because your mom asked me to."

"What?" I asked as I cocked my head.

"She said we could never be together because of my drinking. She gave me a choice: her or the booze. At the time, as much as I loved her, I didn't think I could give it up. And then there was Nancy. I gave everything serious thought and the best thing for your mom and you kids was for me to leave. I would have been a lousy father. I was messed up back then. Your mom agreed. She was the most caring and selfless woman I'd ever known. It was hard to believe her and Nancy were sisters. She let me go because of you and Stephen. Once I left and got settled, I sent her my address and told her that if she needed anything, to let me know. I received this picture seven months later with your and Stephen's names on it. I cried that day because I couldn't believe I had two beautiful children."

"Spare me the bullshit and the lies. Nancy told me my mother got pregnant after one drunken night with you!"

"That's what she wanted Nancy to believe. She couldn't tell her that we'd been seeing each other for months behind her back. I didn't love Nancy and I wanted to break it off with her, but she was a mess. Finally, after your mom told me to leave, I told Nancy I was sorry, I left, and I never looked back. It took me seven years to get sober."

"And now? You own a fucking bar!" I yelled.

"The bar is part of my sobriety. I haven't had a drink in seventeen years. The piano and the music are what helped me through my rehab. I sent a letter to your mother about ten years ago, but it was returned. I figured she still wanted nothing to do with me. I didn't know she had passed away," he said as he looked down.

The tears wouldn't stop falling and Ian got up and got me some tissues. I didn't know what to think. I wanted my answers and now I had them and I still wasn't sure about anything. "And you kept these pictures all these years?" I asked.

"Yes. Whether you want to believe it or not, I loved your mother very much and I left because she wanted me to. I loved her enough to let her go. I made a copy of the picture of you and Stephen and I have it hanging on my office wall at the bar. There hasn't been a day that has gone by that I don't think about my children."

"Did you ever marry?" I asked.

"No. I never found anyone that measured up to your mom."

I sat there and cried. Ian kept rubbing my back and holding my hand.

"You got the answers you wanted, and now it's time for me to go. I want you to know that I'm happy you searched for me. Believe it or not, I would look at every guy and girl that came into the bar and I would wonder if they were my children. I want to get to know you, Rory. I hope someday you'll give me that chance," he said as he got up from the couch. "I'm sorry about Stephen. He was my son and even though I didn't know him, there's an empty place inside me where I kept him all these years. Maybe someday you can tell me all about him."

Ian got up and walked him to the door. As soon as he shut it, he turned and looked at me. I got up and ran downstairs to the gym. I started punching the punching bag as hard as I could. My knuckles instantly bruised and they were still sore from when I punched Andrew. Ian came downstairs and grabbed me from behind.

"Stop, Rory. You're going to break your hands."

I tried to struggle, but his grip around me was tight. I stopped and lowered my head. Ian loosened his grip around me and I fell to my knees, sobbing as I placed my palms on the floor. Ian followed me down and wrapped his arms around me.

"Sweetheart, it's okay. I know how hard this is for you. I'm here for you, baby. You're safe."

I cried in his arms until I had no more tears left. "Are you okay?" he asked calmly.

I nodded my head, turned, and looked at him. He carefully wiped the tears from my face with his thumbs and took my hands and softly kissed each bruised knuckle. "Come on. Let's go upstairs and get some ice for these."

He helped me up and we went into the kitchen. The staff was gone and it was only Ian and me in the house. He took out some ice cubes from the freezer, wrapped them in a towel, and sat down across from me at the table.

"Give me your hands, sweetheart."

I laid my hands on the table and he placed the towel with ice cubes over my knuckles. I pulled my hands back slightly because it hurt.

"Rory," Ian said.

"It hurts, Ian," I whined.

"I know it does, but you need to keep the ice on them just for a little bit." As he held the ice on my knuckles, his thumbs softly stroked mine as he soothed me.

We sat across from each other at the table and stared into each other's eyes. "I love you," I said.

"I love you more." He smiled.

"What do I do about Jimmy?"

"You need to figure that one out on your own. I can't make that decision for you, sweetheart."

"A part of me feels bad for him, but the other part of me still hates him."

"It's going to take time. You can't change the past, but you can change the future. Just remember that his blood runs through your veins and he is your father."

"The same goes for you too, buddy," I said.

"What do you mean?"

"Your dad and your mom. You can't change the past, Ian, but you can certainly change your future."

"Don't throw my words back at me, sweetheart." He smiled.

He took the ice from my hands and got up and put it in the sink. I stood up from my chair and waited as he walked over and wrapped his arms around me.

"I have an idea," he said. "Let's order a pizza and go eat it on the beach."

"Really?" I asked.

"Yep. We'll spread out a blanket, eat some pizza, drink some wine, talk, and then maybe we can make love once it gets dark."

"I love your ideas." I smiled.

Chapter 25
Ian

A couple of weeks had passed and Rory seemed to be doing better. She still hadn't gone back to the Piano Bar to see Jimmy and, when I'd ask her about it, she would just say she didn't know what she was going to do. I decided to leave her alone about it and, when she was ready, she'd let me know. Thursdays had now become our visitation day at the cemetery for Stephen. Adalynn's wedding was next week and I knew Rory was getting excited for it. As for Richard, I needed to confront him about his illness. Too much time had passed and he still hadn't told me. I was getting angrier by the day and Rory knew it. She was the one who talked me into talking to him. I sat at my desk in my study and opened the top drawer. I pulled out the white envelope and sat back in my chair, debating whether or not to open it. All these years of hiding it and never once gave it a second thought, until recently. Rory had opened my eyes about my own family.

"What's that?" she asked as she walked into the study.

I looked up at her and then at the envelope. "It's nothing," I replied as I put it back in the drawer.

"It looked like you were deep in thought, the way you were staring at it."

"It's nothing, sweetheart." I smiled.

"If you're lying to me, Mr. Braxton, I can promise you there will be no more sex for at least a month."

I knitted my eyebrows at her and I got up from my chair and shut the door. I looked at her as I put my arms around her and leaned her up against the desk. "Is that so? Well, I know for a fact you can't resist me when I do this," I said as my tongue traveled down her neck. My fingers took down the straps of her tank top, exposing her bare breasts. "And I know you can't resist me when I do this." I smiled as I took her hard nipples between my fingers and tugged on them. She let out a moan and threw her head back. My hands lifted up her skirt above her waist. As I undid my pants and pulled them down, I set her up on my desk and inserted two fingers into her, making sure she was ready for me to fuck her nice and hard for her little threat. She smiled at me as she bit down on her bottom lip, turning me on even more. I pushed the edge of her panties to the side and thrust myself into her. We gasped at the same time as she wrapped her legs around me, allowing me to thrust in and out of her faster. "I know you can't resist my cock in you. Tell me how much you love it."

"I love it, Ian," she said with bated breath.

"Are you ever going to threaten me with no sex again?" I asked as I pushed in and out of her hard.

"No, never."

We both were on the verge of an orgasm and I couldn't help but rub her clit before we both came. That sent her over the edge as her legs tightened around me and she let out her sexy moans in my ear. She was trying to be quiet because the staff was throughout the house. I pushed deeper into her as she came, and I spilled everything I had inside of her. She felt so good and making love to her made me forget about everything else. When we finished, I stared at her while I pushed a few strands of hair behind her ear.

"No sex for at least a month, eh?" I said.

"Okay, maybe a month was a little harsh." She smiled.

I chuckled as I pulled out of her and grabbed some tissues from the desk. My phone beeped with a text message from my father.

"I'm on my way over."

"That was my dad; he's on his way over."

"Are you sure you want to do this, Ian?" Rory asked.

"No, but I don't have a choice. He obviously isn't going to tell me, so I guess I'll just have to tell him I found out."

We left my study and went into the kitchen where Charles was preparing dinner for us. Mandy was gathering up her things and getting ready to leave for the night when Richard walked in.

"Oh, Mandy, I'm glad you're still here. I need to speak with you in private."

She looked at him and then over at me and Rory. "It's okay, Mandy. I promise to behave. You have nothing to worry about."

She walked with him in the other room and I looked at Rory. "What the hell is all that about?" I asked.

"I'm guessing he may be apologizing to her for his past actions."

He walked back in the kitchen and began talking to Charles. "I'll be right back. Why don't you two go outside on the patio and sit down?"

I went into the foyer to check on Mandy and she was grinning from ear to ear. "Are you okay?" I asked in a whisper.

"Mr. Braxton, you father apologized to me and then gave me a check for twenty-five thousand dollars."

"What?!" I exclaimed.

"He told me he was sorry and this was to make up for all his horrible behavior the past few years. I told him no, that I couldn't accept it and he insisted. He told me it was for me and Molly."

I smiled at her and put my hand on her shoulder. "I'm happy he did that for you. Accept it and don't give it a second thought. Have a good night, Mandy."

"Thank you, Mr. Braxton."

I went outside to join my beautiful girlfriend and father on the patio. They had already opened a bottle of wine and were talking when I approached the table. I sat down, poured a glass, and looked at my father.

"Why haven't you told me you're dying?" I asked abruptly.

Rory's eyes widened and Richard looked over at her. "No, Dad, Rory didn't say a word to me about it. I had you followed a while back. I knew before you took Rory to lunch that day."

"What the fuck, Ian!" he exclaimed. "How dare you!"

"No! How dare you keep something like this from your only son!" I shouted.

"Ian, calm down, please," Rory said as she reached over and placed her hand on mine.

She was right; yelling was not going to solve anything. My dad looked down at the glass of wine he held in his hand.

"I'm sorry, son. I didn't know how to tell you. I didn't want you upset. It doesn't matter what age you are, I'll always want to protect you from grief."

Those words coming from my father's mouth were something that I'd never heard before. I knew he cared for me, but he was never one to show emotion. My heart sank with his words. I watched as Rory leaned over and grabbed his hand. He looked up at her and gave her a small smile.

"Listen, son. It is what it is. Your old man is dying and my wish is to make the best of what time I have left. I've already started righting the wrongs in my life."

"Is that why you gave Mandy twenty-five thousand dollars?"

Rory gasped and her eyes widened as she looked at me. "You did what?" she asked him.

"I've been a horrible man to Mandy, actually to a lot of women. But with Mandy, I can make things right. I gave her that money for her and her daughter so they don't have to struggle. Have you seen where they live?"

"No, I haven't," I replied.

"Well, son, maybe you should. It's not a safe neighborhood and definitely not suitable for a child to grow up in. Mandy's a good girl and I took advantage of her and I wanted to apologize. So, I did, and I gave her a little something extra to help her move to a better place."

"Dad, I'm calling the doctor tomorrow. There has to be something they can do."

"No use, Ian. The cancer has already started to spread. The doctors said there's nothing they can do except prolong my life by six months to a year at the most with chemotherapy. There's risks with chemo. If the cancer doesn't kill me, another disease I pick up from a weak immune system will. No thanks."

"So you're just going to give up?" I shouted as I got up from my seat and threw it to the side.

"Ian!" Rory exclaimed.

"It's my time, son. I'm not giving up and I'm not afraid. I've already made my peace with this and I need you to do the same."

I couldn't believe what I was hearing. I was sick to my stomach over his decision. My father was dying and there was nothing I could do about it.

"I'll be right back," my father said as he looked at his phone and then got up from the table.

Rory walked over to where I was standing and put her arm around my waist. "Ian, I'm sorry."

"Don't be, sweetheart. He's a stubborn ass."

We heard footsteps on the patio and we both turned around. My heart wanted to jump out of my throat at what I saw.

"Hi, Ian."

Tears started to fill my eyes, but then anger quickly took over and dried them up. I gulped before I could speak and I wasn't even sure if words could escape my lips. "Mom?"

"Mom!" Rory exclaimed as she looked at me.

"Son, keep calm and let me explain," my father said.

As I stared at my mother, I saw that tears were streaming down her face. I couldn't believe this and I desperately needed a drink. I wasn't ready for this; a confrontation with my mother after twenty-some years of never seeing or speaking to her. "What the hell is going on here?"

"Ian, maybe you should sit down. I'll go get you a glass of bourbon," Rory said.

"No, I can get it myself," I said as I stormed inside the house. Rory followed behind. I went to the bar, grabbed the bottle of bourbon, and poured a lot in the glass. I took a drink to try and calm down. My heart was racing and my mind was filled with confusion.

"Honey, I know this is difficult for you. My God, I just went through the same thing. This is unreal. I just can't believe this."

As much as I loved her, she was getting on my nerves. "Rory, STOP! Just be quiet."

"Okay. I'm sorry," she said as she walked away.

God, I snapped at her and none of this was her fault. FUCK! "Sweetheart, I'm sorry."

She left the living room and went back outside. I hurt her feelings and I had no right to. I threw back my bourbon, poured another, and went outside to face my mother. I stood in front of the door wall and stared at my mother, talking to Rory.

"Why are you here?" I asked as I stepped outside.

All three of them turned and looked at me. Rory shot me a dirty look and then looked the other way. I was in trouble with her.

"Son, sit down, please," my dad said.

I went to the table and sat down. "Okay, I'm sitting."

"I've been in contact with your mom since I found out about the cancer. I know this is the last thing you probably expected."

"To say the least," I interrupted.

"We've talked and your mom believes in second chances and that's what she's giving me. Is it because I'm dying? Probably. But she loves you, son. She has always loved you and I kept her away from you all these years."

I scratched my eyebrow and sighed. "What are you talking about?"

"Your mother left because of me. I was battling my own demons at the time and your mom couldn't deal with it, so she left. I didn't know she was leaving until that day I came home from the office and you told me that she went on vacation. I was enraged because I loved her, but I treated her poorly. A week after she left, she tried to come back for you. I suspected she would, so I hired security to watch the house. They caught her, brought her to me, and I threatened her. I told her that she had the choice to come back home and do as I say or never see you again. I don't want to get into the details of the things I said and did because I'm ashamed of myself."

"Ian, I tried to contact you several times. A few years later, I went to one of your football games. I had to see for myself you were doing okay. I disguised myself and sat in the bleachers. Your father never knew I was there. In fact, I ran into you that night after the game. We were walking the opposite way and you ran into me. You stopped, put your hand on my shoulder, and apologized."

I couldn't make sense of any of this. My mind felt like it was in a million pieces and it was trying so hard to put them together one by one. I looked over at Rory and saw the empathy in her eyes and the sadness splayed across her face. She was the only person who understood exactly what I was feeling. She was the only person that I could talk to and reach out to. She got me. I finally felt what she did. I held out my hand to her and she took it. I looked at both my parents in disgust. The only thing I saw was hatred for my father.

"I sent you a letter. I thought that when you were an adult, you would write back or try to contact me," my mother said. "When you didn't, I just sat and prayed every day that we'd be reunited again."

I got up from my seat and pointed my finger at her. "I never opened your damn letter. If you really cared about me, you would've found a way to come and get me. You would have found a way to reach out to me when I was a child. If you were at that football game and we ran into each other that was your opportunity to tell me it was you. But you didn't! You continued to hide and led me to believe that I was never loved. You abandoned me and I will never forgive you for that! And as for you," I said in anger as I pointed to my father, "You're a despicable human being and I don't ever want to see you again. You're getting everything you deserve in life, and I hope you rot in hell for what you did. Now both of you get the fuck out of my house before I call the cops." I stormed back into the house and straight to the bar. I grabbed the bottle of bourbon and a glass and went upstairs to the bedroom and shut the door.

I knew it was only a matter of time before Rory came in and I just wanted to be left alone.

Chapter 26
Ian & Rory

Oh God, I couldn't believe what had just happened. I looked at Ian's mom and dad and shook my head.

"He didn't mean it. He needs time. We all need time to process everything. The two of you better leave now and I'll go talk to Ian."

His mother, Veronica, looked at me and smiled. "You two make a beautiful couple," she said as she put her hand on my face. I couldn't say anything to her, so all I did was give a small smile back.

"Please, Rory, if anyone can get through to him, it's you," Richard said and he took hold of my hand.

"I'll try. That's all I can do for now." I walked them out and then headed upstairs. I put my hand on the doorknob and took in a deep breath. I was nervous because I didn't know how Ian was going to react. I slowly opened the door and saw him sitting on the edge of the bed with the bottle of bourbon in his hand. He looked up at me with cold, dead eyes. I walked over and knelt down in front of him as I placed my hands on his knees.

"I'm so sorry. I know how you feel, baby. I know every emotion you're going through."

"Rory, I love you so much, and I need you to understand that I need to be alone. I don't want you to talk to me. I don't want to hear what you have to say. I just want to be left alone."

His words hurt me. I needed him more than anything when I was going through this. I still needed him. Everybody deals with things in their own way and maybe this was his way, alone. I reached up and kissed his cheek.

"I'll leave you alone. I'm sorry." I stood up, walked out, and shut the door behind me. I went down to the kitchen where I left my phone on the counter. I called Adalynn. I didn't know what else to do.

"Hello, darling," she answered.

"Hi, Adalynn."

I told her what had happened and she was astounded. She wanted to come over, but I told her it wasn't a good idea right now. She told me that Ian had his own way of dealing with things and not to take it personally. It was easier said than done because when you love someone, you want them there to comfort you. I never would have been able to get through these past couple of months without him. After I cleaned everything up from the patio, I laid down on the couch and fell asleep.

Ian

I woke up. I didn't remember falling asleep. When I looked over at the clock, it read two a.m. and Rory wasn't in bed. She had never come to bed. *Why the fuck did I tell her to leave me alone? Why didn't I just let her stay?* I rubbed my face with my hands before getting out of bed, and I changed into some pajama bottoms before I went looking for her. I opened the door that used to be her room when she first came here, but she wasn't in there. I walked downstairs and went directly outside and down to the beach. She wasn't there either. Worry and fear crept inside me that she had left. I walked back inside the house and into the living room, where I saw her curled up, asleep on the couch. I reached down, picked her up, and carried her to our bed. She wrapped her arms around my neck and laid her head on my chest.

"I'm so sorry for shutting you out, sweetheart," I whispered as I kissed her head.

I laid her on the bed and she took off her shirt, bra, and pants. She climbed under the sheets, and as I climbed in next to her, I wrapped my arms around her and held her tightly. I closed my eyes and fell asleep. It was easy falling asleep when I was with Rory, no matter what was going on in my life.

The next morning, Rory and I got up and got ready for our run. If there was ever a day I needed one, today was the day. Rory and I always had good talks when we ran. She didn't say much when we woke up. I thought she was still a little pissed off about last night. I'd be spending eternity making up for it. As we headed out the door and down to the beach, she finally spoke.

"Talk to me, Ian. Tell me what you're feeling."

I silently laughed to myself because she was throwing my words right back at me. We ran along the shoreline.

"I'm feeling really pissed off. I can't even comprehend what my father did. I'll never forgive him."

"Yes, you will."

"No, Rory. I won't."

"You will because life's too short. I need to forgive my father for what he did and you need to forgive both your parents. If I learned anything from Stephen's death, it's that you never know what's going to happen."

I looked over at her. “This is different.”

“No, it’s not. Life sucks, baby, and sometimes you have to bite the bullet and go with what it throws at you.”

“My whole life was a lie,” I said.

“My whole life was a lie too. Don’t forget that. You and I are in very similar boats and we’re struggling to paddle to the shore before we tip over and drown. But see, Ian, we don’t have to struggle, and we don’t have to drown. We have each other and we are each other’s life preservers. We keep each other afloat.”

I stopped and she ran a few feet ahead. Where the hell was all of this coming from? I always knew Rory was an intelligent woman, but this...

“Why did you stop?” she asked as she turned around and ran back to me.

“Because of you. The things you’re saying.”

“I’m only speaking the truth.”

“When did you figure all this out?” I asked.

“It took a while, but eventually, I got it. It helps to talk to Stephen when I visit his grave. Every time I step foot in that cemetery, I think to myself that this could be either one of us lying in the ground.”

“Aw, sweetheart, come here,” I said as I wrapped my arms around her and pulled her into an embrace. “Everything you’re saying is true. Every fucking word of it. But, I don’t know if I can do it,” I said as I kissed her head.

"You can and you will. New beginnings, Ian. It's all about forgiveness and new beginnings. I've decided that I want a relationship with my father. At least you had your mom and knew her for a few years before you never saw her again. I never knew my father at all. Your mom tried to see you. She made attempts and even disguised herself. Don't just disregard that. And, as for Richard, what he did was pure evil, but he regrets it and he's dying. You may not have much time left with him, Ian. Don't let him die and then you never got the chance to tell him you forgave him, because you'll spend the rest of your life regretting it."

I put my forehead against hers and cupped her face in my hands. "I love you," I said as I brushed my lips against hers.

"I love you more." She smiled.

We continued our run and talked some more. Rory was right about everything and it was going to take time, and once I pushed the anger aside, the healing process would begin.

Rory

We were in the kitchen and I grabbed a bottle of water from the refrigerator. I sat down in the chair because I was feeling light-headed. I laid my head down on the table for a second, waiting for it to pass.

"Sweetheart, what's wrong?" Ian asked.

"I'm just a little dizzy. No big deal."

"Well, drink your water. You may be a little dehydrated."

Charles had just taken the blueberry muffins out of the oven and the smell was overwhelming. Overwhelming to the point where I felt like I was going to be sick. Ian took one and started eating it. As I sat there and watched him, the sick feeling became more intense as I covered my mouth with my hand and ran to the bathroom. I didn't even have time to shut the door. Ian came in and looked at me.

"Rory, are you sick?" He asked as he rubbed my back.

"I guess so," I said as I continued to vomit in the toilet.

Ian stood there and waited for me to finish. He handed me a tissue and then kissed my forehead. "Why don't you go upstairs and lie down?"

"I feel better now."

"Are you sure?"

"Yeah, I'm just going to finish my water."

Ian went to his study to do some work and I sat down at the piano. I thought a lot about our talk and I was hoping that I was able to get through to him. I stretched my fingers and began to play. As I stroked the keys and played Chopin's "Grande Valse Brillante in E-flat Major," I became lost in the music. This had always been Stephen's favorite. Ian emerged from his study and stood next to the piano and smiled at me. He even swayed back and forth and moved his head around. I looked up at him and began to laugh as I continued playing. I played faster and he moved with the beat. When the song was finished, he looked at me and said, "I need to fuck you now. Are you up for it?"

"The question is, are you UP for it?" I smiled.

He gave me that playful look and I knew I was in trouble. I quickly ran up the stairs and into the bedroom, where he tackled me on the bed and he showed me how up for it he was.

Chapter 27
Rory

Adalynn's wedding was in a couple of days and I was so excited I could barely stand it. I hadn't been feeling well lately and I tried to hide it as much as I could from Ian because he worried so much about me, especially since Stephen's death. I hadn't been running the past few days because I'd been so tired. With everything that had happened over the past couple of months, I thought exhaustion was finally starting to settle in. Not to mention the fact that Ian and I made love about three times a day. That man was enough to wear anyone out. And he accused *me* of trying to kill him.

"Are you running with me today?" he asked.

"Yes, babe, I am. I'll meet you downstairs."

I felt sick again like I did every morning and I went into the bathroom and threw up. I thought the excitement of Adalynn and Daniel's wedding might have caused some of the queasiness I was feeling lately. I had to go for one last fitting on my dress. After my run, I was meeting Adalynn at the bridal shop and then we were going to lunch. I put on my running clothes and headed downstairs. Ian was down at the beach, waiting for me.

"It's about time," he said.

"Sorry, I couldn't find my shoes," I lied.

We ran and talked about the wedding. "Wait until you see how beautiful Adalynn looks in her wedding dress."

"I can hardly wait," Ian replied sarcastically.

I bumped his shoulder and he almost fell over. "Oops, sorry!" I laughed.

"Now you're in trouble," he said as he tried to grab me, but I ran way ahead of him. He was faster than I was and he caught up to me in no time. He grabbed me, picked me up, and swung me around before we went down on the sand. He hovered over me as he tried to catch his breath.

"See what happens when you push me?" He smiled.

"I like what happens when I push you. I think I might do it more often." I smiled back.

He stared into my eyes as he pushed some stray hairs out of my face. "I love you, Rory Sinclair."

"I love you more, Ian Braxton."

"Not possible." He smiled as he lowered his lips onto mine.

"We need to head back. I have to shower and meet Adalynn."

"Ah, that's right. You're going to pick your dress up today."

He got off of me and held out his hand to help me up. Instead of running back to the house, he put his arm around me and we walked back.

"I love spending my mornings like this. Just me and you, the beach, our runs. It's perfect, Rory, and I don't want it any other way."

His words made me melt, but then again scared me. What did he mean by he "didn't want it any other way"? I laid my head on his shoulder until we got back to the house. We showered together and then he left for the office. As soon as I was finished getting dressed, I drove to the bridal shop to meet Adalynn.

"Hello, darling," she said as she gave me a hug and kiss.

"Hi." I smiled.

The sales lady had my dress hanging in the fitting room. I stepped inside, put on the dress, and tried to zip it.

"Adalynn, can you help me?" I yelled from the dressing room.

"Sure, sweetie. What's wrong?"

"I can't seem to zip this up all the way," I said in a panic.

"Hold on, let me do it. These zippers are tricky. Rory, you're going to have to suck it in. Have you put on some weight?"

"NO!" I said. "They sewed it wrong."

Adalynn called in the sales lady and told her that the dress was too tight. She looked at the slip that was stapled to the garment bag and then measured me.

"It looks like you put on a few pounds," she said.

I was horrified that she said that. "I most certainly did not and with all the vomiting I've been doing, I've barely been eating."

"Wait, hold up, Rory. What do you mean with 'all the vomiting'?"

"I think I'm really nervous about the wedding because I've been throwing up every morning."

Adalynn and the sales lady looked at each other. "Is there a way to get this fixed before my wedding? I'll pay triple to have someone work on it all night."

"I can do it. Don't worry. It will be done before your wedding."

The sales lady left and I stood there speechless. "Rory, when was your last period?" Adalynn asked.

"Oh God, I don't know. With everything going on the past couple of months, I haven't been keeping track. Why?"

"Are you pregnant?"

"WHAT?!" I exclaimed. "No, I'm not pregnant."

"Are you sure?"

"Yes, I take my pill every day."

"Were there times when you didn't take your pill because you forgot with everything going on?"

"Well, yes. But I just doubled up the next morning or two," I said as I bit down on my bottom lip. "OH MY GOD, Adalynn. Do you think I could be pregnant?" I started to cry.

"Don't cry, please. Change out of your dress and we'll talk about it over lunch."

Adalynn left the room and, after I finished getting dressed, I stepped out of the dressing room and handed her my dress with tears in my eyes.

"Aw, darling. Don't cry. You don't even know for sure if you're pregnant."

She handed the dress to the sales lady, who promised to have it finished by tomorrow afternoon. As we walked down the street to the café for lunch, we passed a drug store.

"Let's go in here and get you a pregnancy test," Adalynn said as she led me inside.

"I don't want to know." I started to cry.

"Rory, you have to know. If you are, then you have to get to a doctor."

I started bawling in the middle of the store. "What if I am? It's going to destroy mine and Ian's relationship."

"Aw, sweetie, no, it won't. Ian loves you. If anything, it will bring you closer."

I shook my head. "No, no, you don't understand. Ian doesn't want children. He point blank told me that he wants nothing to do with them. He won't even hold Connor and Ellery's daughter, Julia, when we see her. This will destroy us."

"Stop. Let's not get worked up until we find out for sure. Come on; let's pay for this and we'll grab some carry out and take it back to my house."

As we were at the register, paying for the pregnancy test, my phone rang. It was Ian.

"Hi, honey," I answered, all cheery.

"Hi, sweetheart. How's your day going?"

"It's great. Adalynn and I are just about to grab some lunch."

"Good. Are you feeling okay?"

"Yeah, I'm feeling great," I lied.

"Okay, I'm on my way to a meeting, sweetheart. I love you."

"I love you too."

I hung up and looked at Adalynn and started crying again. She put her arm around me and asked me if I was okay to drive to her house. I nodded my head and we got into our cars and I followed her home. I was a nervous wreck. *What if the test comes back positive? What was I going to do?* Ian hated kids. I couldn't live with someone who would hate his kids. Panic started to settle in again.

****

I took in a deep breath as I peed on the stick. Adalynn was in the bathroom with me and watched the window as I laid the stick on the counter. I closed my eyes because I didn't want to know. I didn't want to hear it. I was already sick to my stomach as it was.

"Oh, Rory," Adalynn said.

I knew by the sound of her voice that it was positive. I opened one eye and peeked. Yep, sure enough, there was the plus sign as plain as fucking day. I started to sob as I closed the lid on the toilet and sat down. Daniel knocked on the door and asked if everything was okay.

"Rory's pregnant," Adalynn yelled.

"OMG!" I cried even harder.

"Why is she crying?" Daniel asked as he opened the door.

"Because of Ian. She's scared of him."

"I am not scared of him. I'm scared of what this baby will do to our relationship."

Daniel put his arm around me and helped me up. "Come on, Rory. Let's go to the living room. I think Ian will be happy. It might take some time, but he'll adjust."

"No, he won't. He doesn't want kids."

I finally calmed down and sat at the table while Adalynn and Daniel ate Chinese food. I couldn't eat. Every time I thought about it, I got sick to my stomach. My phone beeped with a text message from Ian.

"Are you on your way home? I'm surprised you're not home yet."

"I'm on my way now. I'm sorry."

"There's no need to apologize, sweetheart. I'll see you soon. Be careful driving."

I hugged Adalynn and Daniel goodbye. "When are you telling him?" Adalynn asked.

"Not until after the wedding. I'm not having your wedding ruined."

"Don't think like that, darling. He'll be happy. He loves you."

"Keep giving him that praise," I said as I walked out the door.

How was I going to hide this from him for the next few days? I needed to call the doctor first thing tomorrow morning.

Chapter 28
Ian

Rory walked through the door and it looked like she'd been crying. I couldn't imagine what had happened and, instantly, I grew worried.

"Sweetheart, what's wrong? You've been crying," I said as I wiped her eyes.

"I was on the way home and I heard a song that reminded me of Stephen, that's all."

I pulled her into an embrace and rubbed her back softly. "I'm sorry. I know it's still hard."

"Thank you," she said as she pulled back and gave me a kiss. "How was your day?"

"I saw my dad."

"What? Where?" she asked.

"Come on; I'll pour us a glass of wine and we'll talk about it."

"Umm, no. I don't want any."

"Why?" I asked. "You love wine."

"My stomach has been upset since lunch."

"Oh. Something you ate?"

"Yeah. I think so." She smiled.

"Okay, then, I'll just have some. Anyway, he stopped by the office. When I saw him, I thought about our talk and the things you said. I told him that I didn't hate him, but I was still angry for what he did. I said it was going to take some time, and I know he doesn't have a lot of it, but just to be patient with me. As for my mom, she wants to have dinner with us. Just the three of us."

"Are you okay with that?" she asked.

"To be honest with you, I don't know. I guess we'll never know unless we try it, right?"

She gave me a small smile and agreed.

"I got Connor's property for his art gallery today. He was thrilled when I told him the news."

"That's wonderful, Ian."

"It's a multi-million dollar deal, sweetheart. Oh, I forgot to tell you. After Daniel and Adalynn's wedding, we're taking my dad's plane and were flying to Walla Walla."

"Walla what?" she asked.

"Walla Walla, Washington, sweetheart."

"Oh. Why? What's there?"

"There's a company called Nocking Point Wines. As you can tell by the name, they make wine. They're just starting out and I'm thinking about becoming an investor. From what I've heard and seen, they're going to do very well and I want to be a part of that. Plus, I know how much you love wine. Maybe we can get a bottle named after you." I winked at her. "It's about a four-and a-half-hour flight from here, so we'll get a hotel room and get some sleep before we take the tour."

"Okay," she said.

"That's it? Okay? We're talking fine wine here, sweetheart. You should be excited!"

"I am excited! I'm just a little tired. Had a long day and then with the crying and everything."

I cupped her face in my hands. "You know what I was thinking?" I smiled.

"What?"

"I was thinking about taking a month off from work after Adalynn gets back from her honeymoon and taking you on a trip. We could visit a couple of different places. Just me and you, alone for an entire month."

"That sounds great. I would love that," she said.

"Consider it done, then. I want you to pick out where you want to go. I'm doing this all for you, sweetheart. I love you."

"I love you too, Ian," she said as she hugged me.

Rory went upstairs to take a bath. Something was off with her. She seemed really sad and upset. I thought that taking her on a month-long trip was what we both needed to get away from the bullshit we'd had to deal with lately. First Stephen's death, her dad, and now my parents. It was all too much to deal with at once. I was really looking forward to spending time with her alone. Just the two of us and no one else.

Chapter 29
Ian and Rory

It was finally Adalynn's wedding day. I rolled over and found that Ian was still asleep. As I lay there and watched him, I couldn't stop thinking about our baby. This should have been the happiest moment of my life, but it wasn't. I should have been able to share the news with him, knowing that he'd be excited, but he wouldn't be, so I couldn't. I loved this man so much and I wanted him to be excited about our baby. Ian had grown so much as a boyfriend, lover, and best friend since I met him, and I honestly didn't know what I would do without him. He opened his eyes and saw me staring at him.

"Good morning, sweetheart. Is something wrong?"

I wanted to tell him that everything was wrong, but I just smiled and said no.

"I was just watching you sleep. You looked so peaceful and sexy."

He reached out his arms and pulled me on top of him. "Let's have a good morning fuck." He smiled. "You can tell that I'm already hard."

"You're always hard when you wake up." I laughed.

"That's because I spend the entire night dreaming that I'm fucking you."

I giggled as he tickled me and when he rolled me on my back and hovered over me. "Yes?" he asked.

"Yes." I smiled.

We ended up making love twice. I didn't want to get out of bed and, apparently, neither did he because he called Charles and had him bring us up breakfast in bed. I started to feel nauseous and I ran to the bathroom.

"Rory, what's wrong?"

"Nerves, Ian."

"You're throwing up because you're nervous about the wedding?"

"Yes. I'm very nervous about it."

I wiped my mouth and climbed back in bed. Ian was eating his omelet. I was trying so hard not to throw up again. He handed me a piece of toast.

"Here, maybe this will make you feel better."

"Thanks, honey." I smiled as I took it from his hand. I took tiny bites and managed to keep it down. I got up from the bed and threw on some yoga pants and a t-shirt. I had to meet Adalynn and the other girls at the hair salon for hair and makeup. I leaned over and when I went to kiss Ian goodbye, he pulled back.

"What?"

"Did you brush your teeth?"

"Of course I brushed my teeth. You know what? You're not getting a kiss. Goodbye, Ian."

As I went to walk away, he grabbed my wrist and pulled me on the bed. "Get over here and kiss me." He smiled as his mouth smashed into mine.

"I will see you later at the church." I smiled.

"See you later, sweetheart."

Ian

I stood next to Daniel at the altar. The church was filled with people: family, friends, and acquaintances.

"Are you nervous?" I asked him.

"Nah. I can't wait to make Adalynn my wife." He smiled.

The minister stepped onto the altar and asked Daniel if he was ready. He nodded and the music started to play. The first girl down the aisle was Rory. My God, did she look gorgeous. I felt myself getting hard just looking at her. Her hair was done in an elegant up-do with cascading curls. She smiled at me when she saw me looking at her. She took her place across from me and I winked at her. We watched as a couple of the other girls walked down the aisle and Adalynn followed behind. I looked at Daniel and he was beaming from ear to ear. Adalynn looked beautiful and so happy. I looked over at Rory as she watched her walk down the aisle. She didn't look nervous anymore; she looked excited. Her eyes were full of light.

When the ceremony ended and we walked up the aisle, I kissed Rory's cheek and told her how beautiful she looked.

"You look amazing and incredibly gorgeous." I smiled.

"So do you in that tuxedo. In fact, I'm incredibly horny right now," she whispered in my ear.

"Ugh, Rory, stop. Because I'm going to have to take you in the bathroom over there and fuck you right in this church."

"Down boy." She smiled.

After taking endless pictures in the courtyard, the bridal party gathered in the limo and we headed to the beach for more pictures before the reception started. When Rory and I were done being photographed, we climbed in the back of my limo and headed to the reception. I opened a bottle of champagne for us and poured some in a glass for Rory.

Rory

Ian handed me the glass of champagne and I didn't know what to do. I had to think of something quick. He held up his glass to mine.

"To a beautiful day, a beautiful woman, and the love of my life."

Oh God, what am I going to do, I thought to myself. I smiled as we clanked our glasses. He took a drink. I didn't.

"What's wrong? Why aren't you drinking your champagne?" he asked.

Shit. I was going to have to dodge these questions all night. "I haven't eaten anything. Remember, I wasn't feeling well this morning? I don't want to drink and take the chance of becoming tipsy before we even make it to the reception. Once we get there and I eat, then I'll have a couple of drinks." I smiled.

"I don't like you not eating, Rory. It's not healthy."

"I'm not doing it on purpose. I just wasn't feeling well this morning. You know, I was really nervous."

"Can I kiss you?" he asked with a smile.

"Yes. Why are you asking?"

"Because I don't want to mess up your pretty lips."

"Oh, well in that case, you can kiss right here," I said as I point to the side of my neck.

"Even better." He smiled.

We arrived at the Beverly Hills Hotel, where the wedding reception was taking place. Our limo was amongst a line of limos at the curb. Ian climbed out first and then took my hand and helped me out. We walked arm in arm into the beautiful hotel and headed straight to the room where the reception was. The décor was beautiful. In fact, the entire room was stunning. This was where everyone's wedding should be held.

"Wow. This is beautiful," I said.

"Yeah. It is pretty nice."

The way Ian said that was almost as if he was saying "Don't get any ideas." The wait staff was walking around with trays of appetizers. Ian grabbed a couple and handed them to me.

"Here, sweetheart, eat these. I'm going to go get us a couple of drinks."

A few moments later, Ian came back with a glass of wine and handed it to me. I brought the glass to my lips and pretended to sip the wine. It went as far as my lips. Ian smiled and then we were interrupted by the announcer announcing that Adalynn and Daniel had arrived. Everyone clapped and cheered as they walked in. Adalynn walked over to me and took me by the arm.

"Excuse us, gentlemen, but I need to talk to Rory for a moment." She smiled.

We stepped a few feet away so the guys couldn't hear us.

"What are you doing with that drink?"

"Ian won't stop pushing alcohol on me and I think he's getting suspicious."

"Just play along for now and when you get a chance, dump it somewhere. In fact, give me that glass."

She drank more than half of it and handed it back to me. "There, now maybe he'll stop." She smiled.

We walked back to where they were engaging in conversation and Ian put his arm around me. Adalynn and Daniel went and greeted their guests while we took our place at the bridal table. After an amazing and delicious dinner, it was time for the dances to begin. First Adalynn and Daniel danced and then it was my and Ian's turn.

"I love dancing with you," he whispered in my ear.

"And I love dancing with you." I smiled.

"Are you excited to go to Walla Walla?"

"Yes, I am. I can tell you're excited too," I replied.

"I sure am. I think it's going to be an amazing business opportunity."

"I bet it will be, honey," I said.

The dance was over and I was feeling exhausted. I guess that's what being pregnant does to you. A couple of hours later,

Ian looked at his watch and asked me if I was ready to go. We kissed Adalynn and Daniel goodbye and headed to the airport. We were only going to be gone a couple of days because Ian had to get back to watch over *Prim* while Adalynn was on her honeymoon. We boarded the plane and I lay across Ian's lap on the couch.

"What a beautiful wedding," I said.

"I guess. If you get into that sort of thing."

"What do you mean? It was perfect."

"Yeah, it was nice, Rory," he said as he played with a few strands of my hair. "Let's not talk about the wedding anymore. You look really tired. Why don't you try and get some sleep?"

I closed my eyes as he lightly rubbed my forehead. How was I going to tell him that we were going to have a baby? He didn't want kids and he certainly didn't want anything to do with marriage.

Ian

Our plane finally landed at the Walla Walla Regional Airport. I grabbed our bags and we climbed into the car that was waiting to take us to the hotel. Once we arrived, I set our bags down and we climbed into the king-sized bed to get some sleep before touring Nocking Point Wines in a few hours.

The buzzing alarm had Rory in an uproar.

"Ian, turn that damn thing off!" she exclaimed as she put the pillow over her head.

I reached over and shut it off and then turned back to Rory, who still had the pillow covering her.

"Sweetheart, why are you yelling?"

"Because I'm tired and that alarm was annoying me! Why do we have to set an alarm? Why can't we just wake up when we want to?"

"Because people are expecting us. They're waiting for us."

She threw the pillow at me and got out of bed. "Well, you're stupid for scheduling this right after Adalynn's wedding. I'm tired."

I looked at her and shook my head. I didn't know where this was coming from. Rory never acted like this. "Sweetheart, calm down."

"I'm sorry, Ian. I'm just tired," she said as she stared out the window.

"You've been really tired lately. I hate to say this, but I think you may be depressed. I mean with everything that has happened over the past couple of months, it's understandable. Maybe you should schedule an appointment with Dr. Neil when we get back."

She walked over to the bed, climbed in, and snuggled against me. "Yeah, maybe I will."

I kissed her head and told her to go back to sleep while I showered and got dressed. She didn't have any problem with it as she rolled over and instantly fell asleep.

Chapter 30
Rory

Ian kept handing me little cups of wine to try on our tour. I would take it and, when he wasn't looking, I'd pour it on the ground.

"What did you think of that one, sweetheart?"

"It was great!" I smiled.

"Really, Rory? Because it was very bitter. You didn't taste it, did you? In fact, have you tasted any of the wine I gave you?"

Shit…shit…shit…What was I going to do? I couldn't lie to him; he'd know. He was already suspicious.

"No, Ian. I didn't taste it," I replied as I walked away. There was nothing but orchards and open fields.

"Why not? You've been acting really strange the past few days. At first, I thought it was the wedding. But the wedding's over and you're acting crazier than ever. What the fuck is going on with you, Rory?" he yelled.

"Nothing is going on with me. I just don't want any wine. Is that okay? Is it a sin not to want any? Jesus Christ, Ian, get off my back."

"Don't talk to me like that," he said as he lightly took hold of my arm. Whatever you're hiding, you better tell me right now."

"You want me to tell you right here? In front of people? Okay, Ian. I'm pregnant!" I exclaimed as I threw my hands up in the air. He stood there and stared at me. His eyes went dead. "That's right, you're going to be a father. We're having a baby."

The blank look on his face scared me. "We'll talk about this later," he said as he turned away from me.

Why did I feel like this was the end of my life? I knew his reaction wasn't going to be good, and I hadn't even experienced his full reaction yet. A few moments later, he walked over to me and told me that we were leaving. I got into the car and he took off like a maniac. He wasn't saying a word to me about it, so I guessed he was going to wait until we got back to the hotel room. I was already a nervous wreck as it was and it intensified when we pulled into the hotel. Ian threw the car in park and got out. He just went right into the hotel. He didn't open the door for me or even wait. Asshole. He was kind enough to hold the elevator doors open until I got in.

"Gee, thanks. You should've just gone up without me."

He shot me a dirty look. He inserted the key card into the door and walked inside. As soon as the door shut, he put his hands on his hips and turned around and looked at me.

"How the fuck did this happen?" he instantly yelled.

"Gee, Ian. I wonder. When two people have sex—"

"Stop being a smart ass. I'm talking about your birth control. Did you just throw it away?"

Now I was angry. How dare he! "I forgot to take a pill here and there since Stephen died. I thought if I doubled up the next day, I'd be safe."

"Well, you thought wrong, didn't you? Fuck, Rory, I told you that I don't want kids, period! How could you not be more careful!" he screamed.

That was it, the gloves were coming off now and I wasn't holding back. There was no way in hell I was going to let him talk to and treat me that way.

"ME? What about you? You made this baby too. I didn't do it by myself. I'm sorry that my brother passed away and I'm sorry that you found my father. I'm sorry that I had so much going on in my head that I was on the verge of a nervous breakdown that I didn't remember my pill every day."

He turned away from me and looked out the window. "Answer me one question. Did you get pregnant on purpose?"

"Fuck you, Ian," I said as I grabbed my purse and stormed out the door. His question hurt me more than anything that was said. I couldn't believe that he thought so little of me that he would think I would get pregnant on purpose. To be honest, a baby was the last thing I wanted right now. The timing was horrible, but it happened and I was dealing with it. I stormed out of the hotel and didn't know where the fuck I was going. I sat down on a bench just outside the hotel. I pulled my phone from my purse and sent Adalynn a text message.

"He knows and he's pissed as hell. We got into a huge fight and he accused me of getting pregnant on purpose."

"Don't listen to him, Rory. He's upset right now and he's going to say things he doesn't mean. Do you want me to talk to him?"

"No. I don't want you or Daniel involved. I'll talk to you later."

"Take care and don't stress. It's not good for the baby."

The baby. I placed my hands on my stomach and looked down. I had to think about my baby. Just like I always had to think about Stephen.

"I thought you took off. It wouldn't have surprised me," Ian said as he had our bags in his hand. "Let's go. The plane is waiting for us."

I got up and followed him to a limo that was waiting for us at the curb. I slid in the back and Ian climbed in next to me. He didn't sit close to me like he always did. I needed to fix this. I needed to talk to him, but I didn't know if it was a good time or if I should wait and let him cool down.

"I'm sorry this happened. I'm sorry to have put you in such a position to make you hate me."

"I don't hate you, Rory. Don't ever say that again."

"I know you don't want to talk about it, but we have to. This is our child, our baby; a human being that we both created out of love," I said as I reached over and touched his hand.

He pulled away. "I was very specific when I told you that I never wanted children. I relied on you to prevent that from happening. I take care of you. I give you everything you need and you can't even do one simple thing for me."

Those words were like a dagger that just stabbed me in the heart and killed me. Instantly, I felt dead. My eyes filled with tears and there was nothing I could do to stop them. They fell down my face and Ian looked over at me.

"I'm sorry, Rory, but that's how I feel."

I turned my body towards the window and cried until we got on the plane. He sat in the front, and I sat in the back. I didn't want to be anywhere near him. I needed to make him see that this baby was the best thing that happened to us. I was curled up in the seat, looking out at the clouds, when Ian came over to me.

"How long have you known?" he asked sternly.

"I found out two days before Adalynn's wedding."

"The day you came home and you'd been crying and you told me it was because of Stephen."

"Yep, that's the day."

"Why didn't you tell me right away?" he asked.

"Gee, Ian. Look at your reaction. Do you think for once second I was going to let you ruin Adalynn's wedding?"

"I knew something was up with you, but to be honest, I never suspected you were pregnant," he said as he sat down next to me. "We need to have a serious talk. I'm not father material. I can't raise a child. I don't want to raise a child."

"Then I'm letting you off the hook."

"What's that supposed to mean?" he said.

"Exactly what I said. Now go away because I don't want to talk to you right now."

He got up and went back to his seat. The plane landed and Joshua was waiting for us at the gate. I walked way ahead of Ian and Joshua knew something was up.

"How was your trip?" he asked.

"I'm pregnant and Ian's pissed and doesn't want it. Does that answer your question?"

"Rory!" Ian yelled.

We climbed in the back of the limo and it took everything I had in me not to break down and cry. "Why the hell would you say that to Joshua?" he said through gritted teeth.

"It's the truth. Did you want me to lie to him? Oh wait, that's right, I do lie and I do things on purpose just to piss you off."

"That is enough! Do you understand me, Rory?"

"I understand you loud and clear, Ian!"

I turned and faced the window. "Rory," he said in a lowered voice. "I need time. You know my thoughts about kids and I just can't let you think that I'm happy about this. I'm not happy about it at all. Our entire lives are going to change. I wanted us to be a couple together with no one else to worry about. I want you alone and all to myself. I don't want to be responsible for another human being. Sweetheart, I'm only being honest with you and I hope you can understand."

I wiped the single lonely tear that fell from my eye. It represented how I felt, alone. He hoped that I understood. It was the cycle of my life starting all over again, but now I was the adult and going through what my mother did. I needed to be strong for my baby. He could hurt me a thousand times over, but I wouldn't let him hurt our child. I turned my head and looked at him directly in the eyes.

"I know how you feel, but I will never understand. So, I hope you can understand that."

He looked at me and then turned his head and looked out the window as we pulled into the driveway. I opened the door, ran up the stairs, and went into the bathroom, locking the door behind me. I sat down on the toilet, where I brought my knees up to my chest and cupped my face in my hands. I cried as quietly as I could.

Chapter 31
Ian

I took our bags up to the bedroom and then went down to my study. I couldn't believe Rory was pregnant. To be honest, I couldn't explain how I felt. I guess you could say confused and angry. I didn't want kids. I wasn't dad material; never was and never would be. I took in a deep breath and dialed my dad. I just needed to talk to him for a minute.

"Hello, son," he answered.

"Hey, Dad. How are you? I asked with a lump in my throat.

"I'm okay. How was the winery?"

I leaned back in my chair. "It was eventful." I didn't want to tell him about Rory because if I actually talked about it, then it made it real, and I didn't want it to be real.

"Something happen?"

"No. It was fine. It was a good business decision and I'm happy I went with it."

"Good. You're a smart man. I had no doubt that you'd make the right decision."

The right decision. If he only knew how I felt about Rory being pregnant.

"Ian? Are you still there, son?"

"Yeah, Dad. I'm sorry. I have a lot on my mind."

"Do you want to talk about it?" he asked. "Are you and Rory okay?"

"We're fine. Listen, I just called to see how you were and to let you know we were back. Let's have dinner next week if you're up to it," I said.

"Sure, I would like that."

"Good. I'll call you. Have a good night, Dad."

"You too, son," he replied before I ended the call.

I set my phone down on the desk and leaned back in my chair. I thought about Rory and how fucked up all of this was. I needed a drink. I walked over to the bar and poured myself a glass of bourbon and looked at it before I threw it down the back of my throat. I sighed as I poured another. Like the first, I threw that one back as well and slammed the glass down on the bar. It had been a couple of hours since I'd seen Rory. I was sure she was sleeping. I hurt her and I hurt her bad. She had the same look in her eyes that she did when I told her I didn't love her. A look that I never wanted to see again.

I went upstairs to the bedroom and Rory was sound asleep on the bed, holding onto a couple of tissues tightly in her hand. I changed out of my clothes and climbed into bed. As I looked at Rory, my heart filled with sadness because I couldn't be the one thing she wanted me to be. I got up and went into the guest bedroom for the night.

The next morning, my phone alarm went off and when I walked to my bedroom, Rory wasn't in bed. I stepped in the shower, got dressed, and headed downstairs for some breakfast before heading over to *Prim*. As I sat down at the table, I asked Mandy where Rory was.

"I haven't seen her yet this morning," she replied.

I looked around the house for her and called her name, but she didn't respond. I had a feeling that she had left. As I walked down the hallway, I glanced over to the room she stayed in when I first brought her here. I placed my hand on the knob and slowly opened the door. There she was; curled up in a ball and sound asleep. I quietly shut the door and went back downstairs.

Chapter 32
Rory

My eyes opened as soon as I heard him close the door. He thought I was sleeping, but I wasn't. When I woke up last night and saw him sleeping in the other room, my heart shattered even more. I didn't think it was possible for him to hurt me any more than he already had. But he succeeded and he also succeeded in me feeling nothing but hatred for him. After running to the bathroom and throwing up, I threw on a pair of yoga pants and a t-shirt and went downstairs. I had to face him some time. When I walked into the dining room, Ian looked up at me.

"You're up," he said.

"Yeah, I am. I just came down to grab some coffee. I'll be out of your sight in a minute."

"Why didn't you stay in our bed last night?" he asked as Mandy walked in with a cup of coffee.

"Why didn't you?" I replied.

He looked down and picked up his coffee cup. "I just couldn't."

"I couldn't either," I spouted. I picked up the coffee cup from the table and went back to my room. A few moments later, Ian walked in.

"I'm leaving to go to *Prim* for the day. What are your plans?" he asked.

"I don't know," I said as I turned and looked out the window.

"Are you going to tell anyone about this?"

"About what?" I asked.

"You and your condition."

I saw nothing but red as I turned around and looked at him. "My condition? You make it sound like some fucking disease."

"I don't have time for you right now. I have to get to *Prim,*" he said as he stormed out the door.

How did things get so bad so fast? One day, we were perfect and the next, we were torn apart. This should have been the happiest time for us. But instead, it was the most miserable. I took off my shirt and placed my hands on my stomach. I looked at myself in the full-length mirror and moved my hands in small circles. The pain inside would never go away if Ian wasn't around for us. I loved him so much, but at the same time, I hated him for making me feel this way. I needed to be strong and take charge. He'd get used to the idea, I knew he would. If he didn't, then we'd leave and never look back. I'd become a single parent like my mom was. She did the best she could under the circumstances and I learned a lot from her. I would have given anything for her to be here right now. I considered talking to Jimmy about this, but we weren't close. We were taking baby steps and trying to build a father/daughter relationship slowly. Just like Ian was trying with his mom.

As the day went on, I didn't hear a word from Ian. Usually, he'd call me a few times or send me love texts. I grabbed my purse and went to the Piano Bar to see Jimmy. I sat up at the bar and Rosie came from the back room.

"Hey, Rory. It's good to see you, darling. It's been a while."

"Hi, Rosie. I was busy with Adalynn's wedding and then Ian and I went to tour a winery he's partnered with."

"You look sad. How about a cosmo to cheer you up," she said.

"As much as I'd love one, I can't drink."

She gave me a strange look and smiled. "Why? Are you pregnant or something?"

"Yeah, something like that," I replied.

Her face lit up and she screeched and reached over the bar to give me a hug. "Rory, that's fantastic news. You're going to be a mama."

I looked at her, thanked her, and pursed my lips, trying to hold back the tears.

"What's wrong? You're not happy about the baby?" Rosie asked.

I sighed. "I'm happy about the baby. It's Ian. He's really upset and says he doesn't want it."

"What the fuck?!" she exclaimed. "Are you kidding me? He doesn't seem like that type."

"He doesn't want kids. He said he's not father material."

She reached over and grabbed my hands. "He'll come around, sweetie. Sometimes, it's a shock, especially if it wasn't planned." Rosie looked up and whispered, "Here comes Jimmy. Are you going to tell him?"

"Not yet." I shook my head.

"Hey, there's my girl." Jimmy smiled as he sat down on the stool next to me and gave me a hug. "How are you, Rory?"

I faked a smile so he wouldn't suspect something was wrong. "I'm great. How are you?" I asked.

"Things are good. I have this great bar and my daughter." He smiled.

We sat and talked for a while about music and Stephen. Jimmy took me over to the piano and played a new piece of music he wrote. He called it "My Daughter." It was beautiful and it brought tears to my eyes. I told him that I had to get going because Ian was waiting for me. A total lie, because I didn't think Ian would ever wait for me again. I gave him a hug and kiss goodbye and told him that I'd see him soon.

****

I looked at my phone and saw that it was five o'clock. Ian still never called or texted me and he wasn't home. I walked out to the beach to find some peace and to do some soul searching. This wasn't just about me anymore. This was about me and my baby. As I planted myself in the sand and stared out into the blue water, I thought about Stephen. I wished so badly that he was here. As I was in deep thought, I heard a voice from behind.

"There's my beautiful American girl."

I turned my head and smiled when I saw Andre standing by the house. I quickly got up and ran to him, throwing my arms around him. He picked me up and swung me around.

"What are you doing here?" I asked.

"Are you not happy to see me?" he asked in his sweet French accent.

"Of course I am. Why didn't you tell me you were coming to Malibu?"

"I wanted it to be a surprise. Let me look at you." He smiled as he twirled me around. "Beautiful as always."

As happy as I was to see him, this was not a good time. "Does Ian know you're here?"

"No, he doesn't. Where is he?"

"He's not home yet," I replied as I looked down.

As we walked into the house, we heard the front door open. Andre went into the foyer and I followed behind.

"Andre, my friend. What are you doing here? It's good to see you." Ian smiled as they hugged.

"I came to visit my favorite couple."

"Welcome to Malibu."

Ian looked at me and didn't say anything. He didn't even kiss me hello. Andre must've picked up on it because he gave me a worried look. I gave him a half smile and turned away.

"If you'll excuse me a moment, I'm going to run upstairs and change."

"Sure. Go ahead." Andre smiled.

As soon as Ian was out of sight, Andre turned to me and lightly took hold of my arm as we walked to the kitchen. "Is something going on between you two?" he asked with concern.

"Yeah, you could say that."

"What is it? What's wrong?"

"I'm pregnant and Ian isn't happy about it."

"Wh—" He stopped as Ian walked in.

"It's good to see you," he said as he patted Andre on the back. "Where are you staying?"

"At a hotel nearby."

"Nonsense, you'll stay here." Ian smiled.

I had to take a moment to think about why Ian would want Andre to stay with us when things were so bad right now. Then it hit me. If Andre stayed here, then Ian wouldn't have to be alone with me and talk about the baby.

"We have a beautiful guest room that was just redecorated," he said.

"I don't want to put you out or anything," Andre said.

"Don't be ridiculous. Rory and I would love to have you stay with us, right?" he said as he looked at me.

"Of course we would. You're not staying in a hotel. End of story." I smiled.

"Well, then I'll go get my suitcase and be right back."

"No need. I'll send Joshua to collect your things and bring them back. I don't know about you, but I'm starving," Ian said as he put his arm around Andre. "Let's go to dinner. I'll take you to one of my favorite restaurants."

"What about Rory?" Andre asked.

"She'll be joining us. Won't you?" Ian asked smugly.

"Of course. Just let me go and freshen up."

I went into the bathroom and shut the door. The tears that filled my eyes wanted to fall down my face. I wasn't going to cry. Not tonight. I sat on the toilet and looked up at the ceiling, waiting for the tears to dry up. There was a soft knock on the door.

"Rory. I need to speak with you for a moment," Ian said.

Great. I didn't want to fucking talk to him. I opened up the door and stood at the sink while I brushed my hair. Ian walked in and stood behind me.

"Well, speak," I said.

"I don't want you telling Andre that you're pregnant. Do you understand?"

I slowly turned my head and looked him straight in the eyes. "Fuck you! Do you understand that?" I said as I stormed out of the bathroom and down the stairs.

"I'm ready to go, Andre." I smiled as I looped my arm around his.

Ian walked down the stairs with a look in his eye as if he was about to kill me. The anger I saw was consuming him. We climbed in the back of the limo and Andre climbed into the seat opposite of me, leaving Ian to sit next to me. I couldn't even stomach to look at him anymore. That was how hurt, betrayed, and angry I was. We arrived at the restaurant and were promptly seated, thanks to Ian and his status. Andre and Ian both ordered drinks and I drank water.

"No wine for you, my beautiful American girl?" Andre smiled.

"No. Actually, I can't have any wine for a while."

"Why's that?" he asked.

I looked at Ian and he was giving me a stern look. I didn't care. Fuck him and his looks. I was done with him at this point.

"Because I'm pregnant." I smiled.

"That's wonderful news! Congratulations, my friend." Andre smiled as he shook Ian's hand. You will have the most beautiful children."

Ian partially smiled and then looked at me with anger in his eyes. I raised my eyebrow at him as I smiled. We had a very uncomfortable dinner and then we headed home.

The next week was hard. Ian and I hadn't spoken one word to each other since the restaurant. He slept in our bed and I slept in the other room. I spent the days with Andre while Ian was at *Prim.* I kept Adalynn informed of how things were going because she kept texting me and telling me how worried she was about me. I told her that I was fine and to stop worrying. It was Andre's last night with us and we were taking him out to dinner. Ian was in the bedroom getting changed. He was in the closet in his boxers and nothing else. I missed him. I missed making love to him and I missed feeling loved. He turned and looked at me.

I stepped into my side of the closet and grabbed my black dress. I took off my shirt and shorts and laid my dress on the bed. I glanced in the full-length mirror and noticed my stomach was already swollen. It was too soon to start showing. Ian walked over and looked at me and then down at my stomach. I quickly turned away because I didn't need him making a remark about it.

"How far along are you?" he asked.

"I don't know."

"How can you not know? Haven't you been to the doctor?"

"Yeah. I think I'm about six weeks."

"It looks like you're already starting to show. Isn't it a little early for that?"

I turned around and looked at him as I took in a deep breath. "You haven't spoken two words to me in a week and now you want to carry on a conversation about me showing? I already told you that you're off the hook, Braxton."

One…two…three. Here it comes. Fuck…fuck…fuck. I couldn't hold back. "In fact, I'll be moving out soon, so you don't have to look at me or my stomach and be reminded how I fucked up your life. You're free to go back to the way things used to be. In fact, why don't you give Andrew a call? Maybe the two of you bastards could rekindle your man-whore relationship."

"THAT'S ENOUGH!" he yelled through gritted teeth as he gently took hold of my arm. "I have heard enough of that smart ass mouth of yours. If you want to move out, then fine. Go. I don't care anymore, Rory."

"And I don't care either! Tell Andre that I'm not feeling well and I won't be able to go to dinner," I said with tears in my eyes.

Chapter 33
Ian

As Andre and I sat in the booth, we talked about Rory and the baby. I was honest with him and told him that I didn't want it.

"Ian, my friend. You're going to be a father. One of the greatest gifts of all. God has given you a gift."

"I didn't ask for it and I certainly don't want it."

"Why are you scared? Do you know what I'd give to have a woman like Rory and a baby on the way? Family is what life's all about."

"Not my life, Andre. Not my life," I said as I swirled the brown liquid in the glass and downed it like a shot.

"I think you need to go talk to that therapist Rory was seeing. You need to get yourself straightened out. Your judgment is clouded, my friend. For some reason, you can't see the best thing that's in front of you. What's it going to take this time to make you see that Rory and your baby are the most important things in your life?"

I looked down because I didn't want to talk about this anymore. I just wanted it all to go away. We finished our dinner and went back to the house. It was late. Andre went up to his room and I went to check on Rory. When I opened the door, she wasn't in bed. I searched the house for her and she wasn't anywhere to be found. I tried to call her phone and it went straight to voicemail. I walked back upstairs to her room and saw her phone lying on the nightstand. I went to the garage and her car was gone. I immediately flew up the stairs and to our bedroom. I opened the closet doors and let out a sigh of relief when I saw all her clothes hanging there. I grabbed my keys and drove to the Piano Bar. I bet that was where she went. As I walked through the doors, I looked around, but didn't see her. Jimmy was over by the piano, so I walked over and asked him if Rory was there or had been there tonight. He gave me a worried look and told me no.

"Is something going on, Ian?" he asked.

"We just had a disagreement and now I can't find her. She left her phone at home."

"Is there a special place she goes to when you two have an argument?"

I stood there and thought about it for a minute. She usually went down to the beach, but I checked and she wasn't there. Then it hit me.

"Thank you, Jimmy. I think I know where she is."

I left the bar and drove to the place I was pretty sure she was at. When I pulled up to the curb, I saw her lying there, on the ground, in front of Stephen's grave. I got out of the car and walked over to her, only to find her asleep. When I carefully picked her up, she opened her eyes and looked at me. Her eyes looked red and swollen as if she'd been crying for hours.

"What are you doing?" she asked in a whisper.

"Taking you home."

She wrapped her arms around my neck and laid her head on my chest. I put her in the car and drove home. I picked her up from the seat, carried her upstairs, and laid her down in our bed.

The next morning, Rory was up and showered before the alarm went off. After I finished getting dressed, I joined her and Andre downstairs for breakfast. She looked at me when I entered the dining room and quickly looked down. I didn't want to say anything about last night in front of Andre.

"Good morning," I said.

Andre replied with a good morning and Rory didn't say anything. I sat down while Mandy poured some coffee in my cup.

"Joshua will drive you to the airport."

"Thank you, Ian. I appreciate it."

I finished up my coffee and muffin and looked at my watch. "Well, it was great to see you, Andre. Have a safe flight home and keep in touch," I said as we hugged lightly.

"Thank you for taking me into your beautiful home. Good luck with everything."

I left and headed to *Prim*. When I arrived at the office, I sent Rory a text message.

"We need to talk about last night."

"There's nothing to talk about. I visited my brother's grave and fell asleep. Leave it alone," she replied back.

I sighed as I threw my phone across the desk. This situation was getting worse by the minute. My phone began to ring and when I picked it up, I saw that Adalynn was calling. Great. I knew exactly why she was calling.

"Hello, Adalynn. How's the honeymoon going?"

"Don't you think for one minute that I don't know what's going on between you and Rory," she yelled into the phone.

"Adalynn, I'm in no mood for this right now."

"I don't care. You're an asshole, Ian. As much as I hate to say this, you're worse than Andrew and I didn't think that was possible. What the hell is the matter with you? What demons are you hiding?"

I rolled my eyes before answering her. "This is none of your concern. Rory knew exactly how I felt about having children and she let me down. I can't be a father to that baby, Adalynn. You know me."

"I thought I knew you, Ian. I thought you were a better person than that. I guess it's true what they say: a leopard can't change its spots. You're a perfect asshole example of that. I'm ashamed of you, Braxton." Click.

As I shook my head, I threw my phone across my desk and cupped my face in my hands. *What the fuck was I going to do?* I loved Rory. She changed me. Or at least, I thought she had. I had my reasons for not wanting this child. Reasons I wouldn't admit. It was better for the baby that I was not in its life.

Chapter 34
Rory

A couple of weeks had passed and Ian and I were still a mess. We did sleep in the same bed, but he stayed on his side and I stayed on mine. My pants were getting hard to fit into and it seemed like I was getting bigger every day. Ian left for the office every morning and I stayed in bed until he left. He didn't call or text and he didn't come home until late. This relationship had fallen so far out of reach that it was time for me to move out and get on with my life; just me and my baby.

I spent the day looking online for apartments out of state. I didn't know where I wanted to go, but I knew I couldn't stay in California. It would be too painful. I would be able to afford my own place for a while, but I would have to start looking for a job. The money Ian put in my bank account wouldn't last forever. I had decided that when the baby was born, I wasn't putting Ian's name down as the father. He didn't want anything to do with this baby, so I was going to make sure there were no ties to him at all. As I searched online, my phone chimed with a text message from Andre.

"How's my beautiful American girl? Is Ian still being a dick? If so, move to Paris and I will take care of you and your baby."

I smiled when I read his text. He was such a sweet and great friend. But that was all he was.

"Thank you, Andre. I'm okay and yes, Ian is still being a dick. I would love to move to Paris and I've considered it, but I would never allow you to take care of me and the baby."

"Friends, Rory. Friends take care of each other. I would see to it that you got a job and I could help out while you're at work. Give it some thought. Raising a baby here would be a wonderful life."

"I'll give it some thought. Thank you, Andre."

"You're welcome. Take care of yourself and your beautiful American baby."

I continued looking at the map of the United States to figure out where I wanted to move. Maybe Paris wasn't such a bad idea after all. I wouldn't be completely alone there with Andre, and I loved Paris. I could rent a furnished apartment and not have to worry about moving anything but my suitcase. I could buy all of the baby things I needed once I got there. It was settled; I was moving to Paris. I purchased a one-way ticket for the day after tomorrow.

I went to the bedroom and pulled the suitcase out of the closet. I figured it would be best to start packing. As I began to pack, Ian walked into the bedroom.

"What are you doing?" he asked sternly.

"I'm packing because I'm moving."

"Where are you moving to?"

"I don't think that's any of your business. You will never see me again once I leave. It will be easy for you to get back to your normal life and forget that you ever met me."

"Bullshit! It is my business," he yelled. "That's my baby you're carrying."

I turned around and stared him straight in the eyes. My blood was on fire and all I saw was red. "Your baby?!" I screamed. "The baby you don't want and the baby you can't be a father to? How dare you, after all these weeks of ignoring me and pushing me out of your life, you say that! Who the fuck do you think you are?!"

"Do you think that it's going to be easy to forget you? To forget everything we've shared? You've hurt me deep down, Rory. You let me down," he screamed.

"I let *you* down? No, it's the other way around. You let me down, you heartless bastard!"

I was in tears and I was so angry. The words were on the tip of my tongue and they were about to spew out of my mouth. I shouldn't have said it, but it was how I felt and I had no choice.

"I hate you, Ian Braxton. I want you out of my life. You don't deserve someone like me. You deserve a ruthless, heartless bitch that you can control."

He stood there in anger. "You're right, Rory. It will be easy to forget you," he said as he turned and started to walk out the door.

Suddenly, I felt a sharp pain in my abdomen and I let out a scream and doubled over. Ian turned around and looked at me.

"Are you okay?" he asked as he ran to me and took a hold of my arm.

"I have to go into the bathroom for a minute," I said as a tear ran down my cheek.

"Let me help you," he said.

As I jerked my arm out of his grip, another pain shot through me. I doubled over again.

"Rory, sweetheart, please let me help you."

"Stay the fuck away from me," I whispered as I went into the bathroom and shut the door. I pulled down my pants and noticed there was blood. I started to panic. I opened the door and looked at Ian.

"I'm bleeding, Ian."

"I'm taking you to the hospital," he said as he walked over, picked me up, and carried me to the car.

When we arrived at the hospital, Ian helped me out of the car and grabbed a wheelchair. Once I was registered and explained what was happening, the nurse immediately wheeled me up to Labor and Delivery.

"Hi there, Rory, I'm Carol, and I'm going to be taking care of you while you're here. This must be Mr. Sinclair." She smiled.

"No, I'm Ian Braxton, the baby's father."

"Oh, I'm sorry."

I was consumed with worry as I changed into the cloth gown and lay down on the bed. Carol, the nurse, asked me some questions and took my vital signs.

"The doctor will be in shortly. I want you to stay calm and relaxed. The more relaxed you are, the better for the baby." She smiled and then turned and walked out of the room.

Ian walked over and sat down in the chair next to the bed. He placed his hand on mine.

"Everything is going to be all right, Rory."

"You don't know that. You can't tell me that. That's what they said about Stephen and looked what happened."

"Shh, sweetheart. Don't get worked up."

"You can leave now. I don't want you here," I lied.

I did want him there. I wanted him to hold me and kiss me and tell me that he loved me. But I knew he couldn't do that as long as I was carrying his baby.

"I'm not going anywhere. I'm staying here with you. End of discussion."

"I'm moving to Paris," I blurted out.

"You mean you're moving there to be with Andre."

"NO! I'm moving there for you," I said as I turned my head.

"For me? How the fuck is that for me?"

"So you won't ever have to worry about running into me or the baby."

"Rory," he said as he grabbed my hand.

"The ticket is already bought. I leave the day after tomorrow."

Just as Ian was about to say something, the doctor walked in.

"Hi, Rory, I'm Dr. Klein. When did your pain start?" he asked as he examined my stomach.

"A couple of hours ago," I replied.

Dr. Klein asked Ian to step out of the room for a moment while he examined me. Ian got up and kissed my forehead.

"I'll be right outside the door," he said.

Dr. Klein finished up his examination and told Ian he could come back into the room.

"How is she?" he asked Dr. Klein.

"I'm going to do an ultrasound. Rory, have you been under a great deal of stress lately?"

I looked away from him and closed my eyes. That was when Ian spoke up.

"Yes, doctor, she has been under a lot of stress."

"Well, the first thing you need to do is eliminate all stress." Dr. Klein smiled.

"I will be in a couple of days," I mumbled.

"I'll send the nurse in to wheel you down to the ultrasound room and I'll meet you in there." He smiled as he walked out of the room.

Ian's thumb was softly moving back and forth across my hand. "Why are you doing this?" I asked.

"Doing what?"

"Staying here. Are you hoping that I'll lose the baby and then things can go back to normal with us?"

"How the hell could you even say something like that?" he sternly asked. "My God, Rory, I know you're worried and upset, but that was totally out of line."

"Whatever, Ian."

Carol walked in and helped me into the wheelchair. Ian walked beside me as I was wheeled into the ultrasound room. She helped me onto the table and Dr. Klein walked in. Ian sat down in the chair on the other side of the table.

"Okay, let's take a look at your baby."

He squeezed the warm gel onto my stomach and began moving the wand around slowly. He stopped and pressed some keys on his keyboard.

"There's your baby's heartbeat. It's a strong one too. That's a good sign, Rory, and there's your baby."

Ian grabbed my hand and squeezed it. I turned my head and looked at him. He was staring intently at the monitor.

"Well, I'll be damned," Dr. Klein said.

"What. What is it, doctor?" Ian asked before I had the chance to.

Dr. Klein turned his head and looked at both of us. "See this right here?" he asked. "That's another baby. Congratulations, you're having twins."

I swear my heart stopped beating when he said that. I was speechless. I didn't dare look at Ian because he was already pissed about one baby and now there were two. Oh my God, I was going to be a single parent to twins, just like my mother.

"Rory," Ian said.

I turned my head and he kissed my lips and smiled. I didn't know what was going on and I didn't want to know. All I could focus on at that moment were my babies.

"Everything looks good with the babies. I don't see any problems. I'm going to send you home and I want you on complete bed rest for the next forty-eight hours. There is to be no stress in your life during the next six and a half months. Do you understand?" Dr. Klein asked.

"Yes, doctor." I smiled.

"Good. I'll take you back to your room and I'll get your discharge papers ready. I'm going to contact your OB doctor and tell him what's going on and I want you to make a follow up visit with him next week."

Ian took my hand and helped me from the table and into the wheelchair. Dr. Klein took me back to the room and I sat on the end of the bed, waiting for him to come back with the paperwork. Ian was quiet and I was worried. He stood in front of the window and looked out onto the beautiful day. Suddenly, he spoke.

"I guess this means you won't be moving to Paris the day after tomorrow. You heard the doctor, you are to be on bed rest for the next forty-eight hours, so that means no Paris."

"We'll see," I said.

He turned around and looked at me. "You're wrong, Rory. There is no 'we'll see.'" He walked over and sat down next to me on the bed. He put his arm around me and pulled me close to him, kissing the side of my head. "It's not a request. It's a command, Rory."

I didn't respond. I sat there enjoying the warmth of him and the tender touch of his lips pressed against my head. I missed him so much and every time he touched me, I became weak for him. But this wasn't about me anymore. I had two babies to think about. I pulled away from him.

"Rory, what the hell?" he exclaimed.

I remained calm for the sake of my babies. I pointed my finger at him and spoke softly.

"You don't get to do this anymore. You don't get to comfort me whenever it suits you. I needed you the past few weeks and you totally shut me out. You hurt me in ways that I never thought possible. You were the only person in my life I needed the most and you turned your back on me. I don't know if I can ever forgive you for that. I'm sorry, but I'm still moving to Paris," I said with tears in my eyes.

He didn't say a word, but his eyes started to fill with tears. He got up from the bed and headed towards the door.

"I'm going to pull the car up. I'll meet you downstairs," he said with his back turned.

A few moments later, Carol came into the room with the papers for me to sign. She helped me into the wheelchair and wheeled me down to the exit where Ian had the car waiting along the curb. He got out and opened the door as I climbed in. The ride home was silent.

Chapter 35
Ian and Rory

My mind was filled with excitement and yet confusion. Twins. I should have known. Rory said she'd never forgive me. *What the fuck am I going to do?* Seeing my babies on that screen changed me. I couldn't live without Rory. I needed her and I needed my children. I was wrong before. I got scared and I basically ran. I shut down and I shut her out. Give me those moments back and I'd change everything. The thought of her moving to Paris consumed me and was basically killing me. I felt like I was slowly dying inside and I needed to make things right. We pulled up in the driveway and Rory opened the door before I even had a chance to take the keys out of the ignition. She walked into the house and began walking up the stairs. I felt like she was walking away from me forever and it was too much to bear. Everything I feared flooded my mind at the same time and I couldn't control it. I began to sob and fell to my knees in the foyer. Rory turned around and stared at me from the stairs.

"Please, Rory. Please forgive me. I can't bear to lose you or my children. I need you," I sobbed as I placed my hands in front of me on the floor.

Rory

I couldn't believe what I was seeing. I walked over and put my arm around him.

"Ian, stop," I whispered.

He turned his head and looked at me. I'd never seen him like this before. His eyes were soaked with tears.

"It's okay," I said as I kissed his head.

"No, it's not okay, Rory," he continued to cry.

We both stood up as he picked me up and carried me up the stairs. He stopped in the hallway and leaned me up against the wall, burying his head into my neck and sobbing like a baby. The only thing I could do was comfort him. I hugged him tightly as we both fell to the ground. I couldn't hold it in anymore. I began to cry with him as he poured his feelings into me.

"I'm so sorry, sweetheart. I know I've overused that in our relationship, but I am. I need you to forgive me for everything. I was scared to be a father because my father wasn't exactly a good role model and I didn't want my child to turn out like me. I was so scared that I would fuck him up and his life and I couldn't bear the thought of that. I'm so scared that I'm going to be a bad father and that's why I pushed you away. Just like I did before you went off to Paris. I was so scared of loving you. I'm not a man, Rory, I'm a coward. And you're right, I don't deserve a woman like you. I don't blame you for hating me. I hate me."

My heart broke, hearing his words. "I don't hate you, Ian. I could never hate you. I was angry, so angry."

"I know you were and I'm so sorry. I would give anything to go back in time and start over. I need your love, sweetheart. I'm nothing without it."

The tears poured from my eyes. "You have my love, Ian. I love you so much," I said as I cupped his face in my hands.

"I can't live without you. I want our family. Please say you'll stay with me and not move to Paris. I love you so much, Rory, and I love our babies," he said as he put his hands on my stomach. "I need all three of you."

"We need you too, baby," I cried.

Ian hugged me and we both stood up. He picked me up and carried me to the bedroom, kissing me the whole way down the hall. He laid me down on the bed and hovered over me, kissing me passionately.

"I want to make love to you so bad, but I know we have to wait. I miss you, sweetheart," he said as he lay next to me and I curled up into him. "This is good enough. I just want to hold you forever. No more stress, sweetheart. I promise you there will be no more stress."

I looked up at him and softly kissed his lips. "Twins, really?" I laughed.

A large smile grew across his face. "Two beautiful gifts from God is what they are."

Ian

"When I saw them on the monitor, they became so real to me. Little human beings are growing inside you, Rory. I'm sorry it had to come to this for me to realize what a bastard I am," I said as I tightened my grip around her. "Adalynn told me off. She hates me now."

"She doesn't hate you, Ian. She's probably upset with you, and you know we say things we don't mean when we're angry."

I sighed. She was right and I was going to spend the rest of my life making everything right for Rory and my family. She got up from the bed and I grabbed her hand.

"Hey, you aren't allowed out of bed."

"I'm only changing into my nightshirt. I'm really uncomfortable in these pants."

I watched her as she changed out of her clothes and slipped into her nightshirt. She was so beautiful and I missed her amazing body more than I'd ever thought I could. I sat up so my back was against the headboard of our bed and I spread my legs, inviting her to lie between them.

"Come here, sweetheart." I smiled as I held out my hand.

She smiled as she took my hand and nestled herself between my legs, lying her back against my chest. She looked up at me and I softly brushed my lips against hers. My fingers drifted down to the bottom of her nightshirt and slowly lifted it above her stomach.

"What are you doing?" She laughed lightly.

"I want to feel my babies," I said as I gently placed my hands on her expanding stomach and slowly rubbed back and forth.

She placed her hands on mine and looked up at me. "I love you."

"I love you more, sweetheart. When are we going to start telling people that you're pregnant?"

"I think we should wait a little while longer to make sure everything is okay," she replied.

"Okay, but you're not going to be able to hide it too much longer. I don't want you to worry because everything will be okay. Think positive, sweetheart."

Rory

I stayed on complete bed rest for the next couple of days. Ian made sure I didn't move except to go to the bathroom and when he wanted me to cuddle with him. The love of my life was back and more attentive than before. Maybe a little too attentive. He worked from home and refused to leave the house. In fact, he brought all of his work to the bedroom because he wouldn't let me out of his sight. I sent Adalynn a text message, telling her that Ian and I were perfectly fine. I didn't go into details because I wanted to tell her about the twins in person. She was due back sometime today and she said that she was coming right over as soon as she landed.

I was in the kitchen, taking my pre-natal vitamin, when I heard Adalynn's voice.

"Where is she?" she asked Ian.

"It's great to see you too, Adalynn," Ian spoke in an irritated tone.

"I'll deal with you later. I need to see Rory."

She walked into the kitchen and immediately hugged me. "How are you?" she asked as she cupped my face in her hands.

"I'm good. How was your honeymoon? I want to hear all about it."

"We can talk about that another time. Wow, look at you. You're already starting to show," she said with a twisted face.

I smiled at her as Ian walked up behind me and wrapped his arms around me. “We’re having twins,” I said.

Adalynn’s jaw dropped and Ian chuckled. “What?! Oh my God! Two babies. I’m so happy for you, Rory!”

“Excuse me! What about me?” Ian said.

“I’m still pissed at you. You couldn’t deal with one baby and now you’re happy there’s two?” she asked.

“Yes, Adalynn. I’m very happy, and I saw my babies on the ultrasound at the hospital. You should’ve seen them. They were tiny humans and they were next to each other. I heard their heartbeats. It was the most amazing thing I’d ever seen.”

“Wow, look at you, Braxton, getting all choked up over your kids. Is he treating you good?” she asked me.

“Yes, he’s perfect.” I smiled.

“Okay, then. Come here, you big idiot,” Adalynn said as she held out her arms to Ian.

They hugged and Adalynn congratulated him. It was great to see that they were good again.

“I’m going to let the two of you visit. I need to run to the office for a bit. Adalynn, will you keep an eye on her for me?”

“I sure will. By the way, how’s my company? You didn’t let it go under while I was gone, did you?” she asked hesitantly.

“*Prim* is doing great. Nothing came up that I couldn’t handle. In fact, we need to have a meeting. I want to run a few things by you that I believe will put *Prim* at the top.” He winked.

She smiled at him as he left the kitchen. “So, it took him to see the babies to finally realize what an ass he was being?”

“Yeah. You should’ve seen him when he got home from the hospital. He broke down the minute we walked through the door.”

“What do you mean, he broke down?” she asked with concern.

“He fell to his knees and started sobbing and apologizing to me. It broke my heart to see him like that.”

“Wait…wait…wait. You’re telling me that Ian Braxton fell to his knees sobbing? Our Ian?”

I laughed lightly as I answered her. “Yes, our Ian did that. And then he carried me upstairs and broke down again in the hallway. God, Adalynn, he was so emotional and broken. He was begging me for forgiveness. He went on about being scared and ruining our children’s lives.”

“At least he came to his senses. I knew he would at some point, but I’m still sorry you had to be put through the ringer with him to begin with.”

We talked for a couple of more hours and then Ian came home. Adalynn kissed us both goodbye and headed out the door. It was good to have her and Daniel back in Malibu.

Chapter 36
Ian

A couple of more weeks had passed and it was time to tell our families that Rory was pregnant. First thing first, Rory and I had a phone call to make.

"Ian, my friend, how are you?" Connor answered.

"I'm great, Connor. Rory and I have some news we'd like to share with you and Ellery. Is she there with you?"

"Yep, she's right here. I'll put you on speaker."

"Hi, Ian. Hi, Rory," Ellery spoke.

"Hi," we both said at the same time.

"So what's this news? I'm assuming it's good?" Connor said.

"Rory's pregnant and we're having twins."

Ellery screeched in the background. "That's wonderful news, Ian. Congratulations, Rory," Connor said.

"Tell Rory I'm calling her right now!" Ellery said with excitement.

Rory smiled at me and left the study to get her phone. Connor took me off speaker and we continued to talk.

"Congratulations, Ian. That's exciting. We have our hands full with Julia. I can't imagine two at the same time."

"I was shocked at first, but it's going to be great. Another reason I called was to talk to Ellery and see if she'd be interested in painting a portrait for the nursery, one for each baby."

"Ah, she would love that. I'll talk to her and let know you'll be giving her a call."

"Thanks, Connor. I appreciate it."

Connor and I ended our call and I went into the living room where Rory was finishing up her conversation with Ellery. I sat down next to her and put my arm around her.

"I was thinking about the nursery," I said.

"You were?"

"Yes and I think we should knock out the wall between both guest rooms and make it one huge nursery."

"But what about when we have guests over?"

"We can add on. In fact, I was thinking about building a small house in the back. That way, when we have guest stay with us, they can have their own place."

She smiled at me with a devilish grin. "That's a good idea. Then you'll have a place to go when I kick you out after a fight."

"I knew that was the first thing you'd think of." I chuckled.

She leaned over and kissed me. "I love the idea."

"Good, because I already called my contractor and went over the plans. It's going to be perfect. Just you wait and see." I smiled. "Now, I need to make love to you, so let's go upstairs. As much as I want to pick you up and carry you, sweetheart,

I'm afraid that's not going to work anymore until after you give birth."

"Is that so? Are you saying I'm too fat to carry now?" She smiled playfully at me.

"No, but you have put on a lot of weight and you're getting really heavy. But in a good way. Please don't be mad at me."

"I'm not and I know it's getting harder."

"Speaking of harder," I said as I took her hand and placed it on my hard cock. "We need to get up to the bedroom now!"

Rory didn't hesitate as she got up, grabbed my hand, and led us upstairs.

****

"Charles, is everything set for tonight?"

"Yes, Ian. Don't worry. I've taken care of everything."

We told both my parents and Jimmy about the twins. Needless to say, they were extremely excited. Richard wasn't doing too well. He had his good and bad days. Rory had finally talked him into getting chemotherapy so he would be around when the twins were born. She had a way of dealing with him. He told me the best day of his life was when I was born and he couldn't be happier that I was going to get to experience that same joy. I wanted to tell him that I was scared, because, to be honest, I still was. I expressed my small fear to Rory and she told me that she was scared too and that we'd conquer it together; one day and one step at a time. Tomorrow was Rory's doctor's appointment for a checkup and another ultrasound. I was so excited to see my babies and see how much they'd grown over the past few weeks.

Rory was out with Adalynn, getting ideas for the nursery, and I had Charles prepare all her favorite foods for dinner. This was going to be a special night because I had some news to tell her. The florist arrived and decorated the patio with a variety of flowers that were all Rory's favorite. I stepped onto the patio to make sure everything was perfect. The candles were lit, the flowers were in place, and the table was beautifully set. The only thing missing was my beautiful girlfriend. I glanced at my watch and then heard the front door open. I went into the foyer and kissed Rory on the lips.

"Hi, sweetheart. I'm glad you're home. I missed you," I said as I took the bags from her and set them down.

"I missed you too. Want to see the cute maternity clothes I bought?" She smiled.

"Sure, but can it wait until later? Charles made us a wonderful dinner and it's just about ready."

"Oh great. I'm starving," she said.

I took her hand and led her to the patio. She gasped when she walked outside. "Oh my God, Ian. It's beautiful out here. What did you do?" she asked with a tear in her eye.

"It's no big deal, sweetheart. Don't start crying."

"Hormones, you know."

I couldn't help but chuckle and kiss her head. "Come sit down, Madame," I said as I pulled out her chair.

Charles served us our dinner and Rory's eyes danced with excitement. "This looks amazing. So what's the occasion?" she asked.

"Does there need to be an occasion to cook the mother of my children her favorite foods?"

"I guess not. But, you didn't cook." She winked at me.

"But I thought up all your favorite foods, sweetheart. Next time, I promise I'll cook." I smiled. "Anyway, I wanted to tell you something. We are going on a little trip, providing the doctor says it's safe for you to travel. I have a meeting I need to be at in New York."

"Oh, goodie, I'll get to see Connor and Ellery," Rory said in excitement.

"Yes, sweetheart, we will see Connor and Ellery. But then once we leave New York, we need to fly to Paris for *Prim*."

Her beautiful face lit up with a bright smile. "Paris? Are you serious? We get to go back to Paris?"

"I knew you'd love the idea, but that's only if your doctor gives you clearance to go."

"Would you go without me?" She pouted.

There was something about the way she asked that made my heart hurt. I got up from my chair and walked over to her. I knelt down and kissed her expanding stomach. "I would never go anywhere without you or the babies. I'm never leaving you, Rory. Not even for a day. Wherever I go, you and the kids go." I gently laid my head on her stomach as she ran her hands through my hair.

"Ian, I love you to pieces, but can I finish eating? We're hungry."

I chuckled as I shook my head. “I love you too. Now feed my kids.” I winked.

Chapter 37
Rory

I smiled as I felt light kisses traveling across my stomach. I opened my eyes to see Ian smiling at me.

"Good morning, sweetheart."

"Good morning."

"I was thinking about something last night. What sex do you think the babies are?"

"I don't know. It would be nice to have a boy and a girl."

"That's what I was thinking too. Do you want to find out beforehand?"

"Yeah, I think I do. It would make it easier to decorate the nursery," she said.

I was happy that Ian wanted to find out the sex of the babies. We got out of bed, made love in the shower, and then got dressed and headed down for breakfast before going to the doctor. When we walked into the dining room, Adalynn was sitting in her seat.

"Good morning, you two." She smiled.

"Good morning, Adalynn," I said, giving her a light hug.

"You're either really early or we're late," Ian said as he kissed her cheek.

"You're late." She smiled. "I just dropped by for a chocolate chip muffin. Rory has me hooked on them. And, to tell you, my darling Ian, that *Prim's* stock went through the roof while I was gone."

"Of course it did. That's what I do." Ian winked at her.

I laughed and rolled my eyes as I ate the fruit cup Mandy set down in front of me.

****

Ian had been on Cloud Nine all morning. The majority of the reason was he couldn't wait for the ultrasound. I was excited too, but nervous at the same time. I always had that "what if" worry inside me. What if something is wrong with one of the babies, what if the doctor can't find a heartbeat, what if they're in danger. It was a never ending line of "what ifs." Another reason Ian was so happy was because the doctor told him that it was perfectly fine for me to travel.

I lay down on the table and Ian grabbed my hand and brought it up to his lips. "You ready?" he asked.

"Yes." I smiled.

The doctor pressed down on my stomach with the wand and, instantly, we saw our babies. Tears started to fill my eyes as I looked at their little tiny hands. Ian got up from the chair and sat next to me on the table.

"Look at them, Rory. They're beautiful. Our children are beautiful."

"Your babies look perfect, Rory. They are growing as expected and they look good. Would the two of you like to know the sex of them?"

"Do you know?" I asked in excitement.

"Yes, I do."

I looked at Ian and he smiled at me and nodded his head. "Yes, doctor. We want to know."

"Congratulations; both babies are girls." He smiled.

I gasped. I'd always dreamed of having a daughter and now I was going to have two. I looked over at Ian as he kissed me softly.

"Girls, Rory. We're going to have two little girls running around the house." He smiled as his eyes began to water and he hugged me.

"I'm so happy, Ian."

Once the doctor finished up the ultrasound and gave us the pictures, Ian helped me up from the table and kissed me. "Our daughters are going to be absolutely beautiful, Rory."

"I hope they look like you." I smiled.

"No, sweetheart, they're going to look just like their mommy. Let's stop by *Prim* and tell Adalynn the great news."

Ian was so thrilled. You could see the happiness all over his face, but his eyes were where you could really see it. While we drove to *Prim*, Ian kept his hand on my stomach the whole ride.

"Why are you doing that?" I laughed.

"I'm touching my daughters. I want them to know that I'll always be there for them. We need to think of names for them, Rory."

"I think we have some time to think some up." I smiled.

We pulled into Ian's parking spot at *Prim* and rode the elevator up to Adalynn's office. Her door was already open and she was on the phone when we walked in.

"You tell that asshole that I said it's to be corrected before print and, if he doesn't do it, then I'm coming after him and his job! Got it?" she said as she slammed down the phone.

"Whoa, Adalynn in action. I like that!" Ian winked.

She got up from the chair, walked over, and gave us both a hug and a kiss. "This is a wonderful surprise. What brings the two of you here?"

Ian looked at me. "Can I tell her, Rory?" he asked in excitement.

"Yes, go ahead."

"Tell me what? What happened?"

"The babies are girls. We're going to have two daughters."

"AH! That's so awesome. I'm so happy for both of you!" Adalynn exclaimed as she hugged us again. "Rory, do you know what this means? Shop, shop, shop! I can't wait to shop for baby girls!"

I smiled at her enthusiasm. She was just as excited as Ian and I were and there was something I wanted to talk to Ian about later.

"Come on, sweetheart. We need to get you home and off your feet."

Adalynn looked at me and winked. “I’ll call you later, Rory. Oh, and Ian, about that meeting, the day you set it up for is perfect.”

Chapter 38
Ian

"Are you comfortable, sweetheart?" I asked her as we were in the air headed to New York.

"I'm very comfortable. Thank you." She smiled.

I had a business meeting in New York that I had to attend with Connor regarding the property sale for his art gallery. We were only going to be there a couple of days because Paris was waiting for us. Rory was so excited to see Ellery. I had overheard them talking on the phone last night about the pregnancy and babies. I grabbed us both a bottle of water and sat down next to her on the couch. I leaned over, lifted up her shirt, and kissed her bare stomach.

"Let's talk names." I smiled as I sat up.

"Okay. You first," she said.

"I was thinking we could make a game out of it. I'll say a name and you say another that starts with the same letter."

"Gretchen," I said.

"Gabby."

"Beth."

"Brianna." She smiled.

"Lucy."

"Lexi."

"Madeline."

"Margaret."

"Really, Rory?" I asked.

"Sorry, I couldn't think of anything else." She laughed. Okay, let me say a name first."

"Go ahead, sweetheart."

"Ashley."

"Ariel. Like the princess." I smiled.

Rory's face lit up. "I love Ariel."

"And I love Ashley."

"Ian, I think we just named our little girls."

I leaned over and gave her tummy a light kiss. "Hello, Ashley and Ariel Braxton."

****

Our time was well spent in New York with Connor and Ellery. After Connor and I finished up our final meeting, the four of us spent the day at Central Park with Julia. She was an adorable little girl and she loved to screech. My ears hurt every time she let one out. She was a very happy baby and I hoped to be the kind of father Connor was to her. Ellery and Rory took a walk to the hot dog stand and left Julia with us.

"She's a beautiful little girl, Connor."

"That she is, my friend. She's my little princess and the joy of my life. You'll see what I'm talking about when your daughters are born. Wow, Ian, two babies at the same time."

I chuckled. "I know. It's going to be quite an adjustment."

While I held Julia's hands up as she tried to walk, Ellery and Rory came back with the hot dogs and chips. Ellery put Julia in her stroller and we all sat on the blanket, ate our hot dogs, and had a good time.

****

Up in the air, again. This time, we were on our way to Paris. Rory was so excited to see Andre. I told him we were coming, but to act like he didn't know when he saw us. Instead of staying at Adalynn's, I rented us a suite at the Le Burgundy Hotel. I wanted this trip to be perfect for her.

"Where are we staying? Are we staying at Adalynn's place?" she asked.

"No, sweetheart, we're staying somewhere else. It's a surprise." Little did she know that I had a few surprises up my sleeve for her.

Rory began to shift in her seat. It was almost as if she was uncomfortable.

"Are you okay, sweetheart?" I asked.

"My back is hurting a little bit. It's hard to get comfortable in this chair."

I got up from my chair and took her hand. "Come sit over on the couch and let me give you a massage."

She smiled as I led her to the couch where she sat down with her back to me. I began to massage her lower back and she started to moan. She sounded so sexy and she was turning me on. Suddenly, she let out a scream and placed her hands on her stomach.

"Sweetheart, what's wrong? Did I hurt you? Did I hurt the babies?" I was scared shitless at that moment.

"Oh my God, Ian. I think I felt one of the babies kick!"

"No way! Are you sure?"

She took my hand and placed it on the side of her stomach. I held it there for a few moments and then I felt it. I gasped as she looked at me and smiled.

"See, I told you!"

"Rory, that's amazing." I got down on my knees and placed my lips against her stomach. "Can you do that again for Daddy?"

I waited and waited, and nothing happened. "Well, at least we both felt it," I said as I looked up at her.

Our flight was long, but we slept a good portion of it. As soon as we landed, we took a limo to the hotel. Rory looked exhausted and I was worried about her, between the pregnancy and jet lag.

"You look tired," I said to her as I took off her shoes and gently rubbed her feet.

"I'm fine. Are you saying that I look like shit?"

"Rory, of course not. You just look a little tired, that's all. You could never look like shit, sweetheart."

"Just making sure because I was ready to fight with you." She smiled.

"Fight with me? Well, in that case, yes, you do look like shit and you really need to do something about yourself." I smiled.

Whenever Rory and I fought, there was always the best makeup sex. I was pretty sure that was what she wanted.

"Is that so, Mr. Braxton? Okay, seriously, I'm tired. In fact, too tired to fight with you and then have makeup sex. I'm sorry, baby."

I brushed a few strands of her hair away from her face and smiled. "It's okay, sweetheart. I need you to get some rest because we're hitting the town tonight. So, I want you to climb on this comfortable bed and go to sleep. I have something I need to go pick up. I'll be back in a while."

"Okay," she sleepily said as she lay down.

A couple of hours later, I returned to the room and Rory had just woken up. I hung the garment bag in the closet and walked over to the bed.

"Did you have a nice nap?" I asked as I softly kissed her lips.

"I did, thank you. What did you just put in the closet?"

"Something for you to wear tonight."

She smiled and wrapped her arms around me, kissing me and thanking me for the dress she hadn't even seen yet. She got up from the bed, walked over to the closet, and pulled down the zipper of the garment bag.

"Ian, it's beautiful. Are you sure it's going to fit?"

"It should. Try it on."

"What's the occasion? What are we doing tonight?" she asked in excitement.

"You'll see." I winked.

She took off her top and pants. Her belly was getting so big and she was so incredibly beautiful. "Come here first before you put on that dress," I said.

She walked over and stood in front of me. I placed my hands on her belly and gave my babies tiny kisses. "You're so damn beautiful, Rory. I love you so much."

She ran her fingers through my hair as I laid my cheek against her. "I love you more, Braxton." I looked up at her and smiled. She was my perfect girl.

"Go try your dress on," I said.

She stepped into her dress and pulled it up over her expanding belly. She had to tug at it and I couldn't help but laugh. She turned around and asked me to zip her up.

"Perfect. It fits perfect. I love it, Ian. Thank you so much."

"You're welcome, sweetheart. I'm going to jump in the shower and get ready myself. We have dinner reservations at six o'clock."

****

She looked beautiful. Stunning and radiant, to be exact. We arrived at the restaurant promptly at six and had a wonderful dinner. When we were finished, we climbed into the limo and I had the driver take us to the Eiffel tower.

"Where are we going?" Rory asked.

"You'll see, sweetheart." I smiled as I kissed her hand.

As soon as we pulled up, Rory looked at me and smiled. "Oh, Ian, the Eiffel Tower. I was so hoping we could see it again."

I helped her out of the limo and we walked hand in hand until we reached a few feet in front of the tower. We stood there and looked up and, when I looked at Rory, she had the most incredible smile on her face.

"I'll never get tired of seeing this," she said.

I took both of her hands and turned her towards me. I gently ran the back of my hand down her cheek and smiled. "I love you, Rory, and I never want to lose you."

"You're not going to lose me, Ian."

"You're my everything, sweetheart. You're the reason I get up in the morning and you're the reason I strive so hard to be a perfect man. You make me laugh. You make me smile, but most importantly, you make me happy. Happiness was something I thought I had until the night you laid across my lap in my limo and you looked at me. I'll never forget that night, Rory. I instantly wanted to protect you and I didn't know why. Something inside me needed you, and as hard as I tried to fight it, I couldn't. The need was stronger than I was. You have made me so happy from the beginning. I know we've had our rough patches, and I know I was a complete dick about sharing my feelings with you. Then I screwed up again when you told me you were pregnant. I'm sorry for hurting you so badly because of my fears. I've come to realize that I don't fear anything anymore when we're together. You've given me unconditional love. You've given me courage and strength, but most of all, you've given me two beautiful daughters and I can't wait until they arrive so I can tell them how much I love them, just like I'm telling you now."

Tears sprung to her eyes. "Ian," she whispered.

"Let me finish, sweetheart."

I got down on one knee and pulled a small red velvet box from my pocket. "You're the reason I breathe every day and I love you more than anything in the entire world, and I want to spend the rest of my life loving you and taking care of you and our children. I need you by my side. Will you do me the honor, Miss Sinclair, and marry me?"

Chapter 39
Rory

My heart was beating at the speed of light and tears started streaming down my face. Ian lifted the top of the box, and inside sat the most beautiful princess-cut diamond I'd ever seen in my life. The way it sparkled was incredible. I let go of his hand and placed mine over my mouth. I was shocked because I didn't expect it at all.

"YES! Of course I'll marry you!" I smiled and cried at the same time.

Ian pulled the ring from the box and placed it on my finger. He then brought my hand to his lips and softly kissed my ring.

"You've made me the happiest man alive, Rory." He smiled as he hugged me.

"And you've made me the happiest woman alive, Ian. Oh my God, I can't believe this."

"Believe it, sweetheart, because it's real and you're going to become Mrs. Ian Braxton."

"I love you so much," I said as we kissed.

I couldn't stop looking at my ring. It was stunning and elegant. Ian did the best job picking it out.

"You had this all planned out, didn't you?"

"I sure did and I have another surprise for you, sweetheart."

I didn't know if I could handle another surprise. I was already on Cloud Nine.

"I professed my love for you in front of this beautiful tower once before, and now I asked you to marry me in front of this tower. Tomorrow at noon, you and I will be getting married and becoming one in front of the Eiffel Tower." He smiled.

"What? Tomorrow? Are you serious, Ian?"

"Yes, sweetheart. I have everything arranged. Tomorrow at this time, you will be Mrs. Ian Braxton."

"Oh my God, there's so much to do. How did you—"

"Shh, I've taken care of everything. Adalynn and Daniel are already here in Paris and they're going to be our witnesses."

"But you said you had a meeting here in Paris."

"I do, and that meeting is with you and our nuptials." He smiled. "I had some wedding dresses sent over to Adalynn's place and they're there waiting for you to pick one that you want to wear. So, I think we should head over there so you can see them."

I couldn't stop smiling. I was in awe of this man and how much he'd changed since the first day I met him. We climbed into the limo and headed to Adalynn's apartment. As soon as she saw the limo pull up, she ran to the door and hugged me, but then she pulled back.

"You said yes, right?" she asked.

"Of course I did." I smiled as I showed her my ring.

Ian and I followed her inside and Ian stayed with Daniel while I went to Adalynn's bedroom. "Tell me he said the most romantic things to you."

"He did. He literally took my breath away and I'll never forget this night. I can't believe he arranged for us to get married tomorrow. That's the most romantic thing in the world."

"Can I be honest with you? I didn't know he had it in him and I know he was worried you were going to say no," Adalynn said. "Oh, and by the way, I know nothing about the wedding. The only thing he told me was the he needed Daniel and me here to be your witnesses and he was having dresses sent over. Speaking of which, let me show you these beauties."

She opened her spare closet and it was filled with beautiful white wedding dresses. I felt like I was at the bridal store. I walked over and started to look at each dress.

"This is going to be too hard. I think I love them all," I said.

"Here, let's pull one out at a time," Adalynn said as she stood next to me and pulled the first dress out.

After trying on the first four dresses, and loving each one, it was the fifth dress that made me feel incredible the moment I put it on.

"Oh, Rory. You look like a total princess in that dress. It's gorgeous on you."

I looked at myself in the mirror and stared at the white princess ball gown wedding dress with the sweetheart neck line. Even being pregnant with twins, this dress made me feel as if I was the most beautiful woman ever to wear it.

"This is the one, Adalynn." I smiled.

"Beautiful choice, Rory. Here's the veil they sent with it. It would look perfect with your hair up in curls."

"What are you wearing?" I asked her.

"I'll show you. It's stunning. Ian picked it out and said it would be perfect for me and he was right."

She showed me an empire waist, princess line, strapless dress in a light pink. She was right, it was perfect. We walked out into the living room and Ian smiled at me. I sat down on his lap and put my arms around his neck.

"Did you pick a dress?" he asked.

"Yes and I can't wait for you to see it."

"Tomorrow, sweetheart," he said as he kissed me.

Something dawned on me. "Ian, I don't have a ring for you," I said with worry.

He laughed. "Don't worry, sweetheart. When I picked yours, I also picked my three favorite rings and someone from the jewelry store will be by tomorrow morning for you to pick which one you like the best."

I hugged him and buried my face in his neck. "You've thought of everything. I love you."

"I love you more, sweetheart."

"Okay, you two, time to say goodbye to each other," Adalynn said.

"What?" I asked in confusion as I looked at Ian.

"You're going to stay with Adalynn and Daniel tonight because it's bad luck to see the bride before the wedding and I don't want any bad luck."

"That's not true and I know for a fact you don't believe that," I said.

"Listen, sweetheart. I don't want to be away from you and the babies any more than you do. There will be many people here tomorrow to help you get ready. So, I'm going to go back to the hotel and go to bed, while you're here with Adalynn and Daniel."

I pushed out my bottom lip and gave Ian my sad eyes. "I'll miss you too much."

"I'll tell you what. I'll stay here until you fall asleep. Okay?" he asked as he tapped the end of my nose.

"Okay. I'd like that. I didn't bring any of my things."

"I packed you an overnight bag and had it sent over while you were asleep," Ian said.

This man, my fiancé, my future husband, and my best friend, formulated a plan and executed it with perfection. He was my hero and he'd also be the hero of his daughters. I climbed into the bed I slept in when I stayed here the first time and Ian climbed in next to me. He put his arms around me, kissed me, and softly rubbed my tummy as I fell asleep.

Chapter 40
Ian & Rory

It felt like the longest night of my life. I couldn't sleep a wink because I couldn't wait to make Rory my wife. After tossing and turning, I finally got up and poured a few shots of whiskey. Whiskey always helped me sleep. I felt like I'd only been sleeping a couple of hours before the alarm went off. I got up, showered, made some coffee, and sat down at the table with my phone.

"Good morning, my future wife. I hope you slept well."

"Good morning, my future husband. I didn't. I hope you did."

"I didn't either. Too excited about today."

"Me too. I love you, and I can't wait to marry you."

"I love you more, sweetheart, and I can't wait either."

"Morning, Ian, Adalynn here. I have to take your bride's phone away because it's time for her makeup. She'll see you in a few hours. Love you!"

I rolled my eyes and chuckled at the same time. There was a knock at the door and it was Daniel. The man from the tuxedo shop was going to be here shortly with our tuxes.

"Good morning, Daniel."

"Are you nervous yet?" he asked.

"Nah. I'm fine. Cool as a cucumber." I smiled.

"Good. It's craziness over at the apartment. People were all over the place."

"Did Rory and Adalynn's flowers arrive?" I asked.

"Yes, and I must say, they're exquisite. Rory burst into tears when she saw her bouquet. I can't believe how fast you pulled this off. You've outdone yourself and I can't wait to see the expression on Rory's face when she sees the other surprise you have for her."

"I can't either. She's going to be so happy."

We put on our tuxedos and it was time to head to the Eiffel Tower. When we arrived, everything was set up perfectly in the park that surrounded the tower and the minister had already arrived. I walked around and said hello to the guests that attended the wedding and then took my place where the beautiful floral archway stood. No expense was spared to make this wedding memorable for Rory.

Rory

"I'm so nervous," I said to Adalynn in the limo.

"Don't be. I can't wait until Ian sees you. His cock is going to go straight up and he won't be able to control it." She smiled.

I let out a laugh and she winked at me. "See, did that help you relax?"

We arrived around the corner of the tower and the limo driver told us that he was told to drop us off there. Suddenly, the door opened and a hand reached in and helped me out.

"Andre!" I squealed.

"Look at my beautiful American bride. You are gorgeous, Rory."

"I tried to call you last night, but you didn't answer."

"I was afraid if I spoke to you that I'd ruin the surprise. This is where I begin to walk you down the aisle."

Music began to play and Andre told Adalynn to start walking along the red carpet. "I can't believe this," I said to Andre.

"Believe it because it's real and it's happening. You are a very lucky woman to be marrying Ian. He loves you more than life and those babies too. He told me so."

I kissed him on the cheek and followed Adalynn a few feet behind. Once we reached the entrance, I gasped at the scene before me. Tears started to fill my eyes when I saw Jimmy, Rosie, Richard, Mandy, Veronica, and Connor and Ellery standing by the white chairs that were decorated with flowers.

"You can't cry, Rory. Your makeup, remember your makeup," Andre said.

He was right and I looked up at the beautiful sunny sky to stop the tears from falling. As I looked straight ahead down the aisle, I saw my future husband standing there with his hands crossed and a big smile on his face. My heart was racing with excitement. When we finally reached where Ian was standing, he held out his hand and Andre placed mine in his. He kissed me on the cheek and patted Ian on the shoulder. The minister spoke a few words and then told us it was time to say our wedding vows. I looked at Ian and bit down on my bottom lip because I forgot about vows and I didn't prepare anything. He looked at me and smiled.

"Don't worry, sweetheart. I didn't prepare because I'm just going to say what's in my heart."

"I love you," I mouthed as he took my hands.

"Rory, these are my vows to you. I will love you and cherish you forever. You're the light in my day and the stars in my night. You've held me up during the most difficult times and you've been my rock. I will forever be faithful to you and I will honor you for the rest of my life. You have my word, my promise, and my love forever and always. I will be there for you in sickness and in health until death do us part. You're the sun in my rain and the rainbow that shines after. My love for you is eternal and nothing will ever change that. With this ring, I thee wed."

I tried so hard to hold it together, but I couldn't. I loved him so much and the tears had to fall. He took his thumb and gently wiped them away. "Ian, these are my vows to you. You showed me a world that I had only ever dreamed of. You saved my life and you saved me. You're my rock and solid ground. You have filled my heart and my world with love and I'm going to spend the rest of my life thanking you. You are mine for eternity and I will love and cherish you forever. I will be there for you in sickness and in health and through the good and the bad until death do us part. I also promise to make sure you have blueberry muffins every day. With this ring, I thee wed."

Ian let out a light laugh and smiled at me as I slipped the ring on his finger. "I now pronounce you husband and wife. You may kiss your beautiful bride."

We both smiled as we shared a passionate kiss and everyone clapped. "I can't believe everyone is here," I said.

"Are you happy?" he asked.

"The happiest person alive."

"Good. That's what I wanted." He smiled as he kissed me again.

Ian broke our kiss and leaned down and kissed my tummy. "How are my girls?" he whispered.

"They're very happy too." I smiled.

We walked hand in hand up the aisle. I stopped when I saw Jimmy and he pulled me into a warm embrace.

"Look at you. My beautiful daughter. I never thought in a million years that I'd ever get to see this day. Your mom would be so proud of you."

"I wish her and Stephen were here."

"They are in spirit, Rory," he said. "You've married a very generous and loving man. I couldn't ask for a better son-in-law."

"You made your old dad here cry," Rosie said as she hugged me and then Ian. "Congratulations to the both of you. It was a beautiful ceremony."

"Thank you for dropping all your plans at the last minute to come," Ian said.

"Excuse me for a moment," I said as I walked over to Richard and Veronica. "I'm so happy you're here." I smiled as I hugged them both.

"Not as happy as I am. Seeing my son marry you is the best thing I've ever seen in my life. I'm proud to call you my daughter-in-law. Thank you for everything, Rory."

Once again, being the hormonal mess I was, tears filled my eyes. “Thank you, Dad.” I smiled.

Veronica looked at me with her tear-filled eyes. “You are simply gorgeous and this is the best day of my life,” Ian’s mother said. “To finally be a part of my son’s life and now I have a daughter and two granddaughters on the way. I feel like I’ve finally been blessed.”

Ian walked over and placed his hand on the small of my back. He placed his other hand on my stomach and held it there. “I can’t wait for you to meet your granddaughters, Mom and Dad,” he said.

Connor and Ellery walked over to us, grinning from ear to ear. “Congratulations!” Ellery exclaimed as she hugged both of us.

“You look absolutely stunning, Rory.” Connor smiled.

“Thank you both for coming,” I said.

“We wouldn’t have missed this wedding for the world,” Connor replied.

Ian

After the photographer was finished taking pictures of us, I escorted Rory to the limo that was waiting for us. Adalynn and Daniel, along with the rest of the guests, took separate limos back to the hotel, where I had arranged a small, intimate reception.

“You are so beautiful, sweetheart. When I saw you walk down that aisle, I swear my heart stopped beating. I thought I died and I was in Heaven.”

She placed her hand on my cheek. “Thank you, Ian, my husband. I felt the same way when I saw you standing at the end. You have no idea how hard it was to hold back the tears.”

“Yes, I do, because I had to do it too, sweetheart.”

“How did you pull this off in such a short amount of time?” she asked.

“Anything’s possible when you’re madly in love and you want something bad enough.”

“I want to make love to you right now.” Rory smiled.

“I want to make love to you too, and we will tonight, after the wedding reception. All night long, I will make you come multiple times.”

“God, Ian, stop.” She smiled. “You’re making me wet already.”

“Okay, Rory. We need to stop talking like that. I don’t know if I can hold back. So, tell me about Andre.”

Rory laughed as she held my face and kissed me. We arrived at the hotel and I took Rory to the room where the reception was being held. The wedding cake turned out perfect and Rory was very happy. We shared a wonderful celebration dinner with our family and friends and then Rory and I cut the cake. As we danced our first dance as husband and wife, Rory made a comment to me.

“Have you noticed that Andre and Mandy haven’t left each other’s side since the ceremony? They even sat next to each other.”

"I did notice that, sweetheart. I wonder if they're falling for each other." I smiled.

"Come to think of it, they did talk quite a bit when he was staying with us," Rory said.

"Good for them. I hope they find in each other what we have."

It was finally time to take my wife up to our hotel room and make love to her for the first time as Mrs. Ian Braxton; something I'd been looking forward to all day. I carried her into our room and laid her down on the bed while I hovered over her and stared into her beautiful brown eyes.

"I love you more than anything else in this world, Mrs. Braxton, and now I'm going to show you how much you mean to me and how special you are."

"I'm looking forward to it, Mr. Braxton, because I plan on showing you the same thing." She smiled.

I growled and kissed her passionately as we made love a few times that night and celebrated our marriage.

Chapter 41
Rory
3 Months Later…

I stood in the middle of the nursery and looked around. It was huge. Ian had the wall knocked out between both bedrooms and had them completely renovated. I felt sorry for the workers because Ian was on their asses every second of every day to get the job done. They finished two days early. I slipped them some cash and apologized for my husband's behavior. It turned out exactly the way Ian and I had planned. We decorated with the colors of soft pink and cream. It was perfect and so were the two paintings that Ellery painted for us that hung above each of the girls' cribs.

"It's beautiful in here," Ian said as he wrapped his arms around me.

"It is. Now that it's complete, we just need to wait for our daughters to be born."

"Ah, they'll be here soon, Rory. Filling this room with laughter."

"Laughter won't come for a while, babe. They'll fill the room with cries."

Ian chuckled and kissed my head. "I can't believe all the things we got from the baby shower. People were so generous," I said.

"They always are, sweetheart." He smiled.

Ian and I went out to pick up a couple more things for the babies. As we were walking down the shopping plaza, we ran into Andrew. Suddenly, I felt sick as I held onto Ian's arm.

"Ian, Rory. Wow, look at you. You look great," Andrew said.

"Excuse us, Andrew. We're in a hurry," Ian replied.

We began to walk past him and then stopped when we heard him speak.

"I need to apologize to both of you. I want to apologize to both of you."

Ian turned around and looked at him with anger in his eyes. "How dare you."

"I'm in therapy, and I have been for months. I even met someone that I think is really special."

"Good for you, Andrew," I said. "Keep getting that help."

"I miss your friendship, Ian," Andrew said with sadness.

"Yeah, I miss your friendship too, except the part where you had my wife pinned to the ground on a cold bathroom floor in a club. I hope you get all help you need, and I hope that your relationship works out. Take care, Drew."

Ian took my arm and led me down the sidewalk. He didn't say a word for quite a while after that. I knew there was a part of him that missed Andrew, but he would never forgive him for what he did, even if I had made peace with it.

"I have to pee," I said.

"You just went to the bathroom ten minutes ago," Ian said.

"And? What's your point? Do you have any idea what it's like to have two human beings inside of you, pushing down on your bladder?"

"Good point, sweetheart. I apologize. Now let's get you to a bathroom."

****

Ian and I were lying in bed. He was doing some work on his laptop and I was looking through a *Cosmopolitan* magazine. Suddenly, Ian looked over at me and smiled. "Can I play with my girls?"

I sighed. As much as I loved his attention to the babies, he actually got them all wound up when he talked to them. They would start kicking away and he thought it was funny. "Ian, they're settled for the night."

"Please, Rory. Just a couple little words. Please," he begged.

"Fine. Just make it quick. I'm tired."

He smiled and kissed my tummy. "Hi, it's your daddy. I just wanted to say good night to both of you."

And there it was; the kicks had started. Ian put his hands across my stomach and smiled with each kick. He was so cute, and I had no doubt in my mind that he was going to make the best daddy. He'd kept a close eye on me ever since the first ultrasound, and when he couldn't be with me because of work, he usually had Mandy keep me company. I sighed with each kick because one of them was kicking my bladder and it hurt. I was already feeling the pressure of them down there and he was making it worse.

"I love you, but fuck, Braxton, your children are really making me uncomfortable, and I have to go to the bathroom."

He kissed my stomach three more times and got up and helped me up from the bed. "Rory, it's getting harder for you to get up." He laughed.

"I'm so happy you find it amusing. How about I stick two babies up your penis and see how comfortable you are."

He glared at me. "Right. Sorry, sweetheart. I won't say another word."

I went into the bathroom and smiled when I heard him yell, "Oh, by the way, don't expect me to ever get hard again after what you just said."

"I have no doubt that you'll be just fine." I climbed into bed and Ian immediately put his arm around me and rested his hand on my belly.

"Don't you dare," I warned.

I heard a light chuckle as he inched his hand away from me. "Good night, sweetheart. I love you."

"I love you too."

****

Ian and I left the doctor's office and went to grab some lunch. He said that I could go into labor any day and if I didn't within the next week, then he would schedule me for a C-section. I didn't know if I could hold out for another week. I was so uncomfortable, I could barely stand it anymore. Small cramping pains started and I wasn't feeling well. I was so tired and I just wanted to go home.

"Can we get lunch to go, honey? I'm so tired and I'm not feeling well."

"What's wrong, sweetheart?" he asked with concern.

"I just feel a little sick. I think I need to lie down for a while."

"Okay. I'll just have Charles make something at home," he said as he helped me into the car.

When we arrived home, I walked up the stairs and was startled by a severe cramp in my stomach. A cramp so bad that it sent me to my knees. I let out what sounded like a howl. Ian came running from the kitchen.

"Rory, what's wrong?!"

"I think I had contraction."

He took my hand and helped me up. "I'll call the doctor."

"No, don't. It was just one pain. I'll probably start getting them here and there. We don't have to worry until they come closer together."

Ian helped me up the stairs and to the bedroom. Another contraction started. "Holy fuck!" I screamed.

"Shit, sweetheart, I'm calling the doctor. I'll be right back. I left my phone downstairs."

"Don't leave me, Ian," I whined.

Ian started screaming Mandy's name and, after a few moments, she came running into the bedroom.

"Mandy, I need you to go to the kitchen and get my phone. I need to call the doctor. Rory's in labor."

"Here, Mr. Braxton, just use my phone," she said as she pulled it from her pocket and handed it to him.

Mandy walked over and rubbed my back. "I know it hurts, Rory, but you can do this." She smiled.

"OH MY GOD! It's happening again," I screamed.

Suddenly, I felt a steady stream of water running down my legs. I looked down and gasped.

"Oh, your water broke!" Mandy exclaimed.

"What?! Ian said.

"Mr. Braxton, forget calling the doctor. You need to get Rory to the hospital now."

Ian gave Mandy the phone and both of them helped me downstairs. Ian ran to the kitchen and grabbed his keys and phone while Mandy helped me in the car.

"Mandy, please have Joshua get Rory's bag from the bedroom closet and bring it to the hospital."

"Will do, Mr. Braxton. Good luck, Rory!"

I was scared, in pain, and unsure about everything. Ian took my hand and held it while he drove us to the hospital. Another contraction started and I squeezed Ian's hand as I let out a yell.

"Why does this hurt so badly?" I screamed. "This can't be normal!"

"Breathe, sweetheart. We're almost at the hospital and everything will be fine," Ian said.

"Nothing will be fine until I get these babies out of me!" I yelled.

Chapter 42
Ian

We arrived at the ER in record time. I broke every driving law possible. I went inside, found a wheelchair, and helped Rory from the car. I could see the pain in her face as she held her stomach. The receptionist took us up to the Labor and Delivery unit, where one of the nurses took Rory's information and then called her doctor. The time had finally arrived. My daughters were about to enter the world and I couldn't wait to meet them. I hated seeing Rory in so much pain and I wanted to do everything possible to try and make her comfortable. I helped her into the cloth gown the nurse left for her and then I helped her onto the bed.

"Ian, this pain is unbearable. I don't think I can do this," she said as she laid her forehead on my shoulder.

I clasped her shoulders with my hands and lightly rubbed them. "Yes, you can, sweetheart. Your daughters are depending on you to help them come into the world. They need your help."

She sighed as she laid her head back on the pillow. I could tell she was already exhausted.

"Hello, there. I'm Cora and I'll be your nurse for the rest of the evening."

"Hello, Cora, I'm Ian Braxton. Is there anything you can give my wife to help her pain?"

"I'll have to ask her doctor, but I'm sure he'll give her something." She smiled.

I pulled out my phone and dialed Adalynn. In the midst of all the excitement, I had forgotten to call her. Actually, I didn't call anyone.

"Rory better be in labor, Ian, because you're interrupting sex time," Adalynn answered.

"She is. We're at the hospital now."

"OH MY GOD! I'm on my way. Tell her that I'm on my way!" Click.

I looked over at Rory just as another contraction started. "Look at me, Rory. Focus on me, sweetheart," I said as I held her hands.

She squeezed them as hard as she could while she breathed in and out. Finally, it was over and she let go of my hands. Damn, her grip was hard and it hurt.

"Is there anything I can do for you?" I asked.

"Yes. Have these babies for me, please." She smiled.

"You know I would," I said as I kissed her nose. "Adalynn is on her way. I'm going to call the rest of the family."

I made a few phone calls to let everyone know that Rory was in labor. As I had my back turned to the door, I heard Adalynn breeze in.

"Ugh, Rory, you poor thing," she said as she held her hand. "Is he taking good care of you?"

I sighed as I shook my head. "Yes, I am, Adalynn, and hello to you too."

"No offense, Ian, and hello."

Nurse Cora walked back into the room and asked us to leave while she checked to see how many centimeters Rory was dilated.

"I'm sorry, Cora, but I'm not leaving my wife's side."

"And neither am I," Adalynn snapped.

Rory told Nurse Cora that it was okay for us to stay. She examined her and then looked at Rory. "I'm sorry, but you're already dilated to eight centimeters. It's too late for you to have an epidural."

"Eight centimeters?" I asked. "How did she dilate so quickly?"

"It happens, Mr. Braxton. Just a couple more centimeters and she'll be pushing those babies out."

Rory began to cry. "Another contraction is coming and I want pain meds! Ian, do something. Buy me some pain meds, baby, please."

I put my arm around her as she screamed through another painful contraction. "Sweetheart, I would if I could, but I can't. You know I can't. We can do this together."

"TOGETHER! Are you experiencing this much pain? Are you lying in this bed, ready to explode? No, I didn't think so, buddy."

"Right, sweetheart. I'm sorry."

"OH MY GOD, Ian, another one already!" she yelled.

Nurse Cora looked over and smiled at Rory. "It's almost time. The contractions will start coming closer together."

I went into the bathroom and ran a washcloth under cool water to place on Rory's forehead. "Here, maybe this will help you."

"Thank you. I love you so much, Ian."

"I love you too and I'm here for you."

Rory's doctor walked into the room and examined her. "Well, it's time. You're at ten centimeters, Rory. Let's have these babies." He smiled.

Excitement poured throughout my entire body. Finally, my babies were going to be here. I took Rory's hand and softly kissed it.

"Me and you are a team, sweetheart. We're going to do this together. I'm going to be here to help you with every push and every contraction. I love you so much and you can do this."

"Wow, you're one hell of a husband," Nurse Cora said.

Adalynn knew that Rory and I didn't want anyone else in the room during the delivery, so she kissed Rory on her head and wished her luck before going out to the waiting room to wait with Daniel and the rest of the family.

Rory took in a deep breath as the doctor put her feet in the stirrups and the pushing began.

Chapter 43
Rory & Ian

It felt like I was being ripped apart. Ian was so supportive and so loving and tender that he made it so easy to focus on him. The contractions were seconds apart and the pushing was the hardest thing I'd ever done. I yelled with each push and Ian was right there, helping me through it.

"That's it, sweetheart. You're doing great. I'm so proud of you. Stephen would be so proud."

"Who's first?" I asked as I gave another push.

"What do you mean, sweetheart?"

"Ashley or Ariel? Who's first?"

"I don't know. I didn't think about it. You pick."

"Doesn't matter, honey."

"We'll decide when we see her," Ian said.

The last push was the hardest. "Rory, I see the baby's head. One more push. Come on," the doctor spoke.

"Rory, our first baby girl is right there. You can do it, sweetheart."

I closed my eyes and pushed as hard as I could. Suddenly, I heard the cries of my baby girl.

"You did it, sweetheart. She's beautiful. Look at how beautiful she is," Ian said with tears in his eyes.

I looked at my baby as the doctor held her up. “Ashley. She’s Ashley,” I whispered and then let out a scream.

Another fucking contraction. “We have one more baby to deliver, Rory. I need you to push again,” the doctor said.

I was so tired and it felt like my body had been hit by a truck. I felt paralyzed and I just couldn’t do it.

“Ian, I can’t. I’m so tired. I just can’t do this anymore.”

He looked at me as he wiped my forehead with a cloth. “Rory, you are to push right now. It’s not a request; it’s a command. Do you understand me?”

I nodded my head and pushed with every last ounce of strength I had left. “Rory, you did it!” Ian exclaimed.

I threw my head back on the pillow and tried to catch my breath. I heard the cries of Ariel and smiled. The nurse had just handed Ashley to Ian, and the doctor handed me Ariel. My girls were finally here and they were perfect. I looked at Ian, who had a tear streaming down his face.

Ian

“Our little girls are beautiful, sweetheart. I’m so proud of you,” I said as I kissed her head.

It was hard to believe my little girls were finally here. Rory did such an incredible job bringing them into the world and I’d never been more proud of her. As I held Ashley, I reached over and softly rubbed Ariel’s little hand. These two little girls that I stared at had instantly changed my life. The love that poured out of me for them was astounding. I had three beautiful girls in my life and I couldn’t have been happier.

"I think they look like you." Rory smiled.

"You think? Because when I look at them, all I see is their beautiful mother. I'm going to go to the waiting room and tell everyone the girls have arrived. I'll be right back, sweetheart," I said as I kissed her head and carefully handed her Ashley.

I walked out to the waiting room where Adalynn, Daniel, Mandy, Jimmy, and Richard were sitting and waiting for the news.

"Ashley and Ariel have arrived, and they're very healthy little girls," I announced with a grin on my face.

Adalynn stood up and hugged me with tears in her eyes. Smiles graced everyone's face as congratulations were said.

"Can we see Rory and the babies?" Adalynn asked.

"Sure. She'd love that." I smiled.

Adalynn was the first one to run in there and coo over both girls. Both she and Daniel held them and I could tell Adalynn was loving it.

"I see that look on your face," I said to her.

"What look would that be, Daddy?"

"The maternal look. The look of 'oh I want a baby now.'"

She looked up at me and smiled. "Don't get me wrong, I love kids, but I don't want any of my own and neither does Daniel. We already discussed it before we got married."

"Look at me! I didn't want kids either." I smiled.

"Nah, you were just waiting for that special woman to give you one or two." She winked.

After everyone took their turns with congratulating us and holding the girls, they said their goodbyes. Rory looked exhausted, so I took Ashley and Ariel from her and laid them down in their hospital cribs. Both girls were asleep, so I climbed next to Rory and held her close.

"I love you, sweetheart, and I want to thank you," I said as I kissed her head.

"Thank me for what?" she asked.

"For coming into my life, marrying me, and giving me the best gift any man could ever ask for: two little girls."

"I love you and you're welcome. But don't forget you had a big part in helping me make those little girls. So thank *you*." She smiled.

"Get some rest, sweetheart."

"Will you stay with me?" she asked.

"Of course I will. I'm never leaving you or my girls."

She closed her eyes and, within seconds, she was sound asleep. I couldn't help but smile every time I looked at my little angels. I was tired, so I figured I'd get a little rest with Rory while Ashley and Ariel were asleep. I closed my eyes, and I could feel myself drifting to sleep, and then, it happened: they both started crying at the same time.

Chapter 44
Rory
One Month Later…

The girls were one month old now and I wished I could tell you that it was a walk in the park. Adjusting to parenthood wasn't as easy as I thought it would be. Ashley and Ariel were only getting up one time a night now versus the every hour and a half they were when we first brought them home. I tried to breastfeed, but it became too impossible for me to keep up with both babies, and my milk wasn't coming in the way it was supposed to, so their pediatrician put them on baby formula. Ian wasn't happy about that until I said a few choice words to him. He quickly changed his mind. He was an amazing father. He got up with me every night. Usually, both girls would cry and want to be fed at the same time, so he would feed one and I would feed the other. Watching the way he was with his girls was so surreal. He was the perfect daddy as far as I was concerned, and nobody could say anything different. Both girls were finally sleeping and I wanted to take a shower. I also wanted to make love to my husband. I hadn't gotten clearance yet from the doctor, but I didn't care. I needed Ian, and I knew he needed me. I got up from the bed and stripped out of my panties and nightgown before heading into the bathroom. I opened the shower door and Ian looked at me and smiled.

"What are you doing, sweetheart?" he asked.

"I think you know what I'm doing." I smiled as I stepped in the shower and closed the door.

"But—" he said.

"Shh," I said as I brought my finger to his lips.

He placed his hands on my hips and smiled as I took his cock in my hand and started stroking it. "Ah, sweetheart. Are you sure?"

"I'm very sure. I need you and I want you. It's been far too long."

His hands traveled from my hips and up to my breasts as he cupped them gently. "I don't want to hurt you."

"You won't. I promise. Now fuck me!"

He moaned as his lips brushed against mine, going from a soft, light kiss to a passionate, deep one. His hard cock was ready and I couldn't wait any longer to have him inside me. I turned and placed my hands on the shower wall.

"Oh God, Rory," he said as he grabbed my ass firmly. "You don't know how much I want you right now."

"Stop talking, babe."

"I'm going to go slow and, if at any time you're uncomfortable, we're stopping."

He took his hard cock and placed it between my legs, gently inserting himself into me. I could tell he was nervous because he was going too slowly.

"Ian, I love you, but if you don't speed it up, I'm afraid the girls will wake up and we'll lose our chance."

That lit a fire under him because he pushed inside of me. I felt a little pain, but not enough to make me want to stop. His thrusts were slow and deep, and his moans in my ear heightened my arousal. Once he was fully inside me, he reached his hands up and grabbed onto my breasts, kneading them and pinching my hardened nipples.

"God, you feel so good, sweetheart. I feel like I'm already about to come."

"Faster, Ian. I'm almost there."

"I don't want to hurt you."

"Ian, it's not a request; it's a command. Do you understand me?!" I exclaimed.

Those words were enough to make him thrust in and out of me at a rapid pace. His hand left my breast and traveled down to my clit, which he forcefully rubbed. I let out a howl as my body tightened and he sent me over the edge with an amazing orgasm.

"That's it, sweetheart, come for me because I'm coming now," he cried out as he buried himself deep inside me and held me tightly.

I took in a deep breath as he pulled out of me and turned me around. He placed his hands on each side of my face and stared into my eyes as the hot water poured down on us.

"I love you, sweetheart."

"I love you more." I smiled.

****

We brought the girls down to breakfast with us since they were awake. Ian held Ashley, and I held Ariel as we sat and ate our breakfast.

"See this, Ashley, this is a blueberry muffin. This is Daddy's favorite thing to eat in the morning, and I know you'll love them too. Please tell Daddy that you'll love blueberry muffins," he pouted.

I couldn't help but laugh. "Ian, what are you going to do if she hates them?"

He looked up at me with a confused look on his face. "Well, out of both girls, one of them has to like them. How great is it going to be to share blueberry muffins with my daughters? I can see it now, Rory, all four of us sitting at the table, you eating your chocolate chip muffin and me and the girls eating blueberry muffins and them telling me how wonderful they are."

"Really, Ian? Is that what you're envisioning with your daughters? A breakfast of blueberry muffins?" Adalynn said as she strolled in and kissed us all on the cheeks.

"Are you always just going to pop in like this in the mornings?" Ian asked.

"Of course I am. In fact, I'll probably be here more because I need my daily dose of my goddaughters." She smiled as she took Ashley from him.

"Great." Ian sighed.

"What are your plans for today?" Adalynn asked.

"Ian and I are going to take the girls to visit Stephen's grave," I said.

"That's a wonderful idea, and it's such a beautiful day out. Well, I'm off. I just wanted to say hi to my girls and you, of course, Ian." She winked.

"Thanks, Adalynn, it means a lot to me," he replied.

"I know it does, sweetie." She smiled as she kissed us goodbye.

"She's crazy," Ian said.

"You're both crazy and you both love each other." I smiled. "Let's go get the diaper bags packed so we can get to the cemetery," I said as I walked upstairs.

****

Ian took the double stroller from the trunk and set it up. We put Ashley and Ariel in and pushed them to Stephen's grave. I couldn't have asked for a better day. The sun was shining brightly and there wasn't a cloud in the sky. Ian and I took the girls from the stroller and sat down on the grass.

"Thank you for coming with us, Ian."

"Aw, sweetheart, you're welcome. I plan on bringing the three of you here every Thursday. I miss him just as much as you do, and I know he would've been so happy for us."

"Yeah. He loved kids," I said as I looked down.

Ian put his arm around me. "I know it's still hard, sweetheart, and I'll do whatever I can to help you through it, even if it takes the rest of our lives."

"Life goes on, Ian. Things change and people come and go; it's inevitable and it's the cycle of life. I'm okay. I know Stephen is in a better place. Even though Ashley and Ariel never got the chance to meet him, I'll tell them all about their uncle and how wonderful he was. Minus the little stabbing incident." I smiled.

"Yeah, let's not bring that up. But, that's how we met. What are we going to tell them when they ask us?"

I laid my head on his shoulder. "We'll figure that out when the time comes."

We stood the girls up on Stephen's grave and pointed to his headstone. We introduced them, and I couldn't help but feel an overwhelmingly wonderful feeling. I couldn't describe it, but it felt like Stephen was there with us. We both stood up and, as I turned, I saw Stephen and my mother standing next to a tree that was across the way. They looked at me and smiled, nodding their heads as they turned around and walked away, fading into the distance. I smiled as I kissed my girls and Ian. I finally felt at peace, and my life was fully complete. I had married the man of my dreams and gave birth to two beautiful little angels. I knew my mom and Stephen would always be with us. I was truly blessed, and I thanked God every day for this beautiful and wonderful life.

Epilogue

"Daddy, Daddy, look at what we found!" Ashley exclaimed.

I walked over to them as they stood near the shoreline and held out their hands, showing me an oyster.

"What is it, Daddy?" Ariel asked.

I knelt down in front of them. "It's an oyster," I said as I examined it. "Let's open it."

I gasped as I split the oyster in half and, sitting in the middle, was a white pearl. "Look, girls, a pearl."

Their eyes widened as the corners of their mouths curved up. "It's so pretty! I can't wait to tell Mommy what we found!" Ariel said excitedly.

"I have an idea. Let's keep this our little secret. Mommy's birthday is next week. I'll take both of you to the jewelers and we can have this pearl made into a beautiful necklace for her. Just from the both of you." I smiled.

I held the pearl tightly in my hand as I stared at my two little girls who were now seven years old. It was hard to believe that they were growing up so fast. It seemed like only yesterday that they were born and I was holding them in my arms. As I was reflecting on the past, I heard Rory yell to the girls.

"Ariel, Ashley, it's time for your piano lessons. Please come inside."

I turned around and smiled at her as she smiled back and blew me a kiss. Our life was perfect. We barely argued and, when we did, we had the best makeup sex. Sometimes, I argued with her just because. I loved her and my girls more than anything in the world. As I followed Ashley and Ariel to the house, I pulled my ringing phone from my pocket and saw that it was Adalynn calling.

"Hi, Adalynn. I hope you have good news for me."

"Hello, darling, and I have great news. *Prim* has reached the top spot over in Europe as best international magazine. Our stocks have doubled already. We did it, Ian!"

"Excellent news! I knew we would. Why don't you and Daniel come over tonight for dinner and we'll celebrate."

"Will do. Tell Rory I said hi."

Not only was Braxton Development doing extremely well, *Prim* was too. I always knew that Adalynn had a fierce business side, and I'd had no doubt that she'd take the magazine to the top. I followed the girls inside and they went right to the piano. I walked over to Rory and kissed her softly.

"Adalynn and Daniel are coming over for dinner tonight to celebrate *Prim's* top spot in Europe."

"That's wonderful news, my love. Congratulations!" She smiled as she kissed me.

"Where's Leon? I thought it was time for the girl's piano lessons."

"He just went to go get the sheet music out of his car. He'll be right back."

I placed my hands on her hips and leaned in to whisper in her ear. "Good, because I'm going to take you upstairs and fuck you up against the wall." I smiled.

"I was hoping you'd say that." She winked at me.

Leon walked back in the house, said hello, and sat down at the piano in between the girls. Rory looked at me and casually walked upstairs.

"Enjoy your lessons, girls," I said before I followed Rory up the stairs.

****

It was hard to believe that my father had been deceased for about five years. He passed away just before Ashley and Ariel's second birthday. Those little girls brought him great joy and I believe that was why he hung on as long as he did, considering the chemo didn't help him much. I had a hard time when he died and Rory helped me through it. I fully understood what she went through and what she felt when Stephen passed away. I arranged it so that Richard's grave was next to Stephen's so that when we visited, we could visit both at the same time. The girls enjoyed visiting every week because they liked to put the flowers down on each grave.

Rory and her father bonded over the past several years and he ended up marrying Rosie. It was a small, simple Vegas wedding held in a little white chapel. I, too, had become close with my mother. She and Richard had spent quite a bit of time together during his illness. There's always forgiveness somewhere inside us, even if things that are done are unforgiveable.

Rory and I had forgiven Andrew for his past mistakes. He'd been in therapy for about five years and then ended up marrying a girl named Olivia. She was good for Andrew because she was a strong woman who didn't put up with any bullshit. She kept Andrew on a tight leash and that was exactly where he needed to be. We never fully recovered our friendship, but we would occasionally meet up for dinner for a couple of hours and then I wouldn't see him again for months.

Mandy and Andre got married, and she and her daughter ended up moving to Paris. Rory was ecstatic because now it gave us an excuse to go to Paris more often. The two of them had a baby boy of their own. We visited them two to three times a year and we would Skype with them about once a month. Ashley and Ariel loved Paris and were so excited to go every time.

Rory was sitting up in bed reading a book when I climbed in and wrapped my arms around her. I began kissing her neck as she smiled and wrapped her legs around me. Suddenly, we heard the pitter patter of little feet heading towards our room. Rory and I quickly sat up and looked at each other and laughed. The girls always had perfect timing.

"Mommy, Daddy!" they yelled as the door flew open.

"What's wrong?" I asked as they both climbed into bed with us.

"We're scared," Ashley pouted.

"Yeah, we're scared," Ariel said.

"What scared you?" Rory asked.

"Umm…" Ashley said.

"Umm…" Ariel copied.

"Just stuff. We want to sleep with you."

I looked at Rory and she looked at me. We both laughed because we knew they just wanted to be with us. They weren't scared. This was something they did about once a month.

"All right, get under the covers." I smiled as I tickled them both.

I leaned over and gave Rory a kiss, Ashley a kiss, and then finally, Ariel.

"Good night, my queen and princesses."

"Good night, my king," Rory said.

"Good night, my wonderful daddy and mommy." Both girls giggled.

I lay there, in my king-sized bed with the love of my life and my daughters. I smiled because this was exactly where I wanted to be. I turned to face Rory at the same time she turned and faced me. We both extended our hands to each other over the girls and interlaced our fingers.

"I love you, sweetheart."

"I love you more," she whispered.

The End

I hope you enjoyed reading the conclusion of Ian & Rory's story.

Make sure to check out my other romance novels:

The Forever Trilogy:

(Forever Black, Forever You, Forever Us)

Being Julia

Collin (Releasing 8/12/14)

Remembering You

Reclaiming Us (Not yet released)

Love In Between

The Upside of Love (Releasing Fall 2014)

Playlist

Human – Christina Perri

Best Day Of My Life – American Authors

All of Me – John Legend

Talk Dirty (Feat. 2 Chainz) – Jason Derulo

I'm Yours – Jason Mraz

On Top Of The World – Imagine Dragons

Wind Beneath My Wings – Bette Midler

Into Your Arms – The Maine

I'll Follow You – Shinedown

You Run Away – Barenaked Ladies

I Miss You – Blink 182

About The Author

Sandi Lynn is a New York Times, USA Today and Wall Street Journal bestselling author who spends all of her days writing. She published her first novel, Forever Black, in February 2013 and to date has seven books. Her addictions are shopping, romance novels, coffee, chocolate, margaritas, and giving readers an escape to another world.

Please come connect with her at:

www.facebook.com/Sandi.Lynn.Author

www.twitter.com/SandilynnWriter

www.authorsandilynn.com

www.pinterest.com/sandilynnWriter

www.instagram.com/sandilynnauthor

https://www.goodreads.com/author/show/6089757.Sandi_Lynn

28321225R00181

Made in the USA
Lexington, KY
12 January 2019